DANIKA'S TOUCH

WARRIORS, WITCHES AND FAE - BOOK 2

DARCY JAMESON

Danika's Touch

Copyright © 2021 Darcy Jameson

All rights reserved

ISBN: 9798480401097

Published in the UK

Cover content is used for illustrative purposes only, and any person depicted is a model.

This is a work of fiction. Names, characters, places, and incidents either are the product of the author's imagination or are used fictitiously, and any resemblance to an actual person, living or dead, business establishments, events, or locales, is entirely coincidental. The following story has been written in US English. The spelling and usage reflect that. All rights reserved. No part of this book may be reproduced or transmitted in any form or by any means, electronic or mechanical, including photocopying, recording, or by any information storage and retrieval system, without the written permission of the publisher, except where permitted by law. To request permission and for all other inquiries, contact admin@darcyjameson.com

To Emma W.
- you're a star

x

CHAPTER 1

He'd not been fast enough. Fierce heat burned Nyle's skin as the daemon's muscular whip grazed his neck. Gritting his teeth, he ignored the pain and sliced at the feeler. The whip-like instrument fell to the ground, still twitching. The daemon screeched and dropped to its knees, black blood pouring from its shoulder. Beetle-black eyes squinted up at him, pieces of flesh clung to rows of splinter-sharp teeth. It unfurled its wings, about to launch itself into the night, but the warrior's sword flashed, and the creature dropped at his feet, dead. Nyle didn't have time to breathe as another daemon landed a few feet away. He planted his feet in the mud and readied himself.

Fighting was what he lived for. Even now, with the odds against him and a horde of daemons bearing down, he relished the rush of battle. He was the best swordsman, the shrewdest leader; his warriors were the strongest from all the clans. It was to him the chieftains turned when creatures found ways into the Shaman lands, desperate to escape their own hellish Gehenna. However, this was not normal. Today they'd been fighting for hours, fending off feelers, teeth, claws, but the daemons just kept coming.

Why were so many finding a way through? He hated not knowing. He needed to capture one of these hellions and pry the truth from it with the tip of his blade. But for the first time, he was beginning to consider the unthinkable, the possibility of rounding up the other three warriors and calling a tactical retreat.

The snarling daemon advanced. Nyle turned to meet it and found his second in command, Sabre, just behind him, facing down another daemon from the opposite direction. Nyle smiled grimly; Sabre was a good man to have at your back.

Sabre tilted his head back and spoke in his usual gruff tone. "I thought we were just going to head off a few troglets, then spend the evening with a harem of grateful Shaman witches," he paused to parry a blow, "not fighting an *army* of ażote." He wiped something dark and pulpy from his cheek with the back of his hand.

Nyle grimaced as he dodged a claw. "I'd rather be here fighting than cooped up in a dusty library with a bunch of high-bred bookworms."

A whip-like feeler struck out as the daemon attacked again; Sabre turned and caught the feeler in a massive leather-bound fist as Nyle lunged for the creature's heart.

Nyle took a breath and rounded on the next creature. "University women? They'd probably think themselves way above your rank, my friend."

Sabre snorted and raised his massive blade, cleaving

an approaching creature in two. "In my experience, Captain, educated Shaman witches have much lower standards than one might expect."

The onslaught eased for a moment. "You sound like Torin," said Nyle, wiping the sweat from his brow. Torin was Nyle's archer, a warrior who had the power to shoot fire from his hands, as well as the seemingly magical ability to bed any woman he desired.

Sabre heaved his broadsword from the decimated daemon. "I can't compete with Torin on that score, nor would I want to. It must be exhausting. So where is old firefingers?"

Nyle looked around over the carnage. At least twenty daemons lay slain. Yet another was circling, readying to land. A white light crashed into the creature above them, causing it to burst into white-hot flames. A blond warrior came into view through the smoke, rubbing his hands together. "Well… this was *not* what I was expecting."

Nyle wiped his sword on a patch of grass. "Yes, Torin. I know. You were hoping for more pretty witches, fewer death-wielding monsters…" He grunted as another ażote came into view. "Well, this is the life you signed up for. Where's Alyssa?"

Torin reached for a regular arrow and nocked it, giving the power in his hands time to recharge. He let a shaft fly; the *thunk* of arrow meeting flesh confirmed he'd found his mark. The monster hung its horned head and looked at the arrow protruding from its chest, before collapsing with a snarl. The archer nodded to a clearing a few yards away; a large pile of daemon bodies lay bleeding into the earth, and the screams of dying ażote could be heard bouncing off the trees. "She's working out some issues."

Alyssa, the only woman he'd ever trained, hated ażote over any other daemon from the realm of Gehenna. She'd dived into the fray without hesitation; her usual icy demeanor replaced by something that had looked suspiciously like bloodthirsty glee.

Nyle looked up and his blood froze in his veins. Twenty or so ażote were flying through the air towards them. It was as if every ażote in Shaman—from his mountain home in the north to the southern isles—had suddenly converged in this place. *But why?* He gripped his sword firmly and concentrated on relaxing his shoulders. *Kill daemons now, ask questions later.*

Suddenly, the creatures stopped and hung in the air.

Alyssa ran over to them, her preferred choice of weapon, a braided whip, coiled in her hands. Her long, pale plaits hung in clumps, black with blood, and her face was streaked with gore. Her eyes, however, shone with a fierce blue fever. "What are they doing?" She uncoiled her whip. "Why don't they attack?" then louder, "*Come here, you base wretches. Come here so I can flay the leather hide from your bones.*"

Nyle raised his hand and Alyssa fell silent. Of all the weird things he'd seen these last few weeks—the increased incursions, and the patterns in the attacks—this was the weirdest. A trickle of sweat ran over the base of his spine, and he suppressed a shiver.

All four warriors stood in the muddy clearing watching the creatures hover.

"Why don't they attack?" whispered Sabre.

Nyle frowned. He'd spent years tracking creatures like these, through Shaman and the hellish Gehenna. Ażote fought each other, often *ate* each other; they were chaotic and violent and consumed with hunger. But these winged horrors looked like they were listening to something—*but to what?* Another bead of cold sweat traced down his back. If something, *someone*, could organize these beasts…

The creatures stayed twenty feet up in the gloaming sky, floating in a perfect circle with just a slight movement of their scaly wings to keep them airborne.

A thud to his left made Nyle wrench his eyes from the eerie sight.

Torin was kneeling in the mud, his hands over his ears. Nyle bent down towards his archer. "What is it, Torin? Speak to me." He touched Torin's face; the archer was ice cold. Was this a spell, some kind of magic the ażote possessed but had never shown? No, they would have felled him and his warriors many times over if they could have. "What is it, Torin? Tell me."

"A voice… It's talking to the ażote. I can hear it. Ahh, it's like I can feel it speak—as if it's inside me." Torin's voice was strained, and he twitched as he spoke. "It says… the herb witch… at the university. Her magic holds the rift… closed. The pack makes for her… we… the ażote are… summoned." He looked up, as did the other three warriors. The creatures above, as one, turned to the east and sailed silently into the night sky.

"Who, Torin? Who's talking to you?" asked Alyssa, a worried edge to her tone.

But Torin didn't answer. He raised his head and met Nyle's stare. Torin's eyes were pale and blank, like the eyes of a baked fish. The archer grinned, not the handsome smile that usually came so readily, but a wolfish grimace twisting his face into something ugly. But it was his voice that made Nyle take a step back, a bitter rasp that did not belong to his archer.

"The whole of Gehennah is coming! They will own you, use your women, and feed on your children's hearts." Torin snarled and pushed his hand out towards Nyle. A white light flashed, and the captain ducked. A shot of pure energy went just over Nyle's head, scorching a nearby tree.

Sabre fell on Torin, pushing him into the mud and kneeling on his back. Torin struggled for a moment, then stilled.

"Torin?" Nyle barked. "Torin, look at me!" He gestured for Sabre to release him. Sabre hesitated before reluctantly getting up, but he stayed close to the archer, poised and ready.

Torin groaned and rolled over. He faced Nyle, his eyes now back to their usual deep green. He sat up and looked at the smoking tree behind his captain, then down at his own hands. "I... oh Goddess, I'm sorry. Why did I...? I remember but..."

"Don't worry about it now." Nyle stood, and Alyssa helped Torin to his feet. The archer was shaking.

Nyle would need to get Torin looked at by a healer, but that would have to wait. "When you were entranced, you said something about a herb witch?"

Torin ran his hand over his face and nodded. "The voice, it told us... I mean it told the *ażote* to kill her, that she was protecting something... something important, a portal of some kind, a rift." Torin rubbed his forehead and winced.

Nyle frowned and turned to Sabre. "You and Alyssa get the horses. We need to find this herb witch." *And we need to make it to the university before the monsters overwhelm it!*

"We can't ride as fast as they fly," said Sabre as he led the horses into the clearing.

"They may stop to feed." Alyssa's voice was grim as she mounted.

Nyle nodded, taking his horse's reins from Sabre and shifting himself into the saddle. He'd seen the aftermath of an ażote feeding frenzy; such horror would haunt him until his death.

"And if they don't?" asked Sabre from his horse.

Nyle didn't answer, but as he worked his mount up into a gallop, he hoped that there might be a few witches and mages at the university whose power was of the more battle-ready kind—ones that could fight off a horde of daemons.

He doubted it.

~

DANIKA WATCHED THE OLD WOMAN'S FEATURES BECOME less pained as she sipped the broth. Her teacher's migraines were becoming more frequent, and this worried her.

"This is good. You've made it perfectly." The Elder-Sha smiled and leant back in the chair.

Danika took the empty mug from her teacher and

frowned. "You should let me do a proper analysis. If you just let me lay my hands on…"

"No." Elder-Sha Ameena closed her eyes as she spoke. "I will stick to herbs and preparations—your healing gift is better used elsewhere."

Danika shook her head but kept quiet. It would take little effort on her part to use her Goddess-given power to find the root of these headaches and cure them for good, instead of messing around with thistle milk and dried thyme. Her teacher's mistrust of healing magic was frustrating.

Elder-Sha Ameena sighed. "Have I failed to teach you anything over the last seven years, child? You must learn your preparations, Danika, and they will serve you as well, if not better than your magic. Healing power has its limits."

Danika sighed. "Yes, Elder-Sha, but if I could only…?"

"How is Layla? Resting, I hope."

It was a blatant change of subject, but Danika let it slide. "I think so. She went off to bed after supper. She was tired from the trials today."

"Good. She will need all her strength for the advanced trials tomorrow. Elder-Sha Paulo will not have made it easy for her."

Danika nodded. Her best friend was expected to gain the highest level possible in physical magic. For a while now, her power had outstripped even what the Elder-Sha had taught her, much to his ill-concealed annoyance. Danika, on the other hand, hadn't even been entered into a basic trial. She'd dropped it altogether in her first year, without regret, due to the fact that she didn't possess the physical magic required to boil a pan of water. So what if she couldn't lift a boulder? She could mend a knife wound. Not that there were many stabbings at the university, none actually; the closest she'd got to actual battle healing was salving the burned fingers of kitchen maids, but she could—in *theory,* at least.

Elder-Sha Ameena yawned. "Danika, be a poppet and bring me that blanket."

Danika spread the quilt over her teacher and dimmed the light. She would miss this woman most after graduation. Her teacher's love had turned her from a surly, miserable child into a confident healer. Danika looked down at her dark, creased face, so familiar, so unchanging; the face she turned to for counsel, for encouragement.

"Ah, Danika!" Kaine, Ameena's husband, entered the room. Despite being in his sixties, he was still a handsome man, over six feet, with strong shoulders and an easy smile. "You've prepared her tea. Good. I was about to do it." It was Kaine who'd driven her here as a sullen, withdrawn teenager. She remembered fondly how they'd stopped off at a farm on the way and picked strawberries; how he'd not peppered her with questions nor rebuked her for her rude silences, just letting her be. She also remembered how happy he'd been telling Danika about the university and how his eyes shone with love and pride when he'd mentioned his wife; *I think you two will get along*, he'd said, despite Danika's frosty reserve. *You and her are a bit alike*.

"Hello Elder Kaine. Your wife still refuses to allow me to perform a proper examination, despite her worsening headaches." Her voice was light, but it still held a note of frustration. Perhaps Kaine could talk some sense into her mentor. The absence of the Sha in his title denoted that he did not teach. Nevertheless, he was one of the most respected members of the university staff, and he still took the younger students for physical education - a subject Danika was very glad she no longer had to endure.

He walked over to Ameena, snuggled up under her blanket. His face softened and Danika noted, not for the first time, how completely he adored her. "Ah, it's for the best." He cupped his wife's cheek in his hand. "The herbs in the drink will suffice."

"But—"

"Goodnight, Danika." There was a finality to his voice, a dismissal, soft but firm. Ameena gave him a small nod, and he smiled in return.

Neither looked up at her as she left her teacher's chambers. Standing on the landing, she felt torn on which direction to go. Layla was no doubt tucked up in bed in the room they shared upstairs. That was where she should go, Danika thought, to get some sleep and be well-rested for her medical exams tomorrow. But something kept her alert.

The wind whined through the old stone walls of the university, and the rain beat down on the shutters. She thought she detected a soft hum behind the wind, a single breath waiting to be exhaled. She turned, half expecting to see someone hovering in the gloom, but the corridor was empty, just the soft glow of a few low hanging, light spheres. She shivered.

She'd never get to sleep in this storm. Turning right,

she descended a curving flight of stone steps. At least she could get in some last-minute revision, she thought as she made for the library. Tomorrow's exams were going to be the hardest. She'd make sure she was as prepared as possible—no matter what tests she might face.

∼

NYLE IGNORED THE EXHAUSTION CRAMPING HIS SHOULDERS and the biting rain that stung his face. He'd been riding for hours and he kept going, driven by the echo of the daemon's words—*the whole of Gehennah is coming...*

The bulk of the university loomed darkly on the horizon. The airborne creatures hadn't stopped to feed and would get there before him. Regardless, he rode harder, motioning for his company to do the same.

After what seemed like an age, the great edifice grew larger before him. Columns and spires rose high against the lightening skyline. A flash of red illuminated the landscape; whether the source was inside the university or outside, he couldn't tell. Red was the color of witches' magic. Could they hold the gates against the hoard? A handful of teachers and untrained youths?

Sabre rode up alongside the warrior and shouted to him over the beating hooves; his friend's usual relaxed expression was gone, replaced with a grim scowl. "The Shaman witches and mages are putting up a fight! There may still be time."

Nyle kept his eyes on the track. "Healers, stone-smiths, academics. No, Sabre, the Shaman magic does not lend itself well to battle. We'll be lucky if the creatures haven't laid waste to the whole place."

Another flash of red reflected off the clouds.

Sabre nodded. "I believe some can raise shields. She may still be alive."

"Our best hope is that the ażote are distracted by the students and do not go straight for her." It was a grim affair when your most likely chance of success depended on the slaughter of juveniles. Nyle put the thought from his mind. "Tell Torin and Alyssa—our priority is to find the herb witch."

Sabre nodded and fell back.

Nyle could just about make out several winged shapes circling the highest turret. Hoping fervently that the Shaman were, indeed, able to hold out a short while longer, he crouched farther down into the saddle and quickened his pace as dawn tinged the indigo sky.

CHAPTER 2

*D*anika picked up a weighty tome entitled *Antivenoms and the Treatment of Poisons—a Natural Guide* and tried to focus on the scrawling text. Dawn was about to break; the kitchens were probably already busy. She wondered what they were cooking. The thought of soft-baked rolls dipped in syrup or some lightly salted, boiled eggs were crowding out her attempts to focus.

She was on the cusp of giving up when a cry sliced through the silence of the library. She frowned, marked her page, and padded over to the oak door. It had sounded like a child's voice; maybe one of the kitchen boys had been injured. Tightening her robe around her, she heaved open the heavy door and began to climb the stone stairwell that led to the main dining hall.

Something crashed into her, almost knocking her back down the stairs. She stayed upright, but only with the aid of the railing. She looked down at a boy of about ten, who'd practically fallen down the stairwell leading from the upper lobby. Chest heaving, eyes wide with fear, he grabbed Danika, his little fingernails digging sharply into her wrist.

"There are monsters everywhere!" he gasped, his grip tightening. "People are fighting, in the dorms, in the dining hall... The monsters are so fast... they have these teeth and knives on their fingers and, and... a whip!"

The child didn't have the breath to continue; he just panted and shook.

Danika bent down, her arms encircling his shoulders. "It's okay, sweetheart, it was a dream." She held the trembling boy to her. It seemed that she was not the only one on edge this night. Despite her calming words, her earlier feeling of unease now returned as a cold, hard lump deep in her gut.

A second scream sounded from the dining hall, making her jump, followed by more screams. The floor shook, dust and chips of stone rained down from the stairwell ceiling. The dull thud of another blast... another shower. She crouched over the boy. Her mind raced as silt and small stones beat on her back and neck. Who would attack a university—to what end? The boy clung to her, terrified. When the blasts stopped, she raised her head and used her hands to shake out some of the grit. She needed to make a plan, to get the boy to safety, to find Layla and Elder-Sha Ameena, and to form a defense with the other Elders. The only way out of the library was up the stairwell. The boy turned to look upwards, and Danika's gaze followed his. He let out a terrified wail.

In one moment, every nightmare she'd ever had and every terrifying story she'd ever heard took form into the horrifying vision that now descended the stone cellar steps. Panic rose thick and choking in her chest, threatening to overwhelm her. The creature before her was an abomination, a beast belonging to another hellish place. She tried to comprehend the glossy black mass of wings and claws, the rows of needle-like teeth that crowded its hideous face. She failed; her mind froze, numbed. The creature moved slowly towards them. Its huge, glinting mouth dripped with thick drool. It looked first at her, then at the boy. It wheezed as it approached, and Danika realized it had spoken one long, dry, rasping word from its gaping mouth. "Huuuuungry."

She scuffled backwards, dragging the boy behind her, shielding him with her body. At no point did she turn her back on this monstrosity. It stood twice as tall as a man with ragged black wings sprouting from its back, giving it greater height still. It had to bend at the waist and flatten its wings into its back to fit down the stairwell. Its naked chest glittered, dark and oily in the library's dim light. Small black eyes squinted from above an over-wide mouth crammed full of tiny, spiked teeth. And from this slick opening uncoiled a thin black tongue, which bobbed and danced in the air between them.

Danika stood in front of the young boy; he was squeezed up tightly against her, and she could feel him sobbing gently. Dazed with fear, she forced herself to attend to the situation, attempting to put up an energy block between them, concentrating hard on manipulating the particles of air to condense them into a solid shield around their bodies. But the magic was beyond her. Every attempt failed, and she almost screamed with frustration as pathetic scraps of red energy evaporated into air.

The creature gave a rasping cry. Gore dripped from its mouth. It uncoiled a feeler from its shoulder, a protrusion Danika hadn't noticed until now, and whipped it towards the boy. He yelped as the feeler slapped around his wrist and began pulling him away from Danika. The boy's skin hissed and steamed under the feeler, and he howled, his little hands trying to prize off the scalding coil.

The creature pulled harder. Danika grabbed the boy, desperate to do something to keep the child close, her eyes flicking wildly around the room for inspiration. Nothing but shelves of books, rolled up papers, a few candles. The terrified boy wrapped his free arm tightly around her waist, but he was slipping. In desperation, Danika considered shooting a dart of sedation into the boy. It would render him mercifully unaware if this thing began to feed. His death would be painless. The creature tightened its grip, causing the boy to scream louder. He let go of her waist and pulled and pulled at the snake-like feeler, burning his small arm.

She was running out of time.

Danika readied herself to sedate the boy; she drew the power into her palm preparing to deliver the shot, but at the last moment the creature tore the boy from her, free from the contact she needed to deliver the dose. In frustration and fury, Danika flung herself at the creature and forced a huge dose of sedation right into the creature's leathery, bulging chest. She had no idea what effect, if any, her energy would have on the creature's physiology. If she just made it pause for a second, maybe she could get to the boy.

Immediately the creature fell, a dead weight onto the

floor, smashing the side of its head on the flagstones. Black blood like tar oozed from its wound and formed an oily pool around its head. The boy, now free, scampered back to Danika, who caught him in a tight embrace.

"Is it dead?" asked the boy in a whisper. "Did you kill it?"

"I think so," replied Danika, although she wasn't entirely sure.

She gently ran her hands over the boy's burnt wrist, drawing the pain from him, knitting together his broken skin. "What's your name?"

"M-Micah," replied the boy, unable to look away from the fallen creature.

"I'm Danika." She brushed a lock of hair from the boy's forehead and tucked it behind his ear. "You were very brave just now."

"Is this a dream?" Micah asked hopefully. "You said I was dreaming. I was working in the kitchen. M-maybe I fell asleep. Will I wake up soon?"

"I'm sorry, Micah. No, it's not a dream. We need to get you somewhere safe." Danika had to concentrate on slowing her heart; stress was making it difficult for her to heal the boy's burned skin. As she stroked Micah's hand, the welts faded, and the boy's face became less pained. Conscious that she was shaking, she straightened, pulled the boy close, and together they warily circled past the creature.

If she could just make it to the kitchens, she could lead the boy out via the servants' exit and hide him in the woods. Maybe others had the same idea. Perhaps many of the students and staff were camped out, hiding, taking advantage of the low tree cover and dense brush. Layla might be there and Elder-Sha Ameena.

But at the top of the stairs, they met with a scene of carnage. The lobby was strewn with dead and dying Shaman. Two creatures feasted on the still twitching limbs of one of their victims. Danika clutched Micah to her chest, trying to block his view. The creatures left off chewing and turned to face them, each with a look of desire on their twisted, blood-smeared faces. Danika backed up to the wall, keeping herself between Micah and the monsters. There were too many; she couldn't sedate them all. She clutched Micah to her, ready to spare him the pain. This was it; there was nothing more she could do. She raised her hands anyway; she would strike down those she could.

Suddenly, all the creatures turned their heads towards the doorway.

The creatures barely had time to hiss before a band of the largest and fiercest looking warriors that Danika had ever seen burst through the outer doors, led by the biggest and most brutal-looking of them all.

Danika watched in awe as the four warriors attacked fast and hard, hacking into the monsters with long-swords and wicked-looking curved knives.

The creature's screeches were quickly silenced as the warriors sliced through oily skin and sinewy flesh, coating the floor in a grisly black tar.

"Where would the others be? The other witches?" the largest warrior demanded, turning to Danika.

"I don't know. The dining hall, I guess." Danika forced

herself to regain a semblance of composure and met the warrior's cobalt-blue gaze.

"Take us!"

Danika turned and quickly led the troop down the corridor, keeping Micah close as they moved. Danika had heard stories of mountain warriors but never met one before—an elite company taken from the fiercest mountain clans and sworn to fight the creatures of Gehenna. They had a fearsome reputation for brutality and fortitude, as well as other things.

Danika's gaze slid sideways to the leader. He was huge, even compared to his fellow warriors, well over six feet tall with wide heavy-set shoulders and thick muscular arms. His lean, stubbled face was blank and stony. His cold blue eyes flicked from side to side, as if gathering information, assessing in an instant and moving on. She sensed he was absorbing data, planning exit routes, thinking through possibilities, going over the odds. His gaze snapped to hers, grim and stark, like the sharp glint of light on a blade. She looked away and quickened her pace, pulling Micah along behind her.

As they approached the doors, she could hear the growls and shrieks of the creatures mixed with the groans of those being eaten alive. The lead warrior pushed her and Micah firmly aside.

"Stay behind us." He burst through the doors.

Danika followed the warrior into the hall, holding Micah's hand tightly. A pearly translucent dome filled the far end of the hall as a group of creatures prowled the perimeter. In the center of the dome, flanked by four Elder-Shas, was Layla. She stood tall, palms raised, obviously straining to maintain the protective barrier. Other students crouched on the floor under the dome, a mass of scared faces visible through the hazy wall. Some hadn't made it, and the floor was littered with bleeding victims. In one corner, creatures had begun feeding on a student; he was still awake and begging for mercy.

The warriors attacked furiously, their slashing swords cutting the creatures down with brutal efficiency. A female warrior, taller than any woman Danika had ever seen and covered in black blood, used a powerful whip to imprison her adversaries before dicing them with a razor-sharp blade. An astoundingly handsome warrior with blond hair and darkly tanned skin shot energy bolts from the palms of his hands at those creatures taking flight. One creature fell screaming to the ground, so close she had to yank Micah away to prevent him from being crushed under its crumpled corpse.

But it was the lead warrior that Danika found her eyes drawn towards. She watched spellbound as he skillfully dispatched three creatures, moving with speed and grace despite his muscular bulk.

He used the long sword in his right hand to slice cleanly through the torso of the first creature before immediately ripping the second from sternum to gullet with the knife in his left. The third dived on him from the air, and he rolled to avoid the attack. In an instant, he was on his feet, grabbing the creature's thigh as it tried to rise again and wrenching its leg completely from its body before beheading the beast. Although he seemed focused on the grisly job in hand, Danika noticed his gaze frequently returning to her and Micah. The moment a creature swooped down on them from above, the warrior was there to shield them, rending their attacker with fast, brutal strokes. The noise of battle eased. In what only seemed a few moments, every creature lay slain. The polished wooden floor of the dining hall ran slick with oily blood. The warriors stood in the middle of the hall, three men and one woman. The leader, Danika's protector, uttered an abrupt command, and the other warriors immediately began to scour the hall and surrounding rooms.

The force field dome had vanished. The braver students and staff began to venture farther into the hall, some sobbing, holding on to each other, some calling out for friends and colleagues. The hall was littered with the dead and the dying students and staff who had been set upon by the creatures. Danika settled Micah with some of the departing kitchen staff and waded into the horror and gore.

Trying desperately to recall her lessons in battle healing, she moved to the student who moments before had creatures eating his insides. He was close to death; a pale, ginger-haired boy of about sixteen. His left leg and both arms had been torn into, the flesh jagged and raw from sharp tearing teeth. His blood pooled thickly around his body. Danika had never seen such injuries. He looked at her, unable to speak; in his eyes she saw the pain and terror of the past half an hour replayed. She felt for his heartbeat, focused her mind, and reached into him. She sensed what little blood he had left moving weakly through his veins—he could not be saved.

She spoke gently to him. "The Goddess awaits you...

do you wish me to ease your path?" She'd never offered the healer's bequest before. She felt scared of the enormity of what she was offering to do but knew in her heart it was the right thing.

The boy could just nod, tears running down his cheeks.

Gently, she laid her palms upon the boy and released a measure of her power into his chest. Immediately, his tortured expression softened, his eyelids fluttered closed, and he drifted quietly to sleep. His passage from this life would not be spent reliving the horrors of the attack. She bowed her head for a moment in prayer, then stood and surveyed the hall. Healers administered cures, and some prayed over those that could not be saved, easing pain where they could, just as Danika had done a moment before. Danika felt a lump rise in her throat but fought it down. For a moment, she felt frozen by a wave of fury. What were these creatures, and why had they come here? Why here?

A second thought, a cold fear: Layla! Elder-Sha Ameena!

Someone called her name, "Danika!"

Spotting Layla, Danika rushed over and hugged her friend, who collapsed into Danika's embrace. For a moment, the friends just held each other, drawing strength from the other's presence. Danika held onto her friend. She couldn't believe that a day earlier, in this very hall, they'd been eating porridge and chatting about their upcoming placements. Now they were ankle-deep in blood, in a scene straight out of the legends of Gehenna, both exhausted and overcome by shock and bewilderment.

Danika pulled back, noting the weariness etched into her friend's features. "What happened here?"

Layla shook her head, her voice raw. "It happened fast; everyone was confused and yelling. Elder-Sha Ameena woke me. She ordered me to go get the other students and meet in the hall. We thought it was a test, part of the exams... then the creatures..." Layla's eyes met Danika's, and the young healer saw her own shock and terror reflected in her friend's stare.

Layla was sobbing as she spoke. "We tried to force them back with blasts of energy, but they were too quick. We formed a barrier, but..." She closed her eyes to squeeze back the tears. "Once it was in place, we couldn't... let anyone else in. Those coming into the hall last..." She lent down, resting her face on Danika's shoulder. The sobs she'd been holding back broke through.

Danika needed to find her mentor urgently; if she hadn't made it into the hall then... "Where is she - Ameena? Which way did she go?"

Layla's eyes widened, shock giving way to fear. "She and Kaine took some students who were too late to enter the dome. They headed for the southern chambers."

"We need to find her."

"You. With me. Now!" Both girls jumped at the sharp command. The savage-looking lead warrior approached. He stood before Danika, who came no higher than his chest. The healer had to look up a fair distance to meet his eye.

"I need to find an old witch—an Elder. One who

taught herbs. They tell me you were close." He nodded towards some terrified looking students huddled in a corner.

Danika turned and hitched up her robe before replying. "The southern chambers."

"Take me," he snapped, but Danika was already running towards the south entrance. Perhaps her mentor had been able to fight them off, although she had no power that Danika knew of. She ran and prayed, blocking out her aching head and strained muscles. Dear Goddess, in your garden, please hear your daughter's prayer. Let Elder-Sha Ameena be alive.

∼

As Nyle kept pace with the short, red-haired woman, he couldn't help but be a little impressed. He'd assumed the naturally peaceful Shamans would crumble when confronted with battle, especially the gore that had been witnessed today. Even he, who had spent years fighting these creatures, was nearing his daily limit of death and viscera.

The young woman had gone through much, yet she hadn't faltered. She'd been outnumbered when he'd found her but readying to fight—like a female mountain lion protecting a cub. She'd kept her head about her in the ensuing battle and from what he could piece together from Sabre's status report, she'd dispatched an ażote in the library without aid—just this tiny little witch, who couldn't be more than, what? Twenty? An impressive display of courage from such a tiny lass.

"Why the southern chambers?" Nyle asked as they ran.

"I don't know."

Nyle eased the pace. "How did you kill the ażote in the library?"

"I... I used sedation... the thing just crumpled."

Interesting, thought Nyle, healing arts could be used as weapons on the creatures of Gehenna. He hadn't heard of this before; he'd have to talk to the mages about it back at the camp.

They arrived at the chamber, to a scene of eerie quiet. Five ażote lay crumpled and lifeless on the floor around the altar. The entrance to some catacombs had been smashed, and rocks and debris filled the doorway.

Nyle circled the dead creatures. "Someone made a stand here, around the altar." The creatures were well slain. If he didn't know better, he would say a clan warrior had dispatched them, which made no sense.

"So where are they? Where are Elder-Sha Ameena and the rest of the students?" The healer picked her way over the dead creatures. "There are no bodies. Ameena, Kaine, the students—they must have escaped." She turned to Nyle, hope lighting up her soft golden eyes.

Nyle allowed himself a flicker of optimism, but something niggled at the back of his mind. "The Elders must have been quick to kill so many ażote." He'd fought these creatures many times. Their scalding, whip-like feelers enabled them to capture even the fastest prey, and in a group like this, even a seasoned warrior would have difficulty. "This Kaine, was he a warrior? A fighter?"

"Not that I know of." She frowned.

Nyle spoke over his shoulder to the healer. "She must

be a potent witch—the only one who has the power to prevent a major rift in the barrier." He moved around the chamber. The witch couldn't have killed them all simultaneously... the pattern of the bodies was all wrong; they were spread out and had died individually, without rallying to a central point of attack, as if they were each taken by surprise. His mind raced through the possibilities, but he came up with nothing. How did they not see their death approach?

"But Elder-Sha Ameena has no magic, only her knowledge of natural science, of plants and blending," replied the young woman.

A noise disturbed the silence of the chamber. Nyle drew his sword. It sounded like someone crying, but there was no one there.

The healer walked towards the sound. "It's just a bare wall." She raised her hand to touch the rough stone.

"Get back, girl!" Nyle grabbed her and pulled her closer to him. "You don't know what kind of sorcery the ażote brought from beyond the rift." The redheaded girl looked as if she were about to argue; she jerked her arm from his grasp and turned to him, her pale face creased in a frown. Before she could speak, however, a group of terrified looking students suddenly appeared before them, standing in a line with their backs pressed up against the wall. For a moment, both he and the healer just stared at the sudden apparition.

"Can you see us, Danika?" One of the students spoke, her voice shaking and low. "Elder-Sha Ameena... she told us not to move."

"Where is she?" Nyle asked immediately.

"I don't know. She and Elder Kaine were there one moment and gone the next. We just saw the… the… creatures drop down one by one. Then there was a struggle between two or three creatures, a lot of confusion."

"Where? Point, dammit!"

"Over there." The young student pointed a trembling finger to the debris piled up at the altar.

Nyle strode to where the girl had pointed; the healer followed. "Is this a Shaman's power? Can you make yourself and others unseeable?"

"No. I've never heard of any Shaman develop such a power, of any discipline. It must be some form of glamour," replied Danika.

Nyle frowned. There was only one race that could wield the power of glamour, and it was not Shamanic. They picked their way slowly through the rubble that led to the entrance of the catacombs. As he worked, Nyle glanced sideways and watched the little healer pull wooden beams and stones away from the doorway. She was completely focused on her task; her robe was torn and ragged, her boots were covered in dried blood, her fiery hair was caked in grime and dust, which also covered her face. And yet he couldn't help noticing her delicate features; the attractive curve at her nape, her slender form beneath her clothing, her warm golden eyes marred by a worried frown.

The healer stood up straight and stretched. Her robe slid open and revealed a creamy shoulder dusted with a smattering of light freckles. Nyle fought the urge to run his fingers over the freckles to see if her skin was, in fact, as soft as it appeared. He checked himself. Now was not the time for thinking about a woman's skin. He had far more pressing things to think about, like whether the Shaman witch, if indeed she was a Shaman, was still alive, and if so, what could she tell them about the rift.

He scooped up a great armful of rocks and dumped them to the side of the doorway, revealing as he did so a frail and bloody hand beneath the debris.

CHAPTER 3

Danika was stretching out her tight, tired muscles when she heard a soft moan from under the rubble.

"Ameena… Oh, Goddess have mercy! Wait, we are coming for you." She began ripping at the stones and wood with her bare hands. "Help her!"

The warrior was already carefully removing the covering detritus from her teacher's small frame. When the warrior had finished, Elder-Sha Ameena, lay before them soaked in blood. The old woman was very still, her eyes half-closed. Deep gouges and fierce burn marks crossed her arms and legs. Her clothes were in shreds, and Danika could see evidence of many more wounds traversing the old woman's body. Danika fell to her knees by her mentor's side. The warrior did the same.

Danika placed her hands on the Elder-Sha's chest, not knowing where to start, but summoning what was left of her healing reserves—she would heal her mentor no matter what it took—but her teacher grabbed her arm.

"You must listen, Danika," she whispered, struggling to breathe. "The daemons will overwhelm the free lands. You must not let this happen, child."

"Elder-Sha, we can talk later. For now, I must heal—"

"You cannot heal me, child. My magic is fading; we must hurry." Elder-Sha Ameena moaned in pain, then gritted her teeth. "Are the students alive, the one's I hid by the wall? I feared my glamour would not hold out."

"Yes, they're fine. They've gone back to the hall," replied Danika. Glamour? How would her teacher be able to cast such a spell?

"Good… good." The old woman smiled despite her obvious pain. "And Kaine?"

Danika looked frantically around the room. "I can't see him. I—"

"—No matter, child. I will see him soon in the Garden of the Goddess. It was quite a fight we put up against those ażote." She took a deep, rasping breath and looked at Danika with sadness in her watery eyes. "My beautiful Danika, in all my years at the university, you were truly my most challenging student, and… my most satisfying accomplishment."

Danika felt her eyes fill with tears. This couldn't be happening, not after everything else, not after the library and the hall and poor exhausted Layla. Surely, the Goddess had allowed enough misery for one day. Danika looked down into her teacher's face, a face she knew so well, so kind, so calm. "Hold on, Elder-Sha, let me at least try—"

"There is nothing you can do, child. Shamanic magic does not work on me."

"What? Why wouldn't it work?"

"It was my magic that built this chamber. It was my purpose to see the rift... stood firm... 'til now."

Danika shook her head. "This building was built nearly three centuries ago. How could you possibly—"

"I am ancient. I... have been here such a very long time." She coughed again and paused to catch her breath. "I'm sorry, child. I wish I had time to explain. I should have done this earlier, but I thought we had more time. Give me your arm." She held Danika and a warm glow spread through the healer's skin. When she released Danika, an exquisite amber design encircled her wrist, lit from within by some unseen power. "Show this to Prince Jamal. He is the only one who can help." The old woman coughed and winced with the pain. "Tell him it is from his sister, Jasmine. Tell him..." The woman coughed again, this time harder, and her eyes rolled back in her head. With effort she continued, "Tell him I'm sorry I left him all those years ago, but he must heal the rift. Tell him that it was his sister's final wish." She turned her face and looked straight at the warrior. She spoke once more, her voice firmer. "You, Nyle of the mountain clans. My remaining magic will buy you another few weeks of protection, but after that, without more support, the rift will burst and all of Gehenna will flood into Shaman. You must ensure that she reaches my brother. Only Fae magic can seal the rift."

Danika felt the warrior stiffen beside her.

"How do you know my—"

"It is your respons... ability to protect her. In this, you must not fail." She turned back to Danika. "Both of your names are written in the great Book of Ages. This is your chapter. Mine is at an end. Grieve not for me for I have been so blessed." Her voice trailed off, and her eyes became glassy and vacant.

Danika's head dropped, and she rested her forehead for a moment on the arm of her beloved teacher. A cramping in her chest made her want to sob with the pain of loss. Tears trickled down her face, tracking through the dirt on her cheeks. This woman had understood and accepted her. She had taken a restless, angry child and shown her that she had a place in the world, and a purpose. Danika had learnt to embrace her own curiosity instead of being ashamed of it. She'd learnt to utilize her strengths rather than lashing out in frustration. The woman who had inspired her to make peace with herself was gone, and Danika felt like the aggressive, petulant fourteen-year-old that had arrived at the university seven years ago, confused and defensive.

"Look!" said the warrior as he breathed in sharply, and Danika gazed again upon her teacher's face. It was changing, the air around it shimmering like tiny crystal sand in sunlight. It settled into the stunning visage of a woman with white-blonde hair and a pale, youthful complexion, so breathtakingly beautiful it was difficult to look away.

"A Fae," whispered Nyle in wonder. "Did you know this?"

Danika shook her head. She was beyond words.

Looking down at her arm, she gazed upon the shapes that glittered in the light. A snake wound around the stem of a budding rose: the royal seal of Elfain, the realm of the Fae.

She removed her cloak and laid it over her teacher, suddenly feeling all the grief, exhaustion, and fear of the evening rush over her in a wave. She swayed on her feet. Instantly, the warrior was by her side, supporting her. Looking up at him in her exhaustion, a strange idea occurred to her—that she should reach out and touch him, smooth the stress lines etched into his brow. His face relaxed for a moment just inches away from hers, then in an instant it snapped back into the cold professional mask of before.

"Go, get some rest, we leave at noon." He spoke curtly and released her, then turned quickly and strode off in the direction of the dining hall.

∼

"The Fae embassy. Are you kidding me?" Sabre shook his head at the news as he wiped down his long sword. He paused and swept the copper braids from his face. "It's three days ride to Shallaha."

"More like four, as we're forced to take the girl," replied Nyle, his face grim. "It's doubtful she's ridden much, living here."

Three days riding with an untrained girl, and for what? More politics? Nyle hated Shallaha, the capital city of central Shaman. He hated the Fae embassy even more. The Fae. Hiding in their own realm and slipping into Shallaha through a portal in the embassy when they felt like it. They would all go scurrying back when word of this attack reached Shallaha. The Fae didn't age, but they could be killed. They protected their obscenely long lives with a cowardly veneer of neutrality. Nyle had no doubt that if the daemons did find a way into Shaman in larger numbers, the Fae would shut down the embassy portal and cut all ties with this realm.

He surveyed the weaponry he'd managed to cobble together from around the university. Essentially, he had a pile of kitchen knives, cleavers, farm tools, and a few ceremonial swords heavy with ornate trimming. They were setting up the south quad for a combat lesson. All students above the age of sixteen were commanded to attend, and it was going to be a vastly different learning experience to those the students were used to. Nyle could only afford to leave one warrior here until reinforcements came, so the staff and students would have to manage the best they could against any further attacks. The major rift in the south chamber held as the witch had said it would, but that didn't mean that creatures couldn't get through smaller rifts elsewhere and gather here.

It seemed the creatures were following some sort of plan. The idea worried Nyle—what kind of being could rally the forces of hell? Who could persuade creatures of chaos to work towards a single purpose? *The forces of Gehenna are coming.* The ażote's words returned to him. He'd never heard of a daemon powerful enough to command the obedience of the anarchic ażote. He would have to leave a warrior here he trusted - one that would keep his wits about him and find a way to deal with this new threat.

Sabre's voice interrupted his somber speculation. "Even if we get there and back in time, the Fae won't help us. They're safe in their city, hidden behind the portal, protected from the forces of Gehenna."

"The witch says the prince was her brother."

"Bloody stuck up, vain, mincing, good-for-nothing, whiny, pretty boy, mind-magician," Sabre muttered whilst he used a stick to draw out a combat circle in the dirt. Nyle suppressed a smile.

"I agree," replied Nyle, "but with the girl and her tattoo to aid our cause, he has greater incentive to step in."

"How's this for an incentive? If the forces of Gehenna invade the Shaman lands, the Fae have a new set of very noisy, very *ugly* neighbors."

Sabre had a point. The ageless, vain Fae valued beauty above everything else. The misshapen races of Gehenna roaming around the realm closest to them might cause . . . discomfort. Also, the Fae couldn't trade with daemons as they traded with the Shaman.

Sabre paced around the circle. The man was highly strung, as were all Nyle's soldiers at the moment. Attacks had been much more frequent of late. His warrior troops were stretched and ragged. Every time they thought they were winning there was another incursion, another village ravaged by daemons. Sometimes they got there in time. The mages at the camp did a good job of pinpointing rifts, small tears between this realm and the next that allowed handfuls of daemons passage. Sometimes the mages failed, and the pressure was taking a heavy toll. Even Sabre, who usually had the easiest manner of all his warriors, was pacing and snarling like a cornered lynx.

"What of the girl?" asked Sabre, practicing vicious

forward strokes with a large flat broadsword. "Is she up to the task? It'll be a hard journey."

Nyle's thoughts turned to the healer with the red hair. He remembered how she defied him in the south chamber when he had told her to rest, returning to the dining room, throwing herself into helping the injured despite her obvious fatigue. "Aye, she'll be okay."

"And the witch marked her?"

Nyle nodded. "The Fae seal." He paused, suddenly embarrassed. "There was something else. The witch said it was written—" Nyle turned away and reached for a weapon. "—that I had a chapter in the Book of Ages."

Sabre stopped what he was doing and turned to his commanding officer, and his expression changed from anger to surprise. Then he smiled. "No offence, Nyle, but I doubt a common fighter from the mountains has been afforded a place in the Divine Book—even as a footnote."

Nyle laughed out loud; it felt good after the stress of the past few days. He could always count on Sabre to give him some perspective.

"So, this girl, what's she like?" Sabre stretched out his big bear-like frame, rolling his shoulders back to loosen his muscles.

Nyle became intently focused on his task, and he answered gruffly, "Young." Then remembered finding her facing down three ażote. "But . . . gutsy."

Sabre raised an eyebrow. "Tall praise from you, especially for a civilian."

Nyle shrugged and carried on working, avoiding his friend's questioning stare. "She's a good healer."

"That may come in handy on the road. Is she pretty?"

An image flashed through Nyle's mind of Danika's creamy skin, of locks of red hair curling into the soft curve of her neck, her warm golden eyes meeting his as they ran to the south chamber. He picked up a long thin rapier with a soiled edge and began cleaning the blade. "I didn't notice," he said, rubbing vigorously. "I'd more important things to consider, like, the fate of the world." The words came out sharper than he'd intended.

"Okay, brother, okay." Sabre held up his hands in mock surrender. "I was only going to suggest that if she is easy on the eye, you should keep her away from Torin. He brings trouble when it comes to females; they can't get enough of him. Last year, on a supply trip to Shallaha, I swear he worked it so that the prostitutes paid him!"

Nyle grasped the hilt of the now spotless sword tightly and made some slicing practice strokes. "She's her own woman, of age. I am not her nursemaid. If she wants to become the latest in a long line of Torin's conquests, it is not up to me to prevent it." He viciously thrust the rapier into the heart of the closest sack man, straw and sand poured from the gaping wound.

Until now, Nyle had never bothered himself over Torin's amorous exploits. His warriors fought hard and played hard. Torin played harder than most, and Nyle once had to mollify the disgruntled family of a deflowered village girl demanding recompense. After that he'd made Torin promise to stick to brothel houses or, at the very least, choose women with a bit more experience. However, the thought of Torin seducing the redheaded healer made him want to take the rapier and prevent Torin from deflowering anyone, ever again. He impaled the dummy a second time and left the sword buried to the hilt.

Sabre snorted and grinned. Nyle ignored him. The last thing Nyle needed right now, what with the world falling down around his ears and the risk of a daemon invasion of catastrophic proportions, was some kind of infatuation. He would work out his tension in other ways.

The students began to arrive in time for some hard training. Nyle scrutinized the young Shaman students who were filing into the quad.

Sabre whispered in Nyle's ear, "They're a sorry looking crew."

And they were—stringy, bookish, and rangy; not much to work with—but all they had. Nyle sighed. "You need to train these . . . these cadets as best you can, Sabre." Nyle would have loved to leave Torin here in charge of the university, and far away from Danika, but Torin knew Shallaha better than any of the others; he'd been posted there. So, it was with a heavy heart that he delivered the news to Sabre.

"Mark these students well, Sabre. They're your new army."

There was a pause. "I'm the one staying?" Sabre's face fell.

Nyle could tell he wanted to protest, but he knew his friend would accept his duty without complaint. "Aye. Build a defense unit out of this lot, train up anyone that shows an aptitude for battle. There was that student with a real gift for physical magic, the one that cast a protective dome in the hall. She has potential."

"Her name's Layla. She is somewhat of a heroine to them all now."

"Find others with talent and put her in charge of teaching them. Also, reinforce the supply lines and increase stockpiles. If we cannot get back in time, or if the Fae refuse to help—this may become the last stand against the forces of Gehenna."

The two warriors surveyed the small crowd of Shaman; Sabre hadn't much time to turn this raggle-taggle group of academics into a brave and efficient fighting unit.

Nyle raised his voice so the students could hear. "Come and chose a weapon." Then as a skinny, bespectacled youth almost toppled over under the weight of a full-length broadsword, he rolled his eyes and added, "Preferably one you can lift!"

The rest of the students cautiously shuffled over to the piles of knives, swords, and cleavers and began sorting through them. They picked up items gingerly, making experimental swipes and lunges. One student was nearly decapitated by an overly eager girl brandishing a scythe. Luckily Sabre was able to intercede.

Nyle shouted for everyone to stand in a circle.

Training had begun.

~

Increasing noise outside made Danika move to the window to look down into the quad. A mob of students gathered, surrounding the commanding warrior from earlier, whose name she'd discovered was Nyle. He was with another large warrior with similar weather-darkened skin, but long braided hair. The warriors handed out an assortment of swords, knives, and dangerous-looking farm tools.

Danika watched as Nyle conducted a class in fighting. He demonstrated some simple techniques and soon had his pupils confidently blocking and parrying his advances as he passed around the group. She noted how easily he moved, despite his size, smoothly rolling from one position to the next. He carefully controlled his sword to avoid injuring his inexperienced students but made it hard for them, enabling them to increase their ability and confidence on each try. He was good at what he did, thought Danika. Exceptional, in fact.

At that moment Nyle shrugged off his shirt, slung it to the side, and continued the lesson. Danika remained at the window. The warrior's torso looked to have been hewn from stone, every muscle clearly visible under his tanned skin. As he moved, the muscles in his stomach and chest rippled and stretched. Danika couldn't look away, drawn by how his body moved. Mesmerized, she watched his graceful rhythm as he demonstrated a complex sword technique. The morning sun reflected off his damp skin, accentuating his wide shoulders and sculpted back. Intricate clan tattoos with beautiful designs weaved in bands around his body, some of them framing scars.

Layla returned to the dorm. "They're serving food in the lobby," she said as she approached the window. "Come on, Danni, I'm starving. I'm . . . what are you looking at? Oh my!" She, too, remained standing at the window.

"Who is the guy with the braids . . . with the really big sword?"

"I think his name is Sabre."

"He's . . . these mountain-men are very . . . tall. Do you think it is true what they say?"

Danika broke from watching Nyle for a moment and took a sly sideways glance at her friend. "What do they say?" she asked in a mock innocent tone.

Layla blushed. "You know . . . that they have . . . voracious appetites."

Danika smiled and looked back at the sparring warriors. Rumors about men from the mountain clans abounded. It was said they were insatiable sexual partners who often spent days, weeks even, in a haze of carnal pleasure. There were also rumors of bloodletting and branding practices, although Danika suspected—hoped?—these were wildly exaggerated. The reputation of the mountain men as consummate and gluttonous lovers was such that it was rumored that rich Shaman women paid large sums of money for the favors of a man of the clans.

"Maybe you should ask Sabre, whether the rumors are true."

Layla blushed a deeper shade of pink. "I was just wondering. It's not important. Forget I said anything." Then after a pause, "I know you were wondering it too!"

Danika smiled sheepishly, and both girls giggled.

Danika turned back to the warrior's demonstration—she'd definitely been wondering.

Sabre stood aside and allowed a skinny bespectacled youth to take his place against Nyle. The young student hefted a large sword and started swinging it wildly in Nyle's direction.

Nyle stretched back to avoid the artless attack, revealing more of his taut stomach and a flash of something lower; Danika gasped. The warrior's head flicked upwards, his fierce cobalt eyes meeting hers. His face showed an instant of recognition, and his lips twisted into a sly grin before his expression extended into a mask of anguished surprise. He fell to the floor clutching his wounded thigh.

Danika, eyes wide, heart pounding, virtually flew down the stairs, Layla following closely behind. At the bottom, she almost crashed into the bespectacled student who was hovering at the foot of the stairs. He was clutching the bloody blade in his hand.

"I didn't mean to . . . Don't let him kill me!"

Behind him, Sabre was supporting Nyle as he shuffle-hopped into the common room and collapsed into a chair. The common room was crowded, and Danika had to push through a gaggle of students to get to him.

"Everyone out." Frowning, she jabbed her finger at the student still holding the bloody sword. "Especially you!" Layla and Sabre herded the students out. She turned to Layla as her friend was leaving. "Make sure no one comes in." Layla nodded and led Sabre outside.

They were alone.

Danika rolled her shirtsleeves to her elbows. "How much does it hurt?"

"It doesn't," replied the warrior gruffly. "I've had worse, much worse. A few stitches and I'll be fine."

Kneeling by the warrior, Danika examined the wound

through the tear in his trousers. "The wound is deep, but luckily the knife missed the femoral artery." She ripped the cloth farther apart and placed her palms at the top of his solid thigh. "Just keep still. I'll only take a few minutes."

She centralized her healing energy and began the process of manipulating blood and tissue. As she worked, she became increasingly aware of the warrior's closeness; it unnerved her and made it difficult to concentrate. His bare stomach was a mere inches from her face. Muscles and nerves she'd spent years studying, sketching from books, and neatly labelling, were now laid out before her in glorious detail.

As she leant farther towards him to reach the edge of the wound, she could smell the sweat on his skin; it smelt damp and slightly tart like a ripe apple, and she found herself wondering what it might taste like. A wayward part of her mind suggested it would taste good.

Voracious appetites. She shook her head slightly trying to clear her mind. What kind of healer thinks about licking her patient? Get a grip on yourself, Danika!

In an attempt to focus on the job in hand, Danika talked as she worked. "You were giving lessons to the other students." It was a statement—the warrior didn't respond. "It was good of you to do that. I mean, it's good . . . that you would do that." She allowed her power to flow into the damaged tissue trying valiantly to concentrate only on the area affected and not allow her imagination to wander to any of the surrounding areas. She kept her head down as she worked, afraid that her expression might convey something very unlike the cool ministrations of a seasoned healer.

Her hands caressed the wound, and she felt the warrior become very still. Her errant mind flicked back to Nyle giving his lessons; it replayed images of the half-naked warrior working his steel in the sunlight—his back and his shoulders, wet and glistening, the dark line of hair that traced down low on his flat stomach. Danika glanced upwards; yes, the line was still there, marking a path downward. She swallowed hard. She needed to lean inwards and press more firmly to knit the skin. Her face was almost in his lap; she let out a soft breath that she couldn't hold any longer.

The warrior growled deep in his chest, a deep, low rumble as her magic flowed from her into him and her breath caressed his skin. He gripped the arms of the chair till his knuckles turned white, his body tensed. She looked up and met his fierce gaze bearing down on her.

As a healer she had studied every part of the body belonging to both women and men. However, practicing on skinny youths and elders hadn't prepared her for anything like this. She met his blazing stare and tried to sound like she was indifferent. "Sit still, please, I'm nearly there." Her voice instead came out cracked and raspy. She tried to clear her throat. She struggled to ignore the oak tree, almost escaping her patient's trousers.

He muttered something under his breath, it sounded like "So am I!" but she ignored it. As her power continued to flow, he closed his eyes, his head flopped back, and he murmured what sounded like a short prayer.

CHAPTER 4

He was the commanding officer of an elite band of fearsome warriors, he'd faced the creatures of hell on a regular basis, he was a proud man of the mountains from a long line of powerful, respected Northfolk, and he was about to embarrass himself in his trousers like an untried youth if this little witch continued with her infuriating *treatment*. He gripped the chair tighter. The healers at the barracks were gnarly old Shaman men, gruff and battle-scarred. He doubted they would have bothered using magic on a cut such as this; instead, just stitching him up with yarn and sending him on his way.

He was about to go insane. Her soft caress on his inner thigh, her gentle breath on his skin, her warm breast resting on his lap… He groaned again and felt the arm of the chair give a little in his fist. She shifted position, and as she did so, her small breasts strained against the linen of her shirt. Looking down, he could see the outline of a nipple pressed against the thin fabric. He desperately wanted to rub the pad of his thumb over that nipple, feel it grow harder under the linen; he wanted to kneel before her and take the hardened tip into his mouth, gently squeeze it between his teeth before suckling it hard and then feel her writhe and moan in his arms—think about something else, Nyle, anything other than the young woman kneeling before him! Nyle tried to think about the upcoming journey to Shallaha. They would travel light, just him, Torin, Alyssa, and the girl to avoid arousing suspicion. They would—Dear Goddess, have mercy. What was she doing to him now?

It wasn't just her proximity; her magic was somehow erotic. He felt the thrumming power channeling into him. It travelled deep into his groin, a warm thick flow of energy that surged into his bollocks and along his shaft, such an exquisite feeling that he couldn't think of anything other than her body wound tightly around his, her slender arms clutching onto him as he thrust into her warm softness, her calling out his name as she rode climax after climax after—

Nyle stood up sharply. "Enough!"

The little healer tumbled backwards, ending up flat on her backside, her face flushed and her shirt askew.

"We're short on time, and I need to prepare for leaving. I suggest you do the same."

"I was nearly done… it will only take a few more moments. The wound in your thigh…"

But Nyle was already halfway out of the room; the wound in his thigh was the least of his concerns. It was going to be a long journey to Shallaha.

~

The frigid bath was cleaning off the blood and sweat of the morning but was failing to wash away his dark mood. As Nyle scoured his naked body with a stiff, soapy brush, he brooded on earlier events. After his reaction to the healer's ministrations, he'd left her company and sought refuge in the bathhouse. It took half an hour sitting chest high in cold water for the effect Danika had on him to diminish. He again cursed the little healer all the way to Gehenna.

It had been too long since he'd felt the touch of a woman. He had been too busy with all the creature incursions to visit the establishments that littered the villages around the barracks, those that catered specifically to the clansmen and women. He was bitterly regretting his tardiness. Unbonded men of the mountain clans were encouraged to take mistresses or visit brothels from the age of seventeen. Otherwise, they became overly aggressive, their judgement clouded. He'd visited prostitutes many times in the past. He remembered his first bumbling, awkward experience when, as cadets, he and Sabre had visited an infamous townhouse in a local village. He'd been assisted by an older woman, Zepta, with dark hair and deeply tanned skin that was always warm, as if the sunlight of her coastal homeland had been absorbed into her and never left. She'd guided him patiently. Nyle had found the whole experience... satisfactory.

He'd never taken a mistress. His visits to the village, to Zepta, proved adequate, if not wholly fulfilling. A mistress would have taken a certain commitment; he preferred to keep things simple. His commitment was to his work and his duty. Women tended to get in the way. Look at Torin, for example.

And as for taking a kish'la… he'd admitted to himself long ago that the life of husband and father was not an option for him. Family life would conflict with his duty. His wife would be left alone for long periods while he went away to fight, always living with the uncertainty of whether he would return, and if he did, whether he would return unchanged.

What kind of life was that for a beloved one? Never seeing their mate, always fearful, always wary—that was no way to live. Some clansmen had taken on the bond, but bonded men quickly got themselves reassigned, far away from the action. Nyle loved his job, loved fighting on the front line, only felt truly alive and vital when hunting the creatures of chaos. A family would only rob him of the thing he lived for.

He carefully washed his wound, which was all but healed. She'd done her job well—too well! Her delicate little hand massaging his leg, the humming of her magic as it pulsed through his veins and spread into his groin… Nyle squeezed his eyes shut as the memory of her warm breath on his flesh returned unbidden. His cock stiffened despite the cool water. Nyle's head dropped back as he gritted his teeth together in frustration. Again? Really!

Accepting the inevitable, that his lust was not about to dissipate of its own accord, Nyle conceded that he would need to take things into his own hands, so to speak—that little redheaded witch had a lot to answer for. Nyle grasped his heavy shaft in his palm.

There was a discreet cough from the doorway.

Nyle jumped, snatching both hands out of the water and causing a wave of soapy water to splatter onto the bathhouse floor.

"Should I have knocked?" Alyssa approached his bathtub, regarding Nyle with cool blue eyes. Her impassive expression didn't flicker for a moment, despite coming upon her commanding officer in such awkward circumstances. Alyssa, he knew, was used to naked soldiers, since in the field there was often no room for social graces.

"What is it?" asked Nyle, frowning, his hands firmly gripping the edge of the bath.

"A message from the main camp. There have been further attacks. The incursions are getting more frequent, especially in the lands surrounding the university. Warriors have already been dispatched to deal with it."

"And the major rift here at the university?"

"The Elders estimate it will break open—a week, maybe two."

Alyssa's face was blank, as usual, difficult to read, but her pause suggested there was more. "What else did they say?"

"That it will not be like the incursions we normally fight. That if the rift breaks open, it will allow all of Gehenna passage, not just smaller daemons like the ażote." She gave him a hard stare. "We must get help from the Fae. Force them if they refuse."

Nyle's face was grim. "A week. That's cutting it fine."

"More so if the girl can't ride. I don't expect she can."

Nyle paused. Alyssa was right; he'd bet those soft hands were unaccustomed to the bite of reigns and bridle. *Do not think about her soft hands!*

"Are you okay, sir?"

"What? Why?" snapped Nyle, more harshly than he'd intended.

"You looked … erm… nothing." Alyssa backed off a few steps.

Nyle ran his hands roughly over his wet hair. "Pass me a towel, and then check Sabre has everything he needs to stay here. Ready some good horses, the best you can find, pack light; we can get supplies as we go. Be ready to move out in half an hour."

Alyssa turned to go.

"And, Alyssa, one other thing."

Alyssa paused, turned back.

"Make sure the healer is prepared and ready to leave."

She rolled her eyes. "Sure. Ready for a hard, three-day ride, bug bites, drinking from puddles, and getting dressed and undressed in front of a bunch of men from the clans. I doubt she's prepared for that!" Alyssa turned and left the bathhouse.

Nyle sat stone still in the soapy bath, ashen faced, clutching the crumpled towel tightly in his fist.

Dressed and undressed in front of a bunch of men of the clans—Goddess have mercy!

∼

DANIKA LEANED BACK AGAINST THE OUTER WALL THAT marked the boundary of the university. How long would it be before she saw this place, her home, again? She didn't consider the house she'd spent the first years of her life, home. Her life had begun when she'd been accepted here. This is where she'd met the people she loved, those that loved her.

"It's beautiful." Layla was examining her wrist, running her finger over its intricate design. She released Danika, who bent down to stuff another scroll into her already bulging pack.

"Let's hope it convinces the prince we're telling the truth."

"About Elder-Sha Ameena?"

Danika nodded sadly. "I still can't believe she's gone, and Elder Kaine."

The friends stood silently together for a while, the golden afternoon light heating the rough stone. For a moment, Danika just rested, leaning against the warm rock.

"I couldn't save her, Danni, they went straight after her." Layla paused and covered her face with her hands, as if trying to hide away from the memory of the attack. "There were so many I couldn't save. Once the barrier was up, I couldn't risk…"

Danika opened her eyes; the soft honey sunlight was too beautiful to face full on. She turned and embraced her friend, held her tightly, wishing she could be a salve to this kind of pain like she could the physical kind. She whispered in her friend's ear, "It's okay, Layla, it's okay. You did the right thing." They stood together for a long moment.

Layla stepped back and wiped her tears away with her

sleeve. "The warriors have suggested we contact the surrounding villagers and get them to come inside."

"It's a good plan, better to have a stronghold and focus all the protection we have." Danika wished she could stay with her friend. After all they'd been through over the past day, she felt sick at the idea of more upheaval, leaving everything she knew and loved, not knowing when she would be back—or if.

"One of the warriors, the one staying here—Sabre." Layla paused for a moment. "He wants us to stockpile supplies and train up a student guard unit, and he says we need to send messengers to his camp, to call for reinforcements." Danika's friend distractedly ran her hand through her curly brown hair and looked back towards the university. "He does seem to have a vast quantity of opinions, in fact."

Danika saw a small frown crease Layla's brow and wondered how her friend would cope now the remaining Elder-Shas and students were looking to her for direction. She took her friend's hand and gave it a squeeze. "Layla, you may be one of the most powerful witches this university has ever seen, but you can't do this on your own. Work with Sabre, let him take some of the strain."

It was a huge responsibility that now burdened her friend. Danika realized that after last night, they were both very different from the young, carefree women who were supposed to be finishing their last exam in just a few days.

"How is the captain's thigh?" asked Layla.

Danika felt her face grow warm. "Fine." He'd left her sitting on the floor, had just walked out before she'd had a chance to finish the healing. She'd been dismissed without a word.

"Be careful amongst those warriors, Val. They are notorious for their temper and their—"

"And their what?" Both girls quickly turned to face the pale-haired female warrior—the one called Alyssa; she towered over them, her eyebrows raised questioningly. "Bad manners? Coarseness?" she paused and smirked. "Their sexual deviance maybe?"

Both Danika and Layla shifted uncomfortably.

"I just want Danika to travel safely," replied Layla. "I didn't mean to insult—"

The warrior scowled. "Danika won't travel anywhere at all lugging that thing." She gestured to the large, well-stuffed pack on the ground.

"It's just essentials," Danika protested, "clothes and books, and supplies for healing and—" Danika gasped as the warrior coolly opened the drawstring, then upended the sack all over the floor. Her precious possessions: her sketchbook, her bags of herbs, her dissecting knives, her wash bag—*her underwear*. Everything lay in a heap on the floor as the blonde woman picked over it all, selecting one or two items to stuff back into the bag. "I need my healing supplies… put that down. Now!" shouted Danika, trying to scoop up as many belongings as possible.

"Can't you just, you know," she flexed her fingers at Danika, "'shoot' people with your hands when they're hurt? Why do you need—" She picked up a jar and squinted her eyes at the label. "—balm of thistles?" The warrior grimaced and threw the jar onto the growing pile of rejected items.

"It heals bites and stings. My power only works on injuries, not on infections or diseases," snapped Danika, trying to bundle up her underclothes and class notes. "I've spent the last six years studying what to do when I can't just 'shoot' people. Haven't the healers at the gates ever given you a draught or a poultice?"

"No," the warrior paused for a moment, "I don't get on with the healers."

"Really?" replied Danika. "I can't imagine why!" She snatched the jar of thistle balm from the pile, only to have the warrior wrest it from her and toss it back. "We might need it!" said Danika.

"Just don't get bitten," replied Alyssa.

The warrior picked up the practically empty pack and dumped it at Danika's feet. "That's all you'll need. Anything else will slow down the horses." She turned to go, and Danika quietly reached for the thistle balm once more. "Don't even think about it, or I'll make you leave behind the cotton underthings." She spoke over her shoulder, and Danika pulled back her hand, exhaling sharply. Thistles or underthings—what kind of choice was that?

Layla looked at Danika with an expression of sympathy. "I could drop a boulder on her head—make it look like an accident."

Danika smiled, then looked down and sighed. "She's probably right. Just make sure this lot gets back to the dorm." She gestured to her belongings, her life, everything she knew now lying before her in a big messy pile. Layla nodded and began packing it all up.

Nyle came into view, leading two horses.

The warrior stood a hand taller than both horses, his muscular arms holding both beasts securely by the reigns. His face was hard and angular, dark stubble shadowing a wide jaw. He seemed dispassionate and efficient, his cool blue eyes appraising the situation, appraising her. Her heart began to pound; she took a deep breath to calm herself.

"Do you ride, girl?" His voice was as hard as his features.

Danika let out her breath quickly and attempted to match his curt manner. "My name is Danika, and I would be grateful—"

Nyle cut her off. "We've three days' ride to Shallaha. I would be grateful if we didn't have to drag you and the horse every inch of it. Now, do you know how to ride… Danika?"

"I have ridden," replied Danika, meeting his stare, "a time ago."

"Finish your farewells. We need to leave." He handed her the set of reigns belonging to a massive beast. "This is Smoke—be firm with him." With that, he sprung up onto his horse's back in one fluid movement.

Two more riders approached. The evil female warrior rode alongside the handsome archer Danika recognized from the evening before. Nyle greeted them with a nod and turned to Danika. "Alyssa and Torin are coming with us."

Alyssa didn't even acknowledge Danika, pulling up without a word.

Torin smiled widely, producing a perfect pair of dimples and white, even teeth. For a moment, Danika's mind went blank in the presence of such a blindingly attractive man.

"You've a big animal there, red-hair. I hope you can handle him." He gave Danika a playful wink. Danika didn't know quite know how to reply, so she half-smiled and turned away and faced the horse's flank. Smoke stomped and snorted, impatient, it seemed, to be underway.

"Concentrate on your own animal, Torin!" snapped Nyle, reining his horse around and pulling up alongside. "Stop wasting time. The afternoon draws on."

Torin shrugged. "Yes, sir!" He trotted on.

Danika jumped up, struggling inelegantly into the saddle, and somehow managing to face the right way. Despite her brave words, it had been a while since she had ridden, more accustomed as she was to the comfort of a wagon. Alyssa flashed Danika a look of disdain as she expertly brought her mount around and set off at a trot towards the road.

Layla tried to wave, but her arms were filled with Danika's belongings, so in the end she simply nodded. "Take care of yourself. Come back soon."

Danika blew her friend a kiss and readied to go.

"Danika. Danika!" Micah ran from the doorway and flung himself at her leg.

"They won't let me learn to fight. They say I'm too young!" Micah was close to tears. "I thought if you told them how brave I'd been, and how we had beaten back those monsters, they would let me train with the cadets. I'm not afraid. Don't make me stay with the old women."

Danika bent down from her horse to be closer to the

boy. She brushed a lock of hair from his eyes. "I know you're very brave, Micah, but it's dangerous training with weapons. I'm sorry." Danika was touched by the boy's pleas but understood why he'd been forbidden to fight. It would be a sorry state of affairs when Shaman started conscripting children as young as ten.

Danika was surprised to hear Nyle speak. His voice was firm, but it lacked its usual curtness. "I have a job for you, boy. Report to Sabre and tell him you are to be his assistant on my orders. Do you understand?"

Obviously in awe of the great warrior, Micah looked up and managed to stutter, "Y-yes, sir!"

"You are to report to him and only to him." Nyle spurred his horse around and started off towards the road at a trot.

Giving a parting wave, Danika gracelessly and awkwardly followed. Looking back over her shoulder, she watched Micah smiling and waving, his little face aglow, and Layla standing arms laden.

She turned to Nyle, who was staring intently at the road ahead.

"That was nice of you… to help Micah like that."

Nyle faced Danika and shrugged. "A man needs a duty; a boy is never too young to learn that." He leant farther down in the saddle and called out, "Ride on, a three-quarter pace!"

The warriors' mounts obediently streamed forward, sleek, and powerful, thundering along the road. Danika's horse took a more leisurely pace.

Then stopped—for a mid-afternoon snack.

And refused to go any farther.

CHAPTER 5

Nyle rarely made a mistake. But as he shifted again in his saddle to relieve some of the pressure that had been building over the past few hours, he had to concede that this time he'd significantly miscalculated. Trying hard to concentrate on anything other than the contents of his trousers, he considered the chain of events leading up to his serious error.

Firstly, in his defense, the girl had obviously never ridden. From the start, she'd bobbed in the saddle like an unbelted sack of beans. Her mount, taking full advantage of his rider's ineptitude, stopped to graze. This had resulted in the girl pleading with the beast, then threatening him, and finally heaping abuse on him, all whilst the unconcerned animal chewed on. The final straw had been when she climbed down and started physically dragging her horse forward. Alyssa had given Nyle an arched look and rode on. Torin had followed, chuckling to himself.

Aware of the necessity for haste, Nyle had trotted back and dismounted.

The woman was a dirty, flustered mess when he reached her. "He's different from the horses I'm used to," she'd told him. "He doesn't obey my commands. I think he's stupid."

"Aye, lass, he's happily munching on gorse whilst you do all the work. He's definitely stupid."

Before she could retort, he'd taken the little healer firmly by the waist, lifted her, and planted her on his own saddle behind him.

"Ride with me. I have a much cleverer horse."

And there was his mistake!

For the last few hours, he'd endured the delicious sensation of having his passenger's firm, rounded breasts pressed into the small of his back. He was achingly aware that a few pathetically insufficient layers of fabric were all that separated her soft flesh from his. Add to this the rhythmic movement of the horse, and he was quickly losing his mind.

It hadn't been too bad to start off with. She'd sat stiffly behind him, her folded arms forming a buffer between them—a minor distraction perhaps, but wholly endurable. Then she'd dozed off. That's when Nyle had realized his mistake. Her full weight forward with her chest crushed against him, and her arms circling his waist—Nyle had become increasingly aware of his passenger. He fancied he could actually feel her breasts rubbing up and down his back, the friction sending his senses into a frenzy. Increasingly carnal images rolled around inside his head. An image of the healer laid out before him, naked, on a bear-rug. Her delicate wrists crossed above her head, her stiff little nipples raised to the sky. An image of him, naked, leaning down over her small frame, teasing her nipples with his tongue, suckling each swollen tip as she arched her back to meet him. He imagined himself moving downwards, pushing his tongue firmly into the spot between her hip bone and her belly, tracing a line lower towards her thighs, burying his head in her sweet—

"Are you okay, old friend? You seem a little distracted." Torin appeared at his side.

"No, fine. I'm fine. Everything's fine."

"I can take the Shaman girl for a while, give the old boy a bit of a rest." Torin inclined his head towards Nyle's horse, but the archer's smile was sly. A voice in Nyle's mind objected loudly and violently to the idea of putting Danika within ten feet of the seductive archer. He gritted his teeth. "We're fine! As I told you before, you worry about your own animal."

Torin laughed and rode onward to catch up with Alyssa. Nyle shifted in his saddle and tried once again to think about something other than the woman whose delicious body was being rhythmically forced against him.

The evening air was damp and woody, rich with the smell of earth and moss. The plains and forests of central Shaman were good terrain for travelling; the ground was generally even, there was game and forest cover, and the weather was temperate. You could sleep outside in the winter with just a fur and be none the worse for it. All so different from the harsh snows and arid rocky plains of his mountain home. It had been many years since he had set foot on his native land. At fourteen, he'd bid his family goodbye and journeyed south to report for training. It had been a proud day for him when he could write to his family and tell them that he had been selected for the elite squad.

Nyle looked over at Alyssa; the blonde warrior was hunkered down in the saddle, her gaze intent on the road ahead. Nyle didn't know Alyssa's story, except that she had no family—and was the only woman to ever pass the fearsome final tests to join this unit. She was a consummate warrior and had saved his life on a number of occasions. She'd earned the respect of every warrior she fought with, but she rarely fraternized with the other soldiers, preferring her own company.

His thoughts turned to the job at hand. They needed the help of the Fae, specifically, it seemed, the Prince. If he failed, he would go down in the ancient Book of Ages as the man who failed in his duty and caused the apocalypse. The thought left a bitter taste. He could not allow that to happen. That pampered Fae wastrel would fix the gates if he had to force him there at sword point.

Lost in thought, Nyle nearly missed the fallen log on the road. He brought his mount up sharply. There was a gasp from behind him and slender arms clutched tighter around his waist.

"Easy boy." He patted his horse's neck and trotted around the log. Light was low, and there would be no moon tonight. None of his soldiers had slept in days, and he needed them alert. Not to mention he didn't relish having to endure another hour of the frustrating ache in his groin, unable to do anything about it—and there was nothing he could about it—he had no intention of seducing the Shaman woman. Even if she was amenable, he didn't need any messy entanglements. *Would she be amenable?* The thought wedged itself in the back of his mind and stubbornly refused to budge as he trotted into a clearing away from the side of the road. It was an adequate place to make camp.

Stopping the horse, he slid from the saddle and turned to Danika to help her dismount. The woman wore a scowl that could turn milk. Before he could offer his arm, she scrambled off the horse, landing in a heap on the damp forest floor, glaring at him. *Probably not then*.

∼

DANIKA HAD BEEN HAVING A WONDERFUL DREAM. She couldn't remember the details, but she had the impression that at some point it involved a kind of furry blanket. Then she was rudely jerked awake to find herself on the back of a smelly horse holding onto a surly warrior, whom she hardly knew, in the middle of Goddess knew where—reality had definitely burst in unannounced. As memories of recent events settled back into place like a damp shroud, she noted that her legs had cramps, her arms were sore, and her breasts kind of ached, no doubt with all that bobbing about. Maybe she should have strapped her chest before leaving.

She also recalled the warrior's somewhat sarcastic reaction to her horse's obvious defective nature: *I have a much cleverer horse*. The humiliation of the afternoon flooded back. Emotionally drained, her body throbbing from the unaccustomed motion of riding, and nursing a heavily wounded pride, Danika ignored Nyle and dismounted. She misjudged the distance, however, and ended up tumbling to the ground. Getting up with as much dignity as she could muster, she smoothed down her riding clothes and ran her hand through her short, spiky hair.

Nyle raised an eyebrow. "Are you all right?"

"Fine, just… stiff," she answered curtly, turning away.

Nyle grunted and tended his horse.

Alyssa and Torin were already dismounted and busy with various camp building tasks, working with well-practiced efficiency. Nobody spoke. Everyone knew what to do and was busy doing it. Danika felt like an idiot just standing there without a purpose. It reminded her of life with her father—always in the way, always seen as an inconvenience, not to be trusted with anything important, always told to stop asking questions and stop being a bother.

She approached Torin. He'd seemed the friendliest warrior she'd met so far. "Can I help? I mean, is there anything I can do?"

The handsome warrior continued to roll out a leather ground cover, his sensuous mouth curving into a sly smile, and he looked up at Danika with impossibly clear emerald-green eyes. "There is something you could do for me, little red-hair. When I've finished here, I've some very sore muscles in my thighs that require medical attention. Perhaps you could…"

Danika nodded enthusiastically; a medical issue was just what she needed to take her mind off this awful day. "Great!" she replied, adding, "I came top of the class in massage therapy and muscle care."

"Really?" Torin's smile widened. "Then it could be said that you are... *experienced?*"

Danika beamed. "Absolutely! Well, a lot of my experience comes from working on toads. I don't want you to think I'm a master or anything, but it's actually a simple method of manipulating the Sartorius—"

"No one is massaging anyone!" Nyle stepped out from behind a nearby bush, glaring at Torin.

Danika nearly balked at the warrior's glacial gaze, but she held her ground. "It is not up to you whom I treat," she snapped. "I swore an oath! I'm a healer. It's my duty."

"Duty?" Nyle spat out the word like a curse. "You can't be... You didn't really think...? Goddess. He's not injured!" Nyle pointed at Torin but kept his gaze on Danika. "He's soliciting favors."

"Favors?" Danika paused for a moment until realization dawned. "Don't be ridiculous." She turned to Torin. "Go on, tell him how much your muscles hurt."

Torin looked sheepish. "Urm... my leg is a little sore."

Nyle glowered.

"But... it's something I could probably live with."

Danika stood open-mouthed for a moment, feeling her face grow hot with shame. *How did I not realize? These are clansmen; it's all they ever think about! Idiot, idiot, idiot.*

She turned on her heel and started off into the forest, her face burning.

"Where are you going?" asked Nyle to her retreating back, and when she didn't answer, "Don't go far. There could be predators."

Without stopping, she shouted back over her shoulder

at the two warriors. "I'll take my chances." She stomped off into the forest alone.

∽

Humiliation boiled inside her as she marched off in search of a moment's solitude. What was she doing in this filthy, insect-ridden wilderness surrounded by coarse, rude, uncivilized soldiers? This whole thing was such a waste of time. Even if they reached the embassy and were permitted to speak to the prince, how was she going to convince him to help the Shaman? What was she going to say? Up until now, Danika had just assumed she would find the words when the time came. Words and opinions she had plenty of. Tact, on the other hand. Nyle, the tall dark-haired warrior with the steely blue eyes, definitely lacked tact. What was it he said? "You didn't really think? Goddess. He's not injured!" Well, excuse her if she hadn't come across rampant, horny, insincere, deceitful clansmen in her time spent at a Shaman university—insensitive brute.

Danika stumbled on a root and nearly fell. She forced herself to stop for a moment, to calm herself, to breathe. She slowed her pace, then stooped to pick a handful of wild strawberries growing by the path, relishing the sweet juices as she crushed each soft fruit between her tongue and the roof of her mouth. Spying a pod of milk thistles, she stuffed her pockets, careful not to free the hot sap. She would brew them up to make a warming tea.

The woodsy smell of earth and wild garlic that hung heavy in the early evening air conjured up memories of

Elder-Sha Ameena's workshop. Danika allowed her mind to drift back to the round stone room nested in a narrow turret, looking out over the forests to the north and farmland to the west. She smiled at the memory of the little wooden drawers of herbs and plants that lined the walls, each offering up a small, scented gift as she opened it. She remembered the way the dust danced in the evening sunlight filtering through the windows as she worked after lessons. How many hours had she spent bent over the large oak table, mixing potions, curing sick frogs, and perfecting her blends? Five thousand maybe? No, many more. People thought her palm magic was the greatest healing power a healer could possess. She knew otherwise.

Her power was a gift, but it was limited. She couldn't help herself, for example, palm magic had no effect on the wielder. Battle healers would often work in pairs so that if one were hurt, the other could treat the wound. She'd sometimes wondered what it would be like to take on such a job. The chaos, the adventure... the danger. It was not usual for a woman to take on such a role, but not unheard of either. The gift of healing also depended on her own reserves of strength. Every dose she administered depleted her energy, and healers had been known to work themselves to death, attempting to heal too many people or those too far gone to help. She regained her strength quicker than most, but even she didn't have a bottomless supply. A good reason to learn herbal remedies, Danika.

Danika's thoughts returned to her Elder-Sha Ameena. "Pah, it is headaches—nothing more, child," the old woman would say and reach up her hands and rub her own temples. "Just fix me my preparation and leave me to rest." Danika paused as the pang of loss shot through her chest.

Elder-Sha Ameena—that was not even her real name. Jasmine—the princess of Elfain, and she was gone. A cool wind ruffled the trees, and Danika shivered. She noted the fading light. Now she would have to go back to camp and face the archer's attentions, Alyssa's unconcealed disdain, and worst of all, Nyle's patronizing irritation. And she would have to sleep on the ground.

Danika shivered again and began walking back through the gloom, clutching her arms around her body, and comforting herself with the thought that things probably couldn't get any worse.

∽

TORIN FINISHED SETTING UP CAMP AND FLOPPED TO THE ground near the fire. He grinned and unloaded a pile of wild strawberries from his pocket, trimmed them with his knife, and popped them in his mouth. "So, you have a thing for the healer then."

Nyle didn't answer.

"I always thought you and Alyssa might, you know, she seems more your type."

To be fair, this idea had occurred to Nyle a few times over the years. Alyssa was a soldier after all; she understood the warrior way of life, relished it in fact. She was beautiful, muscular, tall, but when he looked at her, he felt nothing but fraternal affection. "No, Alyssa and I are not… compatible," he said, offering some roasted rabbit to Torin. "I'm surprised you haven't tried to include her in your ever-eager harem."

Torin took on a wide-eyed, innocent expression. "I'm shocked you would suggest such a thing. She is my colleague, my friend, my sister. I would never sully that relationship for a quick tumble in a tavern stable."

"So, you invited her, and she declined?"

"If by declined you mean she tried to unman me with her broadsword, then, yes, she declined. But that was a long, long time ago. She's probably forgotten all about it." He paused, his face growing serious. "I'd die for her." The carefree archer gave Nyle a flat stare. "There is no one I would rather have with me in a fight. I respect her more than anyone, man, or woman. I would kill anyone that hurt her."

Nyle nodded slowly; he had long suspected that Torin's feelings for Alyssa went deeper than he let on.

A moment later Torin's expression returned to one of mocking amusement. "Well, if you have no designs on the redhead, maybe I should invite her into my eager harem… unless you have any objections?"

"Yes, I have objections! You know the Shaman see sex as a big deal. She's probably still a maid."

Torin rolled onto his back, put his hands under his head, and closed his eyes. "That's never put me off before—"

"She's young, she's naïve, and she's been living in a university surrounded by academics."

"Still not seeing the problem. She'll probably be curious, enthusiastic even."

Nyle's blood pumped harder in his veins at the thought of Torin and Danika together. His heart rate increased, and the muscles clenched in his jaw. "Danika won't be seduced into rolling around like a harlot in some hay barn on this mission, Torin, and if you try anything, I will *enthusiastically* stop you. Are we clear?"

Torin's smile widened. "Whatever you say. You're the boss."

"I promised the Fae princess I would keep her from harm."

"No problem. I'll back off."

"I aim to keep that promise." Nyle paced up and down the camp. "Harm definitely includes deflowerment."

Torin watched him from under half-open eyes. "I hear you, brother—no deflowering of redheaded maidens in hay barns... or anywhere else."

"I couldn't save the herb witch, but I will protect the healer." Nyle stopped pacing and spoke directly to Torin. "I have a duty to keep her safe, and in this, I will not fail!"

A high-pitched scream pierced the quiet evening.

CHAPTER 6

"GET... THEM... OFF... ME!" Danika was fighting to hold it together, and losing to panic, as the evil-looking insects crawled over her legs and torso. Sporcas—ugly mustard-colored creatures with the body of a hairy spider and the up-curled sting of a scorpion. They also had tiny sharp fangs, Danika noted as her faculties threatened to depart and let madness reign supreme.

"Don't move! They won't sting unless they think you're a threat," said Alyssa, flicking them off, one by one, with her sword.

Danika had a lot of experience with sporcas in the labs and workshops of the university; their blood soothed a fever if correctly administered. But they were generally dead when they got to her, not alive and... investigating. "Hurry, please, please hurry hurryhurryhurry." Danika stood hunched over and still, her arms outstretched, her eyes squeezed tightly shut. *This is not happening, not happening...*

Alyssa picked off two more from Danika's shoulder, as three others scuttled up the healer's leg. "Why weren't you looking where you were going?"

"I was thinking about… other stuff."

Nyle arrived, panting.

"What in the name of the Goddess is going on?" demanded Nyle between laboring breaths.

"Sporcas. Help me get them off her," replied Alyssa.

Nyle joined in. The two warriors flicked the creatures off with the tip of their swords.

Torin, on his arrival, began to shoot others with tiny sparks from his fingers. The creatures fell to the ground on their backs and smoldered.

"What's in your pockets? It's getting them excited," said Nyle.

"Milk thistles."

"Drop them on the ground. Do it gently! No sudden movements."

A group of the beasties scuttled after the spiky plants, but many remained scampering over Danika's flesh, pricking her skin with their pointed little legs.

"I thought girls picked daisies and honey-cups," mumbled Nyle as he picked off the creatures.

"You can't make an effective analgesic from daisies," said Danika testily.

Danika kept as still as she could, trying her best to ignore the feeling of nudging mandibles and prodding proboscides and god knows what else. Oh, Goddess, this is not happening. She tried to think about something else. The image of Nyle practicing swordplay in the quad flashed into her mind—she suppressed it. Now was so not the time to think about that!

"Didn't you see the nest?" Nyle said, breaking into Danika's thoughts and dragging her back to insect-infested reality. Her patience didn't so much snap as shatter into a million tiny glass-like pieces.

"Yes. I saw the nest, but I decided to jump in any way—just for fun!" She jerked around to face Nyle just as he was about to remove the last one.

"Stop moving, woman!"

But it was too late. Likely unnerved by the disappearance of his comrades and in a seemingly desperate attempt to exert some control over his confusing situation, the last remaining sporca, bit down hard, releasing a full dose of venom before meeting his end at the point of a sweeping broad sword.

Danika had never felt pain like it. It was as if someone had thrust a red-hot needle deep into her arm and then begun thumping the area with a mallet. Her knees buckled, and Nyle was there by her side in an instant, scooping her up.

"Come on. Let's get you back to the fire, lass. A sporca bite won't kill you, but it can sting a bit."

When they returned to camp, Nyle laid Danika out gently on a ground sheet and covered her in a blanket.

"Can I do anything?"

Danika gritted her teeth and gestured weakly to her bag. "The jar, the one labelled Thistle Balm, get it for me."

Nyle rummaged in Danika's bag and handed her the jar. Danika unscrewed the lid with her left hand and smeared the red preparation over her inflamed shoulder.

Alyssa raised her eyebrows. "So, you chose this over the underthings?"

Danika shrugged and nodded. For a moment, she thought she detected a look of surprised approval flash across the warrior's face, but only briefly before Alyssa's expression reverted to its usual disdain.

The preparation began to work and the pain ebbed. As it did so, Danika felt fatigue wash over her. Nyle insisted she eat some rabbit and drink a strong draught of something harshly bitter that made her warm inside. She snuggled down under the blanket and watched the fire spit amber sparks into the dark night air. As sleep claimed her, she thought she could feel someone gently brushing her hair from her face and the weight of an extra blanket keeping her warm, but it was difficult to tell what was dream and what was not.

~

NYLE HAD PUSHED THE PACE SINCE DAWN AND KEPT IT UP the whole day. He allowed only a short break for lunch. Now, in the fading light, he'd been forced to ease up to save the tiring horses.

The mood of the small company had started off tense that morning. On leaving the camp, Nyle insisted Danika ride with Alyssa, mumbling about the ill effects of excessive weight on his horse's ankles. It was a lame excuse, and he knew it, but he couldn't face another day with Danika's delicious body pressed up against him; it would send him insane. Alyssa lobbied hard against the extra "burden." Torin had stepped in and offered to carry

Danika but had been immediately denied by Nyle, again under the dubious auspices of "horse ankles." Torin had raised an eyebrow, but Nyle had silenced the archer with a stare. As a compromise, Danika was mounted on her own horse, which was being led by a stony-faced Alyssa.

However, as the day went on and they made good time, things had relaxed a little, and now spirits were surprisingly high. Danika was riding solo, under the watchful eye of Alyssa, and was keeping up the pace tolerably well. Torin kept up a stream of jokes and bawdy stories, some of which made even Nyle blush. He was sure such lewd exploits were inappropriate for young, well-educated healers. He looked across to Danika to gage her reaction; she was doubled up with giggles. Even Alyssa cracked a smile. Nyle envied his friend his ease with women.

Nyle's thoughts returned to the news that incursions were increasing. The creatures of Gehenna had spent thousands of years probing the entrance, slinking around the access points, looking for passage. They found it too, sometimes—small weaknesses in the membrane between this world and theirs, like temporary portals. Some creatures, once through, could summon others, but they could only ever come through a few at a time, and nothing big or powerful. Gehenna was home to creatures of nightmare and many of its inhabitants were massive and monstrous. They made the ażote look like house cats. But they'd need a much bigger portal to get here—like the rift at the university.

"What's life like—as a soldier?"

Nyle returned to the present with a jolt. The little

healer had ridden alongside without him noticing and was now casting him a questioning glance.

Nyle thought for a moment. "Solitary and rigorous but... well ordered," he replied. "It's disciplined, there is a rhythm to life, and everyone knows what is expected of them."

"Have you been doing it long?"

Goddess—what was it with all these questions? "Since the age of fourteen."

"Why did you choose this way of life?"

Nyle sighed and turned to Danika

"In the mountain clans, if someone shows certain aptitudes, they are sent as an apprentice or cadet to one of the training camps around Shaman. From there we are offered positions as peacekeepers or skilled swordsmiths, or sometimes the elite."

"The elite?"

"Yes. Units of warriors who hunt the creatures of Gehenna; those creatures that find temporary passageways from their world to ours."

"And you travel the land fighting these creatures—how do you know where they will be?"

"There are mages whose magic locates the incursions. When a weakness is detected, we ride to its location. Hopefully we get there as, the creatures come through. Sometimes we hear of villages being attacked and that is how we know where the creatures will be." Although recently there have been more passageways than there are warriors. Nyle pushed the thought away. He feared that the increase in attacks and the attack on the princess was not a coincidence. The little healer was still talking. Did she ever stop asking questions?

"And you wanted to be part of an... elite?"

"Aye, it is an honor to be chosen."

Danika nodded. "It seems a harsh life. What do you do, for fun?"

"Enough questions!" Nyle's voice was sharp. A few moments went by in silence. He turned slightly to catch a glimpse of her expression. She was pale and tight-lipped. He inwardly groaned before speaking. "I didn't mean to speak so blunt with you. I was just... I mean..."

"It's fine," she sat, straight-backed, and pulled her horse back and away from his.

None of this was "fine," he thought grimly as he geed up his horse and set about finding camp for the night.

∽

DANIKA SAT QUIETLY, HER ARMS WRAPPED AROUND HER knees, gazing into the flames. The firelight highlighted her spiky red hair and framed her delicate features. She looked like a small bird, thought Nyle, like a robin or a wren. He handed her some rabbit.

"Thanks." She picked at the food, distracted.

She was troubled; even he could see that. He should leave her to her thoughts. That's what he would want, to be left to brood and work out what needed to be done. He should go. So, he was surprised to find himself crouching down near to her and adding some sticks to the fire. She ignored him, carried on staring into the blaze. What am I doing? He thought to himself. The horses needed tending, his weaponry needed checking, and he needed to speak to Alyssa about tomorrow's riding arrangements. He sat for another few moments and stole a sidelong glance at Danika. The rabbit lay untouched in her lap. A soft light reflected in her eyes, the soft sheen of unshed tears.

Dammit! What was he supposed to say? This was just not his style, sympathizing and chitty chatting. He felt ridiculous. He shifted uncomfortably, and the little healer sighed.

He cleared his throat. "What's wrong?" The words sounded irritated, like an accusation. Dammit! He tried to soften his tone. "I mean, is everything okay… with you?" His voice sounded strange, but it was the best he could do —he'd tried.

Danika shrugged and continued looking into the flames. "I'm thinking about the university, about Layla." She turned to face Nyle. "I worry about another attack."

Ahhh, thought Nyle, and let out a relieved breath. Now this was a subject he could talk about with confidence. "Don't worry. Sabre will have the defenses well built up by now. And if there is an attack, he could fight an ażote army on his own. The man is a force of nature, as strong as twenty men." He spoke with pride and confidence; he had absolute faith in his friend.

"You and he are good friends?"

"Aye, we are kindra."

"What's kiiindrrra?"

The warrior settled down next to Danika and threw some more branches on the fire. His warrior senses picked up her cinnamon scent as it mingled with the wood smoke in the air: delicious, like winter feast day.

Did she taste that sweet? She was looking at him now, waiting for an answer. He had to shake his head slightly to clear his thoughts. "You have heard about the mountain tradition known as the trial of rights?"

Danika shifted her position nervously. "I think I may have heard something about it." She looked uncomfortable.

Nyle continued, "Every boy, in his twelfth year, survives for a month in the mountain forests with little more than the clothes on his back and the fellowship of other boys from across the clans. Sabre was in my group. We hunted together, built fires, kept each other warm. At the end of the month, the ties you have with your trialmates are forged in iron, you are brothers, kindra."

"It must have been awful for you, alone in the dark forests, cold, hungry, away from your family."

Nyle frowned in confusion. "Awful? It was the best month of my life! We wrestled and fished and hunted. No one told us what to do. We didn't have to wash—what twelve-year-old boy wouldn't want that?"

Danika sat for a moment, her mouth slightly open, blinking a couple of times. "So, it's not dangerous?"

"Pah! The lower mountains are not as treacherous as you Shaman like to believe. The wildest beasts you are likely to come across are badgers protecting their young."

"And no wolves?" The healer looked relieved.

"Not usually." Nyle's eyes flicked sideways, and he half smiled.

"But sometimes?"

"Once." Nyle leant back on his elbows, basking in the warmth of the fire. "My trial followed an unusually bitter winter. The wolves ventured farther down the mountains than usual in search of food."

Danika gasped. "You fought a pack of wolves—when you were twelve!"

"Aye," said the warrior smugly. "Sabre and I fought like devils. Eventually he killed the alpha male, and the rest fled. The man was a force of nature even at twelve." His voice grew softer. "Believe me when I say your friend is safe in his hands."

Danika nodded, and her eyes, which had harbored such strain earlier, seemed to lighten a shade or two. She turned to face Nyle. "Thank you," she said. "I know that I'm not the kind of girl that you would choose to take with you. I don't exactly fit in out here."

Nyle couldn't help thinking that right at this moment, with the embers of the fire casting a warm glow on her skin and her red hair, wild and untamed. She fitted in perfectly, like a forest spirit. "I'm glad you're here." He hadn't meant to say anything; the words had somehow just slipped from him, unbidden.

A flake of ash floated up from the fire and caught in Danika's hair. Nyle leant over and swept it away. On impulse, he stroked her cheek again, his eyes lowering to her small ruby mouth. She was squeezing her plump bottom lip between her teeth, gently biting the soft pink flesh. What would that lip taste like? He suspected it would be sweet and yielding. He felt a heated need to taste her, to draw that swollen lip slowly into his mouth and suckle it, savoring its sweetness.

The memory of her breasts rubbing hard against his back flooded his mind, and his cock ached and stiffened.

His eyes flicked to hers and, to his satisfaction, he saw his own desire reflected back at him. Her amber eyes were dark, glittering in the firelight, unflinching and intense.

Brave little witch.

She wet her lips.

It was all the invitation he needed.

He leant forward and crushed his mouth to hers, relishing her taste. He was right—Goddess, she was so sweet! He explored her with his kiss, the tip of his tongue smoothly tracing a rhythm over the most sensitive parts of her mouth. She groaned into him, then snaked her hand around to the nape of his neck and pulled him in harder—brave, hungry little witch. He was contemplating dragging her far into the woods and continuing his exploration, with her up against a tree, when noisy footsteps approached the camp. With superhuman self-control, Nyle wrenched himself away from those soft hot lips and attempted to catch his breath. Danika, panting, scooted a little way around the fire and away from the warrior.

Torin arrived and grinned at both of them. Nyle couldn't help but catch the mocking tilt to his friend's eyes.

"The perimeter is secured. Fear not. Nobody's going to fall on us in our sleep—Oh, is that rabbit?"

Nyle could have cheerfully garroted his friend as he passed the meat.

Danika ran her fingers through her hair and smoothed her tunic. "Um… we were just talking… about the trials."

"Ahh." Torin sat down next to Danika. "Best month of my life!" he said through a mouthful of roasted rabbit. "Except for the badgers, ferocious little bastards."

"Where's Alyssa?" asked Nyle. "Perhaps you should go look for her."

"No need, boss, no need. She wanted to go through some practice drills. I left her to it. So, Danika, did Nyle tell you about the time he wrestled a pack of wolves? That story always impresses the girls." Torin winked at Nyle and continued chewing. Nyle gritted his teeth and said nothing.

He looked over to the little healer, but her gaze was focused firmly on the ground. He thought he detected a slight blush on her cheeks, and her breathing was a little irregular. The taste of her lingered on his lips, the way she pulled him in, eager, needful. *She's probably a maid. She's recently been torn from everyone and everything she knows, and you are supposed to be looking out for her—not seducing her in the middle of a muddy forest!*

The voice in his head made some excellent points, but it couldn't quite blot out the memory of Danika groaning as he grazed her bottom lip with his teeth. He brought himself up sharply. No! He would not succumb to this—whatever it was—whether he had been too long without a woman or the Shaman girl had bewitched him in some way. It mattered not. He could not afford distractions on this mission, and she was definitely becoming a distraction.

He looked over to the girl who had retreated to the other side of the camp, trying to change her clothes whilst wrapping herself in a blanket for privacy. The blanket kept slipping, and Nyle was treated to a tantalizing vision of Danika's elegant creamy back, her well-toned shoulders, and the delicate flare of her hips. For a moment he could do nothing but stare; visions of running his fingers gently down the curve of her back, tracing her shoulder with his tongue... He looked away and caught Torin's look of amusement.

"You're taking your protective responsibilities seriously with this one, Nyle," said Torin, his tone light. "It seems you are not letting her out of your sight."

"You should take more things seriously, Torin." Goddess, his archer was getting on his nerves. "I'm going to check the perimeter again. You get some rest."

Torin snorted and collected up the remnants of their meal. "Sure thing, Captain. I'll go get Alyssa." He paused and then spoke quietly, without a trace of the mocking tone he'd had a moment ago. "Perhaps, friend, taking things too seriously is as bad as not taking them seriously enough."

Nyle said nothing, just grunted. Grabbing his sword, he started out into the forest.

∼

Nyle checked the perimeter but didn't go back to the camp immediately, taking a wide detour in the fading light. He didn't want the company of others right now. He'd always known what to do. He'd kept his emotions in check for so long, but now they were surging through him, and he was powerless to ignore them. It all centered on a tiny redhead with an amber gaze that felled him like a poleaxe every time. But she was a well-bred healer, not some bar wench. He could not give her what he was certain she would want—a husband, a house, children—and it wouldn't be fair to even consider it.

His mind wandered back to a previous stealth rescue mission. He and Sabre had tracked the captured warrior through a sulphur-spewing swamp in Gehenna and into a putrid, stonewalled nest of hags. The bound man was hung from a post. He was pale and close to death, but Nyle saw in his eyes that the man was still aware as a hag used him, her belly growing fat and heavy with unnatural progeny. Other hags had birthed already and were jostling for another try, their magic keeping the poor man's member willing even as his face crumpled in pain and disgust as each wrinkled, hairless hag hefted herself onto him.

Nyle and Sabre had killed them all. They'd killed the swollen, lusty hags and anything wriggling in their stomachs. Then they'd slaughtered the mewling baby monsters, already screeching, and crawling towards them, reaching out with their needle-like claws and dripping venom. He'd released the warrior, so close to death, and laid him on the fetid ground. Nyle and Sabre had exchanged a knowing look; the man was too far-gone to save.

"I have a woman, Kaity," the man had whispered. "Tell her I died another way… tell her…"

But he'd gone.

They couldn't take the body back. Those that die in the realm of Gehenna stay there. Bad spirits can latch onto the dead—parasites, like the Vorm, that burrow their way into the flesh of the dead and reanimate the body. It is a fact every warrior who travels through the gates must accept. So Nyle and Sabre had buried the body as close to the portal as they dared—as close as possible to the fresh air and sweet scent of Shaman.

When the body was in the ground, Sabre had turned to Nyle. "This place should be destroyed, every creature in this domain obliterated." He'd spat the words through clenched teeth.

Nyle had never heard Sabre so livid, so inflamed; he'd hardly recognized his friend's face, twisted in cold, bitter rage. He gently placed his hand on his friend's arm, feeling the tension radiate from the other warrior's body. "It is our duty, Sabre, and hatred will not benefit our cause."

Sabre jerked away his arm. "You might be able to witness all this and stay cool and shut down how you feel, but I can't. This man was a brave man. He was to take a kish'la and move south to a different order, live peacefully. Until those monsters did... that. It's just so... wicked."

Nyle sought out the woman, Kaity, when he returned to the camp. A beauty with dark eyes and mahogany hair; she was clutching a handful of prayer coins. She'd stood stoically and received a modified version of events with a graceful nod. It wasn't until she was walking away, into the evening shadows, that Nyle saw her stumble slightly and drop her face to her hands, the prayer coins falling onto the stony ground.

Nyle had gained promotion after that mission, but he took little joy in it. He'd realized at that moment that he would never take a wife.

He reached the camp and all were asleep. He threw

more logs on the fire before laying down. But sleep would not come. Just the steadily worsening beat of raindrops in the increasingly bitter night.

∾

A DEEP, HOT, SOAPY BATH SPRINKLED WITH GINGER AND sweet orange oil, ripples of silky water easing her aching muscles. She could almost feel the dirt and sweat of camping dissolving away, and most of all, the satisfaction of being completely and fundamentally warm. That was what she wanted more than anything else in the whole world.

Instead, more freezing rain trickled past her collar and down her back, soaking every layer from the inside out, condemning her to a prolonged, sticky dampness. She would never be warm again. Her cozy dorm room was but a distant fantasy—murdered by a biting wind and the overpowering smell of wet horse.

This had been the worst day yet. Nyle was treating her with cordiality and respect, no acknowledgement of the kiss they'd shared the evening before, not even a lingering glance. Danika wondered if she'd done something wrong. By the time she had got back to the fire after changing her clothes, he'd gone. He'd returned a few hours later and gone straight to bed without casting her a second glance. She knew this because she'd spent much of the night lying awake wondering what the kiss might have meant, if anything, and trying to ignore the strengthening rain filtering through the tree cover.

Her mind ached with tiredness, as her limbs did with

the cold. She glanced at Nyle from the corner of her eye; he stared ahead, oblivious. *What is his problem?* It isn't as if she kissed him! Maybe she was a bad kisser; she hadn't had much in the way practice. Maybe she was too eager; perhaps mountain men didn't like women who made groaning noises and got all panting and… needy. Danika's face burned as she remembered how she had reacted to his kiss. Hadn't she almost climbed into his lap? So desperate was she to get closer, kiss deeper, feel everything. She geed her horse on, hunkering down low in the saddle to shield herself from the stinging rain spray. Torin's arrival had been well timed, and anyway, where did she think it had been heading? She closed her eyes and tried not to imagine where she thought it might have been heading.

She'd been damp from the rain when she awoke this morning but not soaked. The rain had intensified as the day wore on, bringing with it the untold misery of itchy, clammy wool and chafing. Now evening was nearing, and she was considering the woeful prospect of bedding down. On what—mud?

They approached an inn at the side of the road. Danika paused and looked longingly at the warm yellow glow radiating from the grubby windows. Torin also stopped, like a moth caught by candlelight. "Nyle I—"

"No." The lead warrior barely slowed his horse.

"At least consider—"

"No. We've light to ride another hour at least."

Danika fought the urge to weep. Thinking fast, she blurted, "Torin is right. We might, um… gather information!"

"Yes!" said Torin, picking up the bait and running with it. "Creature attacks, intelligence. Taverns like these are hubs of information."

Nyle gave a snort. "Pah."

Torin continued, his even features settling into a look of concerned sincerity. "I think we could all do with a wash and a good night's sleep." Lowering his voice, he added, "Some of us don't have a warrior's stamina." He gave a tiny nod in Danika's direction and raised his eyebrows at Nyle.

Danika considered rising to Torin's dig, but the possibility of sleeping indoors made her instead look at Nyle with the most pathetic and wretched expression she could muster. "Don't worry about me. I'm okay." She rubbed her bandaged sporca bite and winced.

Nyle scowled, looking from Danika to Torin and then back to Danika. "Fine!"

They led the horses to the stable and entered the inn.

CHAPTER 7

*A*hhhhh. It wasn't scented with sweet orange oil, but it was hot, so, so hot. She slowly lowered herself, twisting and balancing on her knees until her body grew accustomed to the steaming water. A few minutes later, she was on her back, mostly submerged, with parts of her turning pink. Basking in the twin joys of being both clean and warm, her mind wandered. Inevitably, a stern warrior with startling blue eyes settled himself firmly in her mind's eye.

She considered quashing the thought as she had the last few days but surrendered and allowed her mind free rein. She closed her eyes and imagined the kiss once more, the feel of his mouth pressing down onto hers, the taste like sweet cloves, heady, masculine. Relaxed, the images came easily to her; the heat of the water made her languid and giddy. She embellished her memory, imagining him dragging his lips down over her jaw, licking down her neck, pausing to graze her earlobe with his teeth before untying her shirt and kissing down across her collarbone to her breasts below. The image was so real, so sublime, that Danika couldn't stifle the soft moan that rose from her lips nor stop her hand from rising from the water to caress the place where she could almost feel his eager mouth tarry.

A knock at the door shook her from her daydream. She sat up fast, causing a large slop of water to splash over the side of the bathtub.

"Sorry to interrupt, ma'am. I got your laundry 'ere. I just finished pressin' it."

A curvaceous maid with light-brown hair and dark eyes bustled in carrying Danika's clothes and a pile of almost-clean looking towels. Danika tried to squeeze down farther into the bathtub; she didn't enjoy exposing her rather modest assets to unknown serving girls. "You didn't interrupt.

The maid fussed with some ornaments on the dresser and checked her appearance in the mirror. She didn't look like she planned on leaving.

"Um, are my friends already downstairs… er…?" asked Danika.

"Celia."

"Okay—Celia—is my group in the bar?

The maid seemed excited by the question. "D'you mean those two great brutes you came in with? They're clansfolk, ain't they?"

"Mmmm, they are."

"You know what they say about mountain men, miss."

She most definitely did know.

Celia didn't wait for an answer. "That they have… unnatural desires." The maid put the pile of towels on the side and busied herself straightening some cushions on a nearby couch. "What d'ya think they mean by unnatural?" She looked sideways at Danika as she repositioned the same cushion for the fourth time.

"I really couldn't say." Danika tried to sink farther underneath the water.

"Hm, well, I wouldn't mind finding out." The girl gave Danika a cheeky wink. "They're both easy on the eye."

"U… If you could let them know, I'll be down shortly."

"Right-e-o, miss." The girl unashamedly pulled her very low-cut bodice a little lower, allowing her ample breasts to bulge further from their flimsy confines. She obviously had no compunctions about flashing her assets. "I'll let them know personally." And with that, the saucy wench bounced from the room.

Danika stepped out of the bath and dried herself with a soft towel. She took a good long look at herself in the mirror. Okay, so she didn't have the prestigious curves that Celia the maid had displayed, but her chest was rounded and high, her waist neat, and her hips did widen somewhat. She turned to the side. Her silhouette was slender; three days of rabbit and berries hadn't helped. She pinched at the meat on her thigh and sighed. What did unnatural desires even mean? Did she even want to know? The rumors she'd heard at university didn't seem to fit with the men she travelled with… and one man in particular. She ignored the thought and laced her bodice up before leaving the room.

The air was heavy with pipe smoke and the yeasty smell of strong ale. The atmosphere was raucous as Danika entered the bar. A few drunkards were enthusiastically singing along to a badly tuned accordion. Not all of them, it seemed, had chosen to sing the same song. Maids bobbed and weaved through the crowd carrying large jugs of ale, avoiding the amorous advances of their more solicitous patrons. Nyle sat in a darkened corner, alone. Folks were tending to avoid that particular corner, Danika noted as she crossed the room to him.

"Where are the others?" She sat down next to the warrior and gathered food from a platter to an empty plate.

"Alyssa has eaten, then took to her bed. Torin… had something he had to do." He gave Danika a sideways glance.

"Oh. By something do you mean a maid called Celia?"

Nyle's eyes widened slightly. His mouth twisted into a small grin. "Aye."

Danika smiled too as she tucked into some roasted chicken, which tasted divine after three days of burned rabbit and stale bread. So Celia and Torin had got together, how interesting. "What are you drinking?"

"Ale, but they might have some wine out the back." Nyle caught the attention of the nearest maid.

"I'll try the ale."

Nyle looked dubious. "It's pretty strong stuff. Are you sure you wouldn't prefer…"

"Nope, ale please."

Nyle shrugged and ordered the brew. When it arrived, Danika sniffed it. Her nose wrinkled, and her eyes watered; it reminded her of the smell of damp horse. She took a sip and was surprised at how mellow it tasted, earthy and dry. Not acrid as she'd expected.

"Do you like it?" The warrior looked amused to see her wrestle with the large tankard. The jug she'd been given seemed bigger than her head, and she had to use two hands to lift it.

"Very drinkable," she replied and took a large, wobbly swig.

Nyle smiled again, this time a full-blown grin, which made him look, for a moment, like a mischievous teenage boy. "Go easy with that ale, lass."

Danika rolled her eyes. "I know all about alcohol, warrior. I wrote a paper on the effects it has on frogs."

"Oh well, that's fine then—carry on."

"What shall we drink to?" asked Danika.

"It's the tradition where I come from to drink to your mother and father."

"Oh." Danika looked down at the table. "Can I just drink to my mother?"

"Aye, but why not your pa?" Nyle was frowning, and Danika felt exposed under his penetrating stare.

"We don't get on... haven't since my mother died."

"I'm sorry, pet—that you lost your mother." Nyle leant forward in his chair, and Danika felt his presence so close to her. It may have been the ale or the bath or Nyle's warm tone, but much of the stress of the past few days slipped away, and she found herself allowing the words to slip out. Talking about things she usually took pains to avoid.

"It was a long time ago. I was young. I can barely remember her, just images and smells. She was a herbalist, and I remember she smelt of lavender in her hair as she held me." Danika slipped her fingers through her own short hair as she spoke. "She had healing magic but never went to the university. She could heal cuts and burns and would take me with her when she went on visits to the town. When people couldn't afford to pay, she accepted gifts and food. Once a woodcarver gave her a beautiful box engraved with magical birds, and my mother filled it with dried lavender and gave it to me. I still have it at… home." Her voice drifted as she remembered how, as a child, the box reminded her of her mother. How, in her darkest moments, when her dad had been particularly angry or indifferent or she had got herself sent home from school in disgrace, she would open the box, breathe in the light, herby fragrance, and feel her mother's presence soothing her pain.

"And your father?"

Nyle's voice was relaxed, but something in his expression made Danika realize that he was very interested in her answer—a small crease in his forehead, a slight narrowing of his eyes that lent intensity to the question.

She sighed. "He took my mother's death badly. We argued—a lot."

Nyle nodded, waiting for her to continue.

"As I grew older, I stopped trying—we became distant." Danika remembered the heavy blanket of cold silence that had settled upon the house when it was just them. She remembered the pressure to be quiet and good and not make a fuss and the anger and pain she felt each time her father rejected her. She remembered when she tried to hug him and he walked away, or talked to him and he met her words with silence, and when she went, tears streaming down her face, with a gash on her knee and was sharply told to stop fussing and treat it herself. "Later I became angry and sullen. I think, in the end, he found me… unlikable." Danika took another huge wobbly glug of ale.

"I doubt that was the right of it," replied Nyle, his voice soft.

"Really? Why?" Danika peeped over her large tankard at the tall warrior.

"Because, Danika—" Nyle leant closer. He smelt slightly of cloves and of trees after rain; his luminous blue eyes held her spellbound, and for a moment the rest of the tavern, the noise, the smoke, all disappeared as his powerful stare, intent and unwavering, filled her vision, pinning her to the spot. "—you're incredibly… likeable." The last word rolled over her, a deep rumble from his chest.

Danika didn't know what to do or say. She felt at the same time afraid and excited. She swallowed hard and felt a warm flush creep up into her cheeks. To gain some composure and to break away from the almost unbearable heat of the warrior's gaze, she raised her vessel. "I'll drink to that," she said firmly and gulped down more ale.

∼

SHE WAS A PRETTY YOUNG WOMAN WHO DIDN'T DWELL ON her past as some town women he'd met did, wearing their miseries like a martyr's shroud. Nyle felt a stab of anger. No doubt the man missed his wife, but a child should be given a chance to grieve, not be shut out. He leant back in his chair and studied the young woman opposite. Her cheeks were flushed, her eyes bright; no doubt due to the surprisingly good ale they served here. He motioned for the maid to bring some more. He couldn't imagine this sparkling girl as a sullen young child, angry and isolated in a busy town. Where he came from, you couldn't move without some well-intentioned villager checking up on you.

Life in the mountains was hard and loss was common. There was a process that was managed by family and friends. A stream of people carried you along. Nyle suspected that in the towns, where no one knew your business and didn't rely on each other to survive, families became—how had she put it?—distant.

Nyle decided that the little healer had gone through enough for now. She needed to lighten up and enjoy herself a little. "So, Danika, what does a healer learn at university? Apart from how to get frogs drunk."

Danika smiled. "Did you know that if a male blue bush frog ingests even a small amount of alcohol, his mating call doubles in volume?"

"So, if a boy frog gets drunk, his voice gets twice as loud in a bid to meet more lady frogs?"

"Yep!"

"I know some clansmen very much like that."

Danika laughed and Nyle smiled. The healer had a surprisingly deep laugh; it shook her whole body and made him want to join in.

"We had to finish the experiment early." Danika giggled. "The noise kept some of the Elders awake at night."

"Couldn't you have just found them some lady frogs to keep them busy?"

"Hmm." Danika frowned. "Why didn't we think of that?"

Nyle smiled and sipped his drink. The way she lit up when discussing her work and the people she worked with, it was clear she missed them, missed her home. She'd gone there as a withdrawn child and obviously found herself at the university, only to have all that peace and security torn apart by monsters. Monsters you allowed to get to the university—Nyle crushed the guilt-ridden thought as it was still forming. Tonight, he would take Torin's advice: to stop wallowing in past mistakes for a few hours and try to relax.

Danika was proving to be very interesting company. She was talking about milk thistles and the healing properties found therein. He didn't really understand the science of it, but he loved the way her passion in her work shone through. She glowed as she spoke of how to prepare the various remedies. He could listen to her for hours; her enthusiasm was engaging, exciting.

And there was no denying she was easy on the eye, dressed in a fresh linen bodice laced tantalizingly low on her chest. When she leant in to talk and emphasized her words with hand gestures, the bodice rode down ever so slightly, revealing just the hint of the curve of her firm breasts. Was she aware? Did she have him in mind when she dressed tonight? The thought caused a shiver to travel up and down Nyle's spine. She took another sip of ale and licked her lips, making them gleam in the candlelight. Nyle's mind darted back to the kiss they had shared in the woods, a kiss he had resolutely tried not to think about. He remembered now how she'd pulled him in closer, eager to taste him. So brave, so inquisitive, so damned... erotic.

What was the reason he'd given Torin for avoiding her, for not pursuing her, for not seducing her? He couldn't remember, or more accurately, he didn't want to remember. He was relaxed and didn't want to think about consequences for a while. Hadn't he given himself the evening off? He just wanted one evening free from the constant nagging of responsibility and duty that dogged him every waking minute. If she was amenable, and he suspected she was, why shouldn't they share some quality time with each other? The thought made his ballocks tighten and his cock stiffen in his trousers. It was all he could do to choke down a moan.

He picked up his drink and took a swig, smiling as Danika explained how a group of novice students had accidentally burned down part of the classroom in an unsupervised revision session. She leant in towards him, her pale skin shimmering in the flickering light. One evening, he thought, as he stared into Danika's warm golden eyes, where he could let his desires run free.

∽

"So let me get this straight. You push a boulder up a mountain," said Danika a little later when the conversation had turned to his life in the mountains.

"Aye."

"And the first one up wins."

"Yep."

"And gets to be king?"

"Aye. Well… for an evening, anyway."

"So, I'm drinking with royalty." Danika raised her flagon and finished off the remaining ale. Was this her second or third, did it matter? She was feeling better than she had felt since the whole daemon/rift/end of the world misadventure had begun.

Nyle laughed. "Aye. Two-time clan champion and fool king of the winter feast, that's me."

The atmosphere in the bar had quietened. The singers now mumbled into their cups—some snored with their heads buried in folded arms. The accordion player was weaving a softer tune.

Danika's head felt a little heavy. She put her elbows on the table and rested her face in her hands. Nyle lay back in his chair, legs stretched out, his fingers locked behind his head.

"You warriors are nothing like your reputations." Danika was only vaguely aware she'd spoken.

"Ah, so tell me, little Shaman, what reputation do we have? That we are fierce? Brutish? That we sacrifice our young to appease our gods?"

"Yes, all that."

"Anything else?"

Danika giggled. "Oh yes, there's more."

"Tell me, lass, tell me the horrors I am supposed to have committed, the barbaric rites I take part in."

Danika turned pink and avoided the warrior's eye. "I… um… it's not easy to find the right words."

Nyle unclasped his hands and leant forward onto the

table, positioning his face only inches from hers. "Now I really want to know. Come now, tell me or I will force it out of you with my terrifying brutish ferocity."

Danika laughed. "They say you have…"

"Hm?"

"That mountain men have…"

"Hmm?"

Danika took a deep breath "They say you have… unnatural carnal desires."

Nyle smiled - a slow, lazy smile. "Did they give any details?"

"Only that it involves bloodletting and… and a branding iron?" The last part of the sentence, the part about a branding iron, was rushed, and when she said it, Danika took a large gulp of ale.

"Ahhhhh." Nyle rolled his eyes. "They have it a little confused. They're referring to our marriage ceremony. When a man wants to take a kish'la, a wife, they exchange blood in a ceremony, just a small amount, a token, it's a tradition."

"And the branding iron?"

Nyle's eyes fixed on Danika's, becoming serious for a moment. "A mountain man marries for life, and to prove his worth, before his wedding day, he must endure a ritual."

Danika leant closer, fascinated.

"He goes to the clan's blacksmith and forges a unique brand. He presents the brand to his sweetheart as a mark of his bond. On the eve of the wedding, a clan leader prays with the groom, and when the sun is set, the groom is branded with his own iron."

Danika's mouth was gaping, stunned by what she was hearing. It sounded brutal and violent, but also magical.

"We don't take a wife on a whim, as you can imagine." Nyle was smiling again, his eyes glittering in the low lamplight.

"So that's what they meant by unnatural carnal desires."

"I assure you, all my carnal desires are natural." Nyle lowered his voice. "It is said that when a clansman finds his true kish'la his strength doubles. It is known as the power of the lanvi."

Danika's eyes grew wider. "And is it true?"

Nyle's eyes were fixed on some unseen distance and slightly glazed. "Aye, my grandfather could lift boulders when he thought of my grandmother. He didn't speak of it, but we knew." Nyle shook his head as if to clear it. "It isn't always the way. Only a special few get the magic of the lanvi." Nyle finished his drink. "Did they say anything else about us twisted, ferocious mountain men?"

"Yes." She sighed and fidgeted with the candle on the table, letting the melted wax coat her fingertips.

"And?"

Looking up, she said, "They say you have insatiable appetites."

For a moment Nyle looked puzzled, then, as understanding hit home, he smiled again. This time Nyle's gaze was less flirtatious, more intense. "Aye, lass, I shan't argue with them on that point."

For a moment they stared at each other, and Danika felt a feeling she didn't recognize well up inside of her. It felt like when she had watched him from her bedroom window, only this time much, much stronger. The atmosphere at the table changed. Gone was the easy laughter and gentle teasing of a moment ago. Danika was suddenly aware that she was in close proximity to a warrior. Nyle was ten years her senior, a man of the clans, notorious for their passion and animalism.

She was no ardent puritan. She'd no strong opinions on chastity and virtue; it was simply the issue had never arisen. She looked across at Nyle. He was perfectly still, leaning back, no smile now. His square jaw was clenched tight, his cobalt stare fixed hungrily on her. She suddenly had the ridiculous notion that if she turned and started running, he would chase her down. The question was—did she want him to?

As he continued to stare at her in silent concentration, the hot nervousness in the pit of Danika's stomach increased. She could politely excuse herself, retreat to the comfort of a real bed and the luxury of sleeping indoors. A small, wicked voice whispered in her mind: But then you wouldn't know what it feels like. What if it feels good? Nyle leant forward and placed his hand near hers. He lightly brushed his thumb over the back of her hand, causing little shivers of pleasure to run up and down her arm. If the way she felt right now was any indication, it might feel *really* good.

Danika took a deep breath. "Take me outside. I need some air."

Nyle's mouth twisted into a half-smile. He took her hand in his and led her outside.

CHAPTER 8

*H*e'd wanted Danika since the moment he met her. Now he felt the need consume him like tinder fire. Every movement she made, every bold question she'd asked, made an animal within him roar. He was also aware they'd both had a fair amount of ale, and the fact irked his conscience. He should see her to her room and let her sleep… alone. That's what he should do. The animal growled loudly at the thought. No, damn it! Tonight, he would not allow prudence to force his hand. He would not think. He would just feel.

As he looked down into her pale, upturned face, he noticed she was doing that thing with her bottom lip again, nibbling the edge between her teeth. It fascinated him; he paused, just for a moment, focusing on her small pearly teeth squeezing the pink flesh. Her amber eyes were curious, always so damned curious. He ran the pad of his thumb over her plump bottom lip, feeling the silky smoothness of her mouth. The breath caught in her chest, and her eyes fluttered closed.

In an instant, he had her pressed against the side wall of the inn as he smothered her with a hard, punishing kiss. She met his force eagerly, devouring his mouth and his neck. Sharp, needy, biting kisses that scraped along his skin and made him want to roar with approval. He would have her here and now, world be damned!

Danika froze as voices and footsteps passed close by, patrons on their way home. It was enough to enable Nyle to regain a vestige of composure. He looked around and, spying a nearby hay barn, led Danika inside and behind a wall of hay.

Nyle kissed her again, slower this time, running his fingers lightly down her back, cupping her face, and kissing her deeply until she was breathless and urgent with need.

"I never thought my first time would be in a hay barn," she said, peeling off her chemise and tossing it to the side, then leaning back into him.

Goddess help him—her breasts were divine, just perfect and high and perky with ruby tips that made him weak with the desire to suckle on them. *I never thought my first time would be in a hay barn*. Was that what she had just said? No matter. Nyle squashed the guilt trying to reach him. Virgin or no', she wanted him and that all there was to it!

Danika wiggled her underskirt over her hips. "You'll have to be patient with me and show me what to do. I mean, I know the anatomy but in practical terms... Nyle? Why have you stopped undressing?"

The tattoo on her wrist glowed softly in the dark

night, a snake wrapped around a rose—*it is your responsibility to protect her. In this, you must not fail.*

The animal in him roared, but he forced himself to ignore it. He took a deep breath and steadied himself, drawing on his years of discipline and self-control. "I can't take your virginity in a tavern hay barn." His words to Torin returned to haunt him—Danika won't be seduced into rolling around like a harlot in a hay barn on this mission, Torin.

Danika was no harlot by any means, but the hypocrisy cut him just the same. "You've had too much to drink. I would not be right to... take advantage."

Danika's face was flushed, and her eyes glittered in the moonlight. "I have not had too much to drink. I know exactly what I'm doing, and I demand you finish what you started!" The young woman struggled with her skirt as she spoke. Having not, it seemed, undone the laces before trying to remove it, it was fast becoming wrapped around her legs.

Nyle started to put his shirt back on.

"No!" Danika ran to him, half dressed, and grabbed his arm. "You do not get to choose what is good for me. I choose! I want it! Leave if you do not wish to lay with me —do not leave out of concern for my maidenhood!"

A snarl broke loose from Nyle; he yanked the young healer up by the waist as if she were weightless and flung her into a deep bed of hay. She landed in a sprawled heap.

"What do you want, Danika?" His voice was low and dangerous as he stalked towards her.

Danika swallowed, her eyes widening as she struggled

to sit up. "I—I don't... know. I just wanted to carry on. I..." Her voice drifted to silence.

Nyle could feel the need and the unresolved lust radiating from her, mirroring his own. He needed to curb his hunger, and right now his only outlet was to keep control, to be in control.

"Lie down!"

She did so, trembling as the large warrior knelt between her legs. He roughly pulled her skirt off over her hips and knees, leaving it in a pile on the stable floor.

"What are you going to...?"

"Lie still!" He rolled up her underskirt, exposing her to him fully. The sight was incredible; her pale thighs came together at a perfect triangle of coppery curls, liberally coated with silky dew. "You're going to come for me, Danika," he spoke quietly. "I have an insatiable appetite, remember." With that, he drew his tongue hard up the center of her slowly, allowing his tongue to invade every inch, every crease. She gasped, her chest rising off the bed. She tried to sit up again. "I said, lie down!"

She complied, falling back into the straw.

He slowly licked her again, noting the exact spot when Danika bucked her hips from the bed and moaned. With one strong hand holding her still, he focused all his attention on that one spot. He worked in a persistent rhythm, lapping and sucking, savoring her wetness, reveling in her cries and mews. The beast in him was not exactly appeased, but it had found a new focus of attention.

Nyle listened as her breathing became quick and shallow, watched her hands dig into the hay, squeezing it into her fists. He eased back for a moment and watched her tremble before him. He licked his lips. Ahh, Goddess! She tasted like honey mixed with wine. The thought of her coming in his mouth made his swollen cock ache in his trousers—*but not quite yet, pet. I get to decide.* Leaning back down, he placed his arm across her stomach to hold her in place and covered her with his mouth, suckling that most delicious bud.

His inner beast roared with approval. He would show no mercy this time.

∾

DANIKA WAS ABSOLUTELY SURE THAT SHE WAS ABOUT TO GO insane. If the warrior kept this up, her mind would shatter into a thousand tiny pieces. The incredible waves of pleasure coursing through her body would rise and rise and then when she was about to plunge into a perfect release, when she was on the very edge knowing for certain that nothing could stop her, the warrior between her legs would slow the pace, soften his touch, lean back, blow on her gently, kiss her inner thighs, everything but what she wanted. And when she whimpered and moaned and cursed and wriggled and finally came down from that blissful, dizzy ledge, he would start all over again.

She raised herself slightly and looked down at Nyle, his strong arms holding her in place, his powerful shoulders looming over her thighs, swirling black tribal tattoos glistening in the moonlight. He raised his eyes to meet hers, and she felt him smile against her sensitive flesh.

"Please, Nyle... I can't... I need..." Her voice was raspy, sweat beaded on her chest and stomach. Her breath came in ragged gasps.

He raised his head from her, his mouth moist with her dew, and looked her straight in the eye. "You wanted to carry on, Danika, did you no'?" His voice was thick and low, his accent more pronounced. There was playfulness behind his words but hardness in his tone.

Danika didn't feel playful; she felt drawn out like a bowstring set to snap. "I'm begging you, Nyle... you have to..."

"No, lass, I don't have to do anything. But I like it when you beg me, pet." Nyle dipped his head and whispered directly onto her sex. "Just trust me, little witch, it'll be worth the wait." The feeling of his warm breath on her dampness sent a new set of shivers across her flushed skin. He stopped and blew gently on her wetness.

"We could stop... if you really want to, lass."

He drew his tongue firmly over her most sensitive spot, and Danika collapsed back onto the straw, feeling the waves build again, wanting to sob with the overwhelming pleasure mixed with the maddening frustration. He had what she needed, what she craved so much she thought she might die if she didn't get it, but he wouldn't give it to her—damn him to hell! She moaned at the sensation, biting her lip to stop crying out.

"I'll take that as nay then." He lapped at her, tracing shapes on her most intimate parts, then suckling her again, ruthlessly drawing pleasure from her.

She placed her arms above her head, gritted her teeth,

and readied herself to ride the pulsating pleasure, knowing he would snatch away from her at the last moment but unable to resist the glorious sensations rippling through her body.

She was reaching her peak again. Nyle kept up the rhythm and the pressure, pushing her ever nearer the brink. A wonderful ache was building up and up inside her. If he just kept going a moment longer… one more second.

Nyle raised his head from her, and Danika raised her eyes to meet his, ready to beg, to plead—to scream. She felt the warrior ease his thumb inside her, just an inch. The feeling was exquisite, and her breath caught in her throat. His voice rumbled as he spoke. "Come for me, Danika." Lowering his mouth onto her, he rubbed his thumb inside her, lapping at her bud at the same time, his steely gaze never leaving hers.

She was falling with his words ringing within her, plummeting as a white-hot light overloaded every nerve ending in her quivering body. The surge of pleasure was so extreme she was terrified at how deep it would pierce, but she rode the wave, crying out in relief, branded by bliss. Her body bucked against the warrior's strong arms, but he held her fast, anchoring her. She felt her inner muscles clench around his thumb, still rubbing her gently, as he softly kissed her between her legs, and she drifted on a raft of ecstasy where time held no sway.

As the rush abated, she tried to raise herself on her elbows, but her trembling muscles made it impossible.

"Lie still, woman." Nyle took his thumb from her and

sucked it, closing his eyes briefly and sighing as if savoring a rich treat. He licked his lips in the same manner, and Danika blushed. He winked at her and grinned. The grin made him look young and carefree for a moment, and there was a playful light to his eye that she'd never seen from him before. Her embarrassment was replaced by a deep-felt, languid happiness that spread like warm treacle into every part of her. She smiled back, relishing the last remaining shudders that were pleasantly running through her.

Oh my! she thought as her mind flicked back over recent events. People did this all the time. How had she not known about this? Why didn't the books at the university mention any of... this? How ridiculous that they described the anatomy, the correct terminology, the reproductive process, but neglected to include the earth-shattering pleasure.

They hadn't even done... it. Danika turned to Nyle, her mind suddenly alive with questions, a vast void of knowledge waiting to be filled; she would need to do a full study, including lots of fieldwork.

"Nyle, I... Oh, for goodness' sake—where are you going?"

～

DANIKA HAD SCREAMED AS SHE CAME HARD INTO HIS mouth, and he thought he would spill, right there in his trousers. And her taste! Goddess, she was fine. He could have carried on sucking on that sweet nectar forever. He'd held her and drank from her until her movements eased, her breathing slowed. Until he knew she was wrung out. It felt good that she couldn't sit up; he thought for a moment that's how he'd like to keep her, boneless and sated on a bed of straw.

When she finally did manage to sit up and look at him kneeling between her thighs, her hair was mussed and spiky, her skin flushed, and her eyes were drowsy and a little glazed. She smiled.

That languid smile was the most erotic thing he'd ever seen.

He stood and turned towards the door

"Where are you going?"

"For a long walk."

"Wait." Danika rose from the bed of straw and stood close to him. She ran her hands over his abdomen, and reaching into his trousers, she wrapped her small hand around his cock. "Show me what to do."

He drew in a quick breath and allowed Danika to free his swollen shaft. Her soft hand on his tight skin was incredible. Rushes of aching pleasure pulsated through him, making his muscles clench. He bit down hard on his bottom lip and suppressed a groan.

"Like this?" She gently ran her fingers over him, running them up from the base and lingering on the tip before running back the other way.

"Harder." He forced the word out through clenched teeth.

She gripped him in her fist and rubbed firmly, up and down in long, hard strokes. Nyle almost collapsed as waves of exquisite pleasure radiated from his cock. To avoid falling, he leant back, supporting his weight against the stable wall and allowed Danika to work his shaft. Danika's rhythm was perfect and had him speeding towards his release. His breathing quickened. "Ahhh, Danika. In the name of the Goddess, don't stop." She was relentless. He felt his ballocks tighten in anticipation, and he took a deep breath and held it, right on the cusp of orgasm.

Danika stilled. Nyle dragged his gaze to hers in sweet agony, desperate, frantic, and in that moment, wildly dangerous. Her golden eyes gleamed with power. Maybe she would play the same game, denying him his release. She'd be playing with dark forces if she tried. He'd denied himself enough this evening to be toyed with. He would have the girl on her back with him buried deep inside her if she didn't give him release. But she did something else, something he could never have anticipated—something that blew his mind with its impudence.

He felt a jolt of power shoot from her palm and straight into the base of his shaft, like a dart of white-hot ecstasy ripping through his body. The effect was instant and magnificent. Nyle's whole body bowed away from the wall as he bellowed his release. The pleasure was so intense, so sharp, it bordered on pain as he rode wave upon wave of breathtaking sensation. She had used her power on him in some way, and the effect had been instant and excruciating in its ferocity. He thought of nothing but the wicked little healer as his orgasm raged for moment upon divine, excruciating moment.

Eventually his rapture abated and Nyle opened his eyes to find himself slumped on the wall. Danika stood over him, her eyes wide, her mouth slightly open. She was panting, too. For a moment they just stared at each other, then her words tumbled out in a rush.

"I shouldn't have done it, used magic. It was an impulse. Goddess, are you okay?"

"Isssfine." It took a few attempts before Nyle could stand properly,

"I thought I'd hurt you!"

Nyle allowed Danika to support him for a moment; he shook his head to clear it. As he leant on the healer, his energy began to return. "Maybe next time I should at least lie down if you plan to do… whatever you did."

"Next time?" Danika looked up at him, raising an eyebrow.

Though still buzzing, Nyle matched her playful look with his own, loving the way she met his gaze head on. Fearless and so damned enticing. Oh yes, his energy was definitely returning. He dipped down and kissed her on the lips, this time at a leisurely pace, running the pads of his fingers over her face and neck, relishing the small gasp she made as he brushed his thumb over her nipple. He could get used to this little witch, he thought as she leant farther into his touch.

"Nyle!" Alyssa's voice was urgent from the other side of the hay. "You need to come to the inn."

Nyle was away from Danika and yanking on his shirt in a flash. "What is it?"

"A villager. He's been attacked."

"Is he hurt?" he asked, buttoning his fly.

"Yes, badly."

Nyle looked to Danika, who was quickly adjusting her chemise.

It was Danika who spoke first. "Go. I'll be there in a moment."

He nodded and jogged out into the damp night air.

CHAPTER 9

The innkeeper showed Danika into the parlor. The room was overly warm and cramped. The furniture had been moved to allow a space in the center of the room, and a young man lay on the floor; the warriors stood about him.

Danika hitched up her sleeves. "Give me space." The warriors backed off as much as they could in the tiny room. She leant down to examine her patient.

The boy's face was pale. Sweat beaded on his forehead and lip as he clutched his bloody leg. He struggled to speak. "I rode—I just rode as fast as I could. They were chasing me. Dogs - but huge…"

Behind her, Danika heard Nyle speak to Torin and Alyssa. "Go!"

The two warriors were already out the door; Alyssa coiling her whip and sheathing her dagger, offering a brief, "We're on it."

"Where did you ride from?" Nyle leant down, studying the boy intently.

"Westbury." The boy's voice broke into a sob.

"Shhhh, rest," said Danika pushing past Nyle, leaning down and ripping open the young man's breaches to examine the wound. The top of his leg was mashed into ribbons; a white flash of bone was just visible through the pulpy flesh. "I'm going to try to stop the bleeding, but the wound will take a while longer to repair. Lie back. You needn't be awake for—"

"No, wait!"

Danika paused a moment, turning to look up at Nyle. "What is it?"

The warrior spoke in a low tone. "I need to question him—now."

Danika couldn't believe what she was hearing. "It can wait an hour! This is not some hardened warrior. He's a young man, a villager." The boy began to shake, no doubt from the beginnings of shock. Ignoring Nyle, Danika placed her hands near the wound and eased some soothing energy into the boy's tortured nervous system, simultaneously speeding the clotting in his wounded leg. The young man's face went slack as he passed out cold.

"Danika! Westbury is only a few miles from the university. I need him awake. I order you to wake him."

"You order me?" She remained focused for the sake of the boy, but her hands shook as she ran them over the wound. She knew where Westbury was; she'd healed the blacksmith's son of a nasty burn. She couldn't allow herself to think of the fate of the village right now; all she could do was concentrate on the patient in front of her. She took a breath and focused her energy.

Nyle, it seemed, had other ideas. "He has a responsibility, a duty! I need to know what's out there. I need information. He might have news of the university. I need you to wake him up!"

Danika jerked her head up. "He's a civilian, and I am his healer," she hissed the words through gritted teeth, "and he will have rest and treatment before he is required to answer any questions!"

Nyle looked furious and opened his mouth to argue. He stood for a moment, his fists clenched, frowning deeply; his earlier boyish appeal replaced by a tight mask of vexation and rage. Danika stared back defiantly, trying to ignore the tears that threatened to well up.

The captain turned, picked up his sword, and walked out into the night.

∾

After ensuring her patient was as comfortable as possible, Danika slumped into a well-cushioned chair and watched the dying embers of the fire. She tried to arrange her thoughts in some sort of order.

The events of the evening seemed so distant. Had she really shared that astounding experience with a man she hardly knew? Even now, the memory of his warm mouth on her, his voice deep and rough, sent tiny shivers across her skin.

She had no ambitions to become more to Nyle than a lover; he had bachelor stamped all over him and good luck to him. But when he'd shouted at her to wake the young man, ordered her, she felt something more than simple anger; it felt suspiciously close to betrayal. During their evening in the bar, he'd relaxed, and she'd felt close to him. And then he had to go and ruin it by being... *himself*.

Danika rubbed her aching temples. The after-effects of a large amount of ale might account for her fragile emotional state, pared with having to treat this poor wretch. She looked down at the sleeping man. He looked like a farmer's son. Well built and well fed despite his current condition. It wasn't as if he'd signed up for a soldier's life. It wasn't an honor for him to guard the land from the forces of hell; he was just caught up in the battle. She would wager that up until a few days ago all he'd cared about was gathering in the harvest and sweet-talking the dairymaid. What had he said had attacked him? Dogs, but much bigger. Danika shivered.

It would be light soon, and they would be in Shallaha by evening. She had more important things to think about than fierce warriors with blue eyes and heart stopping smiles. She had to work out how to convince the Fae embassy to grant her an audience with the prince. She looked at the markings on her arm—would it be enough?

The embers glowed in the grate, and Danika closed her eyes for a moment. It was not the Fae embassy on her mind as she slipped into a light and fitful slumber; it was the tall, dark warrior with strong arms and a wickedly seductive touch.

∽

Soft dawn light diluted the night's dark. Nyle turned to Torin. "Can you see any tracks?"

Torin paused by a spot on the muddy forest floor. "As we feared—hunters. See the way the mud is pushed out in ridges, and here?" He pointed to a large paw print, like a dog's but four times the size.

Both warriors started to carefully search the undergrowth. Nyle pondered where the creature had come from. Was it tracking the boy? Was it tracking them? Why was a civilian riding about the forest alone at night? At that moment, he wanted desperately to be at the inn, questioning the boy—this was getting them nowhere. Then there was Danika; the way she had looked at him when he asked to speak to the boy, like he was some kind of monster. Maybe he was, but he was sick of fighting an enemy he couldn't see. He wanted answers about what was happening near the university; the wounded man would give him some information at least, even if the news was bad.

The image of Danika's angry face stayed in his mind. Her lips, which had only a short time before shouted out his name in pleasure, twisted into a look of fury and distaste "You order me?" Nyle clenched his hands into fists. Maybe it would have been harsh to wake the boy, but many lives depended on the information he might have. Danika was clouding his judgement and causing him to lose focus; even now he was worrying about her opinions of him instead of the task at hand. He shook his head and continued his search.

Torin shouted from behind a cluster of low bushes. "Here! More tracks."

Nyle ran towards him; the archer was peering into a deep thicket. The warriors leant in. Nyle sniffed the air rising from the dense brush. It smelt of freshly dug earth and something else, something sweet and fetid, like rotting fruit. Nyle watched Torin lean farther into the darkness. The archer had in his palm a sphere of magical light. The light reflected off the branches and mud, but the opening in the undergrowth disappeared down into the belly of the forest.

Torin stood up straight. "It's probably long gone. We should go back to the—"

As he spoke, a mass of muddy fur and claws shot out of the bush and knocked Torin onto the floor, landing squarely on the man's chest. It growled and sniffed the archer with its long snout, the creature's teeth pausing just inches from Torin's neck, viscous yellow fluid dripping from its jaws. Nyle grasped his sword.

"Don't move," hissed Torin.

Nyle stayed his hand. The creature leapt off the archer with its powerful hind legs and bounded towards Nyle at unbelievable speed. Nyle couldn't bring his sword around quick enough, and this time there was no mistaking the attack in the creature's eyes. The creature launched itself towards Nyle and barreled into the warrior's chest. Nyle only had time to protect himself with his forearm, pushing the snapping creature away, the rotting stench thick in his nose and lungs, its jaws just a hair's breadth from his jugular.

There was a strangled yelp, and the creature was yanked backwards away from Nyle, landing in the mud, a whip wrapped around its face and neck.

Alyssa strode out of the brush, clutching the whip handle tightly and dragging the captured wriggling beast along. Torin was on his feet in a flash and fired a bolt at the creature's flank, stilling it for good.

"Danika told me to tell you the boy has rested well," said the female warrior, unwinding her whip from the muzzle of the fallen beast. "She suggests you wake him—if you must."

Nyle grunted. She suggests, does she?

Alyssa coiled her whip and fastened it to her side. "Lucky I was around."

"Thanks, Alyssa. At least one of my soldiers has my back. If I'd had to rely on Torin, I'd be dog food right now." Nyle spoke in jest, but Torin snarled.

"I had to get a clear shot," he said, rounding on the other two soldiers. "I couldn't just shoot it. I would've shot you."

"Torin, I was kidding. I know you would have—" But Torin had already left, striding quickly through the muddy forest towards the inn.

Nyle looked to Alyssa, who shrugged.

The stress, it seemed, was getting to them all.

∽

Nyle found Danika, pestle and mortar in hand, grinding herbs in the kitchen. Dark shadows marred the pale skin beneath her eyes, and she muttered under her breath as she worked, frowning down into the stone mortar.

She didn't look up or stop grinding. "Did you find the creature?"

"Yes. It's dead."

Danika moved to a small table facing Nyle and poured a fine powder from the mortar into a cup. She picked up a copper kettle from the stove and added hot water. She stirred vigorously and the mixture gave off a pleasant berry smell.

"What are you doing?" he asked.

"It's to calm the villager when you wake him." Danika looked up at Nyle for the first time since his return, her fiery gold eyes meeting his. "It will make it easier for him to answer your questions."

It was Nyle's turn to look away. When he looked back, she had returned to her preparation.

"Where's Torin?" she asked.

"In the barn, I think, getting horse feed."

At the mention of the barn, Danika's stirring slowed slightly, and he thought he detected a slight flush appear on her cheeks. It might, of course, be the steam from the potion. Nyle felt like he should say something. Explain to Danika how he shouldn't have let it go that far in the barn. She probably hated him for taking advantage of her when she was drunk, and she was most likely right to. He loathed conversations like this and was tempted to leave things as they were, but the idea that she now had a low opinion of him rankled. He also didn't want her to think it was her fault; he was the one who should have had more self-control.

He moved towards the table she was working at as she crumbled something dry and mossy in the mixture. He paused for a moment. Maybe she was fine about the whole thing and he was worrying unnecessarily.

Nyle cleared his throat. "Listen... about last night...

um—" Ignoring him, Danika picked up the cup and walked off into the parlor. No, thought Nyle as he followed. She was definitely not fine.

A few moments later, they were gathered in the parlor around the sleeping man. Torin walked in; the archer looked tired, but he raised his eyes to meet Nyle's. He nodded, and Torin nodded back. Whatever devils Torin harbored, he was dealing with them.

Danika crouched next to the boy and gently shook his shoulder. At first he didn't move, then he opened his eyes. Immediately he tried to sit bolt upright and began gasping, "What... happened... where are they? They're coming, and I have to lead them away from the other villagers. We must hide!"

"Shhhh, it's okay, it's okay. You're safe now." She offered him the cup. "Sip it. No, not too fast, it's still a bit hot. That's right, take another sip, gently." She dabbed a trickle from his chin with the edge of her sleeve and carried on murmuring to the wounded boy. Nyle noted how Danika's voice had become rhythmic, hypnotic even, and how the patient was already calming under her tender supervision.

A few minutes later, he was breathing normally, although his eyes shifted around the room nervously, and he held his arms tightly crossed across his chest. Danika turned to Nyle. "He's still in a state of shock. Perhaps you should let Torin ask the questions?"

Nyle gritted his teeth and forced himself to give a curt nod. She was right. Torin's manner was less abrasive than his own, but he did not appreciate it being pointed out to him. He turned to his archer and made a point of speaking softly. "I need to know what he knows, Torin. Get as much detail as possible."

Torin knelt beside the boy. "What's your name, son?"

"Logan, sir."

"Logan. I'm one of the warriors sent to protect the university." Torin smiled in encouragement, but Logan backed away slightly, his eyes suspicious.

Torin frowned. "What happened to your village, Logan? Can you tell us?"

Danika bent down and spoke softly. "It's okay, Logan. These men can help."

Logan closed his eyes for a moment, his face creased into a look of pain. Finally, he opened his eyes and nodded. "There were monsters, winged monsters. They came at night. We managed to escape, to flee into the woods. Most of us anyway..." His eyes filled with anguish at the memory. "For two days we've been living in the forests around Westbury, hiding from the daemons. I led a hoard away. I lost them in the forest, but then... the dogs came. They ran me down, and I thought they would kill me... but I managed to stay on the horse." He closed his eyes as if to block the sight. "When the horse finally fell, they were distracted. I climbed a tree, and I was there since last night. The dogs must have left. Some tinkers found me and brought me here." Danika leant down and made the young man sip some more tea.

Nyle caught the eye of the innkeeper by the door. "Is this true?"

"Aye, tis," replied the innkeeper. "Tinkers brought him in."

Nyle sat for a moment, deep in thought. None of this

made sense. Why were the villagers wandering the forests in the first place? He turned to the young lad. "Why didn't you go to the university? Word was sent for you to seek refuge behind its walls. You would have been safe."

Logan shrunk back away from Nyle, and the warrior regretted his sharp words.

Torin lowered his head, so it was close to the boy's. His voice was soft. "Go on, lad, tell us. Why didn't you go to the university?"

The young man looked from Nyle to Torin. "There were... rumors."

Torin nodded. "Go on."

"It was said that the warrior at the university is..." Logan swallowed and looked at Nyle, "that he is... unstable."

Nyle frowned. "What?"

"That he talks to himself, and he has a witch who does his bidding."

Nyle looked at Torin in confusion. "I... I don't understand."

Logan continued, "It is said that the cries of village children echo around the stone walls at night, and that the students are forbidden to speak to anyone outside the university. That the warrior is prone to outbursts and rages."

Nyle stood up perplexed: Sabre? Unstable? Where in the Goddess's name were such rumors coming from?

The man had stopped talking and was sitting quiet and still, staring at the wall.

Nyle frowned. He'd known Sabre all his life, and he couldn't imagine his best friend suffering from any kind of madness. The villagers must have built up the rumors from hearsay and fear.

Nyle loomed over the boy. "Where did your information come from?"

Logan stuttered but met Nyle's gaze. "I heard that one villager escaped from the university. He spoke of daemon raising and sacrifices. He said the university was a trap. So when the monsters attacked the village…"

"You took your chances in the forest." Nyle shook his head. He knew how the whispers of villagers could snowball, but this sounded like something different—there was real fear in his voice. Could Sabre have fallen apart? No. He would sooner believe that the moon had disappeared from the night sky than believe that Sabre could be neglecting his duty. He'd ridden into combat with the man at his side more times than he could count. Of all his troops, Sabre was the least likely to succumb to imaginary fancies. Some kind of daemon magic must be filling the villager's minds with these stories, fanning the flames of fear with poisoned words and thoughts.

Nyle looked over at Torin. The archer's face was flushed, and his hands clenched tightly into fists; he looked as shocked and dismayed as Nyle felt. Alyssa stood cool and expressionless as ever; her face gave nothing away, but her stance was more rigid and tense than usual.

"Anything else?" Nyle barked the question, his voice raw with emotion.

Logan flinched. "No, I… I don't think so."

He turned to the others. "We leave in an hour." Then turning once more to Logan, "I have arranged for you to be provided for here until we get to the bottom of this."

Logan gave a wavering nod. "Thank you, sir." His drawn face softened slightly, and a little color returned to his cheeks. Danika stood over the boy, talking softly and blocking him from Nyle's view. The interview was obviously over.

Nyle made for the door, his mind whirring on the events of the last few hours. Villagers hiding in forests? Hunters roaming the land? His soldiers suffering from, what? Stress?

He needed time to think this through, to work out the facts from the rumors, to clear his thoughts and formulate a plan, to focus on his job. His eyes flicked to the healer standing over her patient, firmly insisting the young man eat the oatcakes she was offering.

To focus only on his job!

~

Danika was confident enough on her horse to eat some breakfast whilst managing to keep up with the brisk trot set by Nyle. Eating the honey-cake as she bobbed up and down, however, was making her feel sick, so eventually she gave up and stuffed it in her pocket.

Danika wondered what was at the root of the rumors. Had Sabre really come unhinged? If so, would Layla allow him to hurt the students? Sabre was a strong man, a warrior, but Danika had seen her friend lift a boulder ten feet into the air and toss it as easy as if it were a paperweight. If Sabre had lost his mind, her friend could deal with him.

Nyle was under the impression that it was all villager

superstition and worried gossip. Danika wondered whether that was all there was to it. Logan seemed sure of what he'd heard. But she had to admit the rural people of central Shaman were often full of ill-informed doctrine and baseless beliefs. She'd once had to stop a young girl from being whipped when the village elders had mistaken a brain seizure for daemonic possession.

Nyle was a little way ahead with Alyssa, while Torin rode at her side. When they'd left the inn, Nyle hadn't spoken a word to her. Her earlier indignation at him had dissolved with her hangover. She could see how hard he was trying, the amount of pressure he was under. He was used to dealing with soldiers, those who were used to the chain of command, who could endure a hard life. To have to rely on a civilian for the only information he had must be driving him insane.

The road ahead stretched off over a hill and into the distance. But as they rode on, villages and hamlets became more frequently dotted around the surrounding hills. The farmhouses grew bigger and grander. Some of the farms looked like villages themselves with so many outhouses and barns. Teams of workers could be seen in the crop fields, and more than once the party was forced to stop as livestock was driven across the road. A small thrill rippled through her at the idea of finally reaching Shallaha. She felt nervous, of course, about the daunting task ahead, but excited at the prospect of seeing the city she'd only heard stories about.

"How far are we from Shallaha?" she asked Torin.

The archer was unusually preoccupied and didn't

respond. Staring off into the distance, he turned to Danika. "Hmmmm?"

"Until we get there, how long?"

"I'd say just before nightfall if we keep this pace and only rest the horses for short periods." He continued staring down the road, and Danika stayed quiet. The archer obviously didn't want to talk.

Over the few days, Torin's company had eased the sting of being alone amongst strangers. He was easy to talk to and charming, so different from Nyle's focus and intensity. The archer's flirtatious ways and his humor had made the madness bearable.

His introspection was worrying.

Then Torin turned his head to face Danika and offered the same cheeky, pearly white smile she'd begun to rely on to cheer her up over the last few days.

"Do you remember Celia?" he asked.

"The maid at the inn. The one who was very, um… friendly?"

"Yes, that's the one. She's agreed to keep a close eye on Logan for me. They got on famously when I introduced them." Torin's grin widened. "In fact, Logan seemed almost cheerful when I left."

Danika laughed. She could well imagine Celia enjoying her own private patient to tend to, and a young farmer would no doubt appreciate such an enthusiastic nurse.

They trotted along in companionable silence for a while. Nyle and Alyssa had ridden on a little way ahead.

Torin turned to Danika again and said in a low voice, "Don't judge him too harshly."

"Who—Logan?" she replied, frowning. "I don't think Celia is all that bad, not exactly subtle in her approach, but—"

"—Not Logan," Torin raised his eyes to the sky and back down to meet hers, "Nyle."

"Oh." Danika looked away. "I don't really—it's just he's so very driven. Sometimes I think he likes me, and sometimes I feel like I'm some kind of burden." It felt good to verbalize what she had been bottling up inside. She looked sideways at the archer and asked, "Why? Has he said anything to you, about me, I mean…?"

"No." Torin chuckled. "Nyle isn't one for pouring out his heart to anyone, but the way he looks at you when you're busy doing something else—I don't think he's seeing a burden."

Danika gave Torin a skeptical look.

Torin sighed. "Just don't give up too easily."

As he spoke, Danika noticed his gaze settle on Alyssa and something that had been niggling Danika in the back of her mind suddenly made sense. "You have feelings for Alyssa?"

Torin shrugged but didn't deny it.

"Have you told her how you feel? She may feel the same way."

"She doesn't."

"Now who's giving up easily. She might be waiting for you to—"

"She isn't."

"But you don't know—"

"I do. Trust me."

Danika was about to continue arguing, but Torin was squinting off into the distance.

"What can you see?" she asked.

"It's probably nothing." He sped up to catch the others. Danika followed.

Nyle turned his head at the approaching hooves. "What?"

Torin peered ahead again, shielding his eyes from the sun. "It looks like a crowd of people coming this way, on foot."

Nyle frowned. "Some kind of procession?"

Torin shook his head and turned to Nyle. "More like a migration."

They all looked towards Shallaha. All Danika could see were a few dark blobs on the road in the distance.

CHAPTER 10

"Why would people be fleeing the city?" asked Danika.

"Stay close and don't draw any unnecessary attention," said Nyle, looking grim. "I'll question some of the refugees and try to assess the situation."

About half an hour later, the first of the refugees began to pass by.

As the first men galloped past on horses, Torin tried to flag down a rider to find out what was happening, but none wished to stop. Then Danika watched as a raggle-taggle bunch of men, women, and children began to filter past, some in coaches or carts, many clutched bundles of emergency provisions, food, and water. Haphazard piles of blankets and clothes lay in many of the carts, dumped there as if in haste.

Nyle could see a small, covered wagon that had become stuck in the freshly churned mud. Pushing the wagon was an old man, but it was clearly stuck fast.

Danika followed Nyle as he carved a path through the burgeoning crowd to the stranded wagon.

"We will help you free your ride, but we need information."

Danika noticed the man's eyes flick from side to side, and his wrinkled hands rubbed up and down his grubby trousers. "Whaddaya wanna know?"

"What is this?" Nyle gestured to the masses.

The man shrugged, and his eyes darted to the wagon. "We're gettin' out. 'Is not safe." He backed up towards the cart and tried again to free the half-buried wheel. "There's bin whispers for some days," his voice strained with effort, "of Fae leavin' the embassy." He gave up and turned back to the group, his red face splattered with flecks of mud. "If they go, then their magic what protects us'll go wiv 'em." He raised a gnarly finger towards the city. "All this'll be overrun by the scum of Gehenna. Gotta go ta the mountains awhile." His gaze slid from the group to the crowded road. "Guess these others 'ad the same idea."

Squeezing past Nyle and ignoring his warning look, Danika asked, "Have you seen any creatures? Have there been attacks?"

The man took a step back and shook his head. "Nope, a'int seen 'em." As he spoke, sweat beaded on his brow, and he wiped it away with his shirtsleeve. "Jus' whispers for now." Danika saw fear in the man's eyes and something else. Was it guilt?

"You gonna 'elp me then?" The man nodded towards the stuck wagon.

Nyle, Torin, and Alyssa dismounted. Danika started to climb down, but Nyle signaled for her to stay seated.

Danika watched the warriors easily push the wagon free. It lurched from the soggy earth and landed with a bump on firmer ground. A groan sounded from within the wagon. Nyle frowned. "Who rides within?"

"No one," the man replied. "Well, 'is me daughter—she's gotta bad leg."

This time Danika did dismount. "Let me see. I might be able to help her," she said, slipping from the saddle and into the mud. Nyle turned towards her angrily. "I thought we agreed you'd stay on your horse."

"No. We didn't," she replied. "Let me see the girl. I have some healing skills. I may be able to help."

"No. She's sleepin' and shouldna be minded." The man spoke quickly, his voice rising in tone.

"Let me see her," demanded Danika.

"No! I'll be gettin' on. Leave me be." The man moved towards the wagon. Nyle blocked his path and narrowed his eyes. He strode to the back of the wagon. He raised the cover and cursed sharply in Clannish. *Bacraut!*

Danika turned to see four young women bound at the wrist to each other. Their dark complexion and pale saris suggested they were southern islanders.

"Slaves!" Nyle spat the word, and Danika could feel the anger radiating from the warrior. "You were keeping these women prisoners." Nyle loomed over the old man, and Danika thought he might strike him down. But he pulled back at the last moment.

"Now 'ang on a moment," the old man stammered. "They's me property. I paid good money—"

"It's illegal to trade in slaves north of the Ivory Ocean, and we are very much north of that stretch of sea." Nyle leant farther down so that his face was inches from the man's.

"Well, yeah, but I reckon you're a clever man," the trader eyed the sword at Nyle's side, "an' I'm sure we can come to some sorta understandin'. I've good coin 'ere." The old man held out a fat pouch and thrust it forwards, his hand shaking. Nyle did nothing.

The man's voice dropped to a whisper, but Danika could still it make out. "Or you could take a turn wiv one of me girls. They're all fresh. I've not tried 'em." He smiled, revealing a couple of yellow teeth.

Nyle growled, his face pale, his stare cold and hard. He grabbed the old man by his shirt and lifted him to face level. He spoke from behind clenched teeth. "You're a filthy toad. I hope the creatures of Gehenna find you and feast on your entrails." Nyle took the coins and dropped the old man to the floor, turning he said, "Go tend to the woman, Danika. See to the injured."

Danika wasted no time. The break was a simple one. The girls spoke in frightened whispers in a language Danika didn't understand. The injured girl flinched from her as she touched her limb. Danika gently rubbed the poor girl's leg and spoke softly until she was finally allowed to knit the broken bone.

Nyle untied the girls and gave one of them the coins. Danika moved to remount, but Nyle stopped her.

"Ride with me, Danika. Give the reins to the girls." She did what she was asked.

Nyle gestured to the wagon's horse and pointed northeastward. Then, to Danika's surprise, Nyle spoke in fluent Ilandish. The girls nodded and mounted two to a horse, hitching up their saris. With a flick of the reigns, the girls headed back towards the east of the city.

"Now 'ang on," the old man said, his voice thin and high, "everyfing I got is in me cart. How'll I move me stuff wivout a horse?"

"Carry it on your back," replied Nyle

"But—"

Nyle's voice dropped low. "Would you rather I haul you back to Shallaha for the courts to deal with? There are heavy penalties for slave trading."

The man slowly shook his head and muttered under his breath. Danika thought she could make out something about "heathen" and "clansmen." If Nyle heard it, he ignored it.

The warriors and Danika mounted and continued towards the city, leaving the old man in the mud.

Danika remained quiet on the journey, resisting even Torin's attempts to draw her out. Nyle rode with her but didn't speak. What he had done was right—the flesh trade had been banned for over twenty years, and no one should be bought and sold like meat. There were always rumors that women were imported from the south and kept secretly for domestic work or as prostitutes. Danika shuddered.

But Nyle had taken the old man's transgression personally. He'd been so angry, so out of character for the brutal yet cool warrior. And how did he know how to speak Ilandish? Did he have a history with an Ilandish woman?

Danika felt tiredness drag her down. Healing the girl's leg had taken some of her energy, but this was a tiredness that went right through to her soul. Thinking about Nyle was exhausting.

Danika rubbed her wrist, and the amber tattoo warmed under her touch. It comforted her. Petitioning the prince was her priority, not worrying about Nyle's prior engagements. He hadn't given her any indication, one way or another, whether he was involved with someone else, and she hadn't asked. It was best that they just forget what had happened earlier in the barn. Danika flushed. They had both been giddy with ale and not fit to make good decisions. It was time to draw a line under the whole business and concentrate on what needed to be done. This wasn't easy to do as she was currently sharing a saddle with the warrior, forced to clutch his well-hewn form to stop from falling off. She wriggled back to allow some space between them, but it was no good; she always seemed to slip forwards in the saddle towards him.

"Stop wriggling," he said over his shoulder. "It's distracting."

She gave in and rested on his back. She wound her arms around his waist and thought for a moment she felt him run his hand gently over hers. It was a fleeting, light touch. I probably imagined it, she thought.

As afternoon passed into evening, the road grew less crowded, and they were able to make better time. Just a trickle of stragglers wandered past in the failing light. They trotted on as the buildings and spires of Shallaha came into sight on the horizon. The anticipation and excitement of earlier, however, had been replaced by a quiet sadness that Danika couldn't really understand.

HE LOOKED AT DANIKA; THE WOMAN WAS LEANING OVER her plate with her face down. She looked exhausted. The last few days, the stress of worrying about the university, and now this, were all taking its toll. He was uncomfortably aware that he might be responsible for some of that stress. He'd resolutely avoided the healer. The night in the inn had taught him that his powers of reason seemed to leave him whenever they were alone together.

On the horse earlier and when they'd arrived, she'd been distracted. Was she feeling bad about what had happened in the barn? He hoped not. He tried not to think about how far it had gone—and how far it might have gone. She'd driven him half-mad with lust. Even now, sitting here in front of him with the pinch of exhaustion on her soft face, he felt the familiar stirrings in his loins. What kind of beast was he? She needed nothing more than solid sleep and here he was imagining taking her to bed for some energetic lovemaking. Nyle pushed the remainder of his stew to the side.

The rest of the company finished their meal in silence.

Alyssa got up. "I need some fresh air. I'm going to scout the area and perhaps investigate the Fae embassy for tomorrow."

"Do you want me to come along with you?" asked Torin. "We can't have little ladies roaming the big city unchaperoned now, can we?" His voice was light, but Nyle suspected the archer's usual cheer was strained.

Alyssa rolled her eyes. "Come if you want. I'll look

after you." She sheathed a broad sword to her back, her coiled whip, as ever, fastened close at hand on her belt.

Torin stood up and turned to Danika. "Get some sleep, healer."

Danika nodded wearily as the two warriors left the room.

After a moment's awkward silence, Danika stood, too. Despite the dark circles under her eyes and the small hunch to her shoulders, she was still beautiful in the soft lamplight, thought Nyle. Her fiery hair framed her features, feathering onto her face in wisps. She looked so vulnerable and shaken that he had to fight the urge to reach out and gather her into his arms, to soothe her. She hesitated as she stood and took a deep breath.

"I should go to bed…" She paused, still looking down at the table.

"Aye." Nyle didn't trust himself to say anything else. It took all his willpower not to suggest she come to his bed. He had an urge to tuck her into him and make sure she got some rest. "Your room is opposite mine. I'll show you up."

In the corridor separating their rooms, there was another awkward pause. Again, Nyle had an overwhelming urge to invite Danika in, but resisted. What would he do if she said no? And, for that matter, what would he do if she said yes?

She turned to her door. "Goodnight then."

"Goodnight," said Nyle.

She entered her room and shut the door behind her. He did the same and sat down heavily on his bed. The room was one he'd stayed in before. It was basic, but serviceable. Two beds stretched along one wall, a dresser and trunk on the other. In the center of the room, a large threadbare rug covered the rough boards, and a lamp sat on a table in the corner. A small window at one end let in a little moonlight, but other than that, the room was in darkness.

Nyle lit the lamp and stripped down to his trousers and vest. After a quick wash, he began a routine kit check. As he laid out his panniers, he gave himself a stern talking to in his head. He was doing the right thing, he thought to himself, by placing his mission above his feelings for Danika, so why did it feel so... wrong?

He cleaned his hunting knife with a piece of mole hide. He thought of Danika and of how she had looked this evening, lost and afraid and a little hopeless. The idea that she was miserable made him uncomfortable and restless. He rubbed the hunting knife until the steel gleamed in the lamplight. Maybe he should go and talk to her again. It was, after all, his job to make sure she was all right, and how could he do that from a different room? He forced himself to resist his temptation, knowing full well his intentions had little to do with his duty, quite the opposite, in fact. To keep himself busy, he began polishing his broadsword. Leave her be, she probably wouldn't...

There was a light tap on the door. Nyle was across the floor instantly to open the door, his heart racing in his chest.

A young man stood on the threshold, a pile of blankets in his arms.

"Sorry to disturb you, sir. Some of the guests have complained of being cold this evening. I was asked to distribute these." The youth offered Nyle extra blankets, his eyes nervously scanning the room.

"I'm fine," barked Nyle and went to shut the door.

"The young lady... I'm to offer her extra blankets. Where does she sleep?" the boy asked.

Nyle gestured to the opposite room. "But if she doesn't answer, then leave her be. She may be sleeping."

"Thank you, sir—" Nyle shut the door in his face.

He listened to the muffled knock and mumbled conversation next door, then quiet.

A few moments later, there was another knock on his door. Nyle put his sword aside and wrenched open the door, expecting to see the boy again. "What?" he demanded.

Danika stood in the hallway, her eyes wide, her face pale. "I'm sorry. I thought..." She turned to go back to her room. "It doesn't matter, forget it."

"Danika, wait."

She stopped but didn't turn around.

"What is it?" asked Nyle. "What's wrong?"

"I can't sleep and... I wanted some company. I'm sorry if you're busy."

"No, it's not a bother. I didn't mean to imply..." He cleared his throat and stood up straighter. "Come in."

Danika turned to him, her face pink. He stood aside and ushered her in.

She perched stiffly on the end of his bed, her arms folded in her lap, glancing awkwardly around the room. "What about Torin?" Danika asked as Nyle latched the door.

"I doubt he'll be back before dawn," replied Nyle. "He has a knack for finding places to sleep."

Danika nodded and stared at the wall. Nyle noticed her eyes were red rimmed and strands of hair clung to her damp cheeks.

Nyle had little experience of people crying, especially women. He had the niggling suspicion he was supposed to do something, only he was at a loss as to what. He wanted to know the exact words to ease her heart, but life as a soldier hadn't equipped him with that particular set of skills. As he looked down at her, she gave a small sad sniff, which made his chest hurt. He decided to jump in any way, regardless of his inexperience. He sat next to her on the bed and leant down so his face was level with hers. "What is it, lass? Talk to me," he asked, softly.

Danika's lips quivered as she answered, fresh tears welling in her eyes, "I miss the university, I miss Layla, and I will never see Elder-Sha Ameena again." She broke into sobs. Big, fat tears traced a slow path down her cheeks. Nyle put his arm around the healer's trembling shoulders, tentatively at first then, when she seemed to be calming, he pulled her in closer.

Danika continued, "When Elder-Sha Ameena put this mark on my arm, she had faith that I'd be able to convince the Fae aristocracy to help us." She turned to face Nyle. "But what if I can't? What if they refuse and the university falls? All the healing power in Shaman will not help if we're overwhelmed. It's going to be terrible, and there's nothing I can do…" She lapsed into silence, punctuated by the occasional sniff.

Nyle could identify with her. It was his nature to take his duty to heart, and he feared failure above anything. He was aware that throughout the camp, he was known as the hardest taskmaster with the highest standards. Every one of his soldiers knew that he expected complete commitment and focus. Sloppy mistakes were never acceptable. But sitting here on the bed with Danika and listening to her berate herself, he found himself murmuring something he would never have expected to hear himself say.

"Some things we cannot control, Danika. We fight and we try harder, but if we fail despite our best efforts, we fail with honor." He pulled her in closer to his chest. She was warm and comforting when she pressed her damp face into his shoulder. "I left Sabre at the university, and it seems there is a possibility that he is struggling with his task—putting our mission at risk. I don't like to believe it, and deep down I still don't, but if it is the case, then it is nothing I could have predicted—he has never failed before." He gently kissed the top of her head. Her hair smelt of lemon soap, and he liked it so much he nuzzled in closer.

His voice dropped to a whisper. "I can't take responsibility for things I could not have foreseen, Danika. Just like you can't take responsibility for the idiocy of the prideful Fae." He stroked her hair, enjoying the way it brushed softly through his fingers. They stayed like that for a few moments.

"When did you get so... clever?" Her voice was muffled by his shoulder, but to his relief, she sounded less pitiful and more like her usual self.

He pulled back and looked gravely into her honey-gold eyes and whispered, "Since everything I thought I knew started falling apart, since the university turned out to be a gateway to hell—" He smiled. "—since I was bullied into submission by a gutsy healer over her patient."

Danika smiled. The knot in Nyle's chest eased. He wanted to kiss her. To kiss away the tears and any lingering doubts she might have about her failures. Really, he thought to himself, he wanted to kiss her because he remembered how good she tasted.

Looking into her upturned face, he thought she probably wouldn't stop him either. But would it end at a kiss? Odds—zero.

At that moment, Danika stifled a huge yawn. Nyle rolled his eyes and let her go, leaning back on the bed. Kissing her would not end with a full night's sleep—it would end with a full night's lovemaking and with her in the morning, too exhausted to move. Nyle sent a small prayer to the Goddess, asking her to help him ignore the idea of Danika in the morning light, supine and sated, aglow with sweat and limp with satisfaction.

"I should probably go back to bed," said Danika, wiping her face on her sleeve and attempting to stand.

"Mmmm, probably," replied Nyle, grabbing her by her waist and dragging her towards him. He tucked her into his side as he lay down, keeping her firmly in his arms. "But if you promise not to try anything inappropriate, I'll permit you to stay with me."

Giggling, Danika tried to wiggle away, but her resistance was half-hearted. Soon she surrendered and cuddled back into the warrior's embrace, curling up against him and yawning again. "Your virtue is safe, warrior, as I'm too exhausted to fight you for it."

Nyle smiled as he held the healer close and closed his eyes. Danika drifted off almost immediately, so didn't hear the warrior's reply. "I've seen you fight, lass. I doubt my virtue would stand a chance."

CHAPTER 11

Danika woke to the smoldering stare of two hundred and fifty pounds of lean, well-muscled warrior. His eyes bore down into hers, his face just a few inches away. He had his weight balanced on his palms, each side of her shoulders. Tiny shocks of adrenaline surged to every part of her body, and her heart began thumping to an irregular beat.

As she met his gaze, the side of Nyle's mouth curled into a half-smile. He leant down towards her lips, so close she was certain he was going to kiss her, but he moved slightly at the last moment, and his lips brushed her ear as he murmured, "Good morning, lass."

His warm breath stroked her ear and tiny shivers travelled down her neck and across her back. She swallowed hard. "Good morning. Is it late?"

Nyle didn't move from her ear. More soft words, more shivers. "No, it's early. The city has yet to rise." He planted soft little kisses down her neck, which made her eyes roll back and a warm ache settle between her legs. Her breath came out with a quiet moan. Nyle stilled his mouth on her neck mid-kiss. He groaned low in his chest, a rumble that Danika felt vibrate through her whole body.

"Would you like to get up, or stay in bed awhile?" His tone left no doubt as to what staying in bed might entail.

A voice in her head told her she was out of her depth. She didn't have a skinful of strong ale to embolden her this time. Images of the night in the hay barn came flooding back. She remembered the feeling of bliss as he took her into his mouth, the rolling waves of pleasure as he coaxed her orgasm from her. She remembered the feeling of power as he came in her hand.

"Well?" He kissed her neck again, this time hard, scraping his teeth over her sensitive skin. Her hands entwined in his hair as she pulled him firmly into her. Responding to her writhing encouragement, he wrapped his arms around her, and lying on his side, held her length against his and kissed her mouth hard.

"I'll stay awhile," she said, answering his passion with her own.

Her doubts and fears evaporated—there was only him in this moment. He gripped her lower back and squeezed her closer. She could feel the ridge of his shaft hard against her thigh and found herself rocking against it, wrapping her legs astride his as he plundered her mouth with his tongue. She rose to meet him, pressing her body against his and causing him to groan again deep in his chest. He ran his hand up underneath her chemise and ran his hands over her breasts, the rough skin on his palm making her nipples achingly tight. Danika's head swam with desire. She was about to run her hands down and feel Nyle's hard shaft in her hand when a loud thump sounded outside the door, followed by the smashing of glass. They both froze.

Nyle broke away, cursing, and was on his feet in an instant. Pausing only to pick up his sword, he yanked open the door and sped into the room opposite. Danika hurriedly followed, her heart pounding, and her face flushed.

The room opposite was a scene of carnage and confusion. Furniture lay in pieces on the floor, along with shreds of ripped fabric. And in the center of it all stood two of the largest and most savage dogs Danika had ever seen.

Standing roughly the height of pit ponies with lean bodies and long pointed muzzles, they were coal black and terrifying. Their squinting eyes held tiny points of white, which glowed in the semi-dark room. But it was their teeth that made Danika want to turn and flee. Huge fangs jutted from their upper jaws like four-inch daggers, each dripping with yellow saliva. Snarling and growling through their fangs, they pawed at the floor with jagged yellow nails.

"Get back—now!" Nyle shouted at Danika. The closest dog swung its ugly muzzle towards the healer and sniffed. It howled, a guttural roar that turned Danika's blood to ice. She jumped back as it lunged. She held out her arms to fend it off and closed her eyes. Robbed of the ability to think, she waited for the moment those fetid jaws would rip into her. She felt its breath on her face, but then heard a thud, and opened her eyes.

The creature lay at her feet—it let out an agonized

whine as the end of Nyle's sword emerged from its stomach, dark blood pooling around its body. Nyle was on his feet in an instant, extracting his sword and raising it towards the second snarling creature, ripping it open from tail to chest. He bent and severed the creature's head from its body. He remained crouching next to it, hardly out of breath but frowning deeply.

Danika was struggling to get her own heart rate under control. She stepped over the mass of blood and fur towards Nyle. "Are you okay? Are you hurt?"

Nyle shook his head but barely looked at her.

"What are these… these things?"

"Hunters." He turned to Danika's bed. The blankets and mattress were in ribbons.

"W-what do you mean? Why here? Why this bed?"

"They follow a scent marker?" said Nyle. He bent over the torn bed and reached down to retrieve a scrap of blue fabric. "Extra blankets."

"What about the extra blankets?"

"Hunters rely on scent to mark their prey. This pack was meant for whoever slept with this blanket." Nyle held up the ragged cloth.

"So, if I'd stayed here…in this room last night."

Nyle didn't say anything. He turned on his heel and made for the stairs.

Danika looked again at the creatures dead on the floor. If she'd been alone, they would've ripped her apart.

Downstairs they found the innkeeper overseeing breakfast preparations in the kitchen.

"The boy—the one that handed out the extra blankets," said Nyle. "I need to speak with him urgently."

"What blankets?" replied the innkeeper with a frown.

"There was a lad of about sixteen. He delivered some blankets to the top floor last night."

The innkeeper's frown deepened into a look of annoyance, but he called over his shoulder, "Goran, come here."

The same boy who had delivered the blankets came in from the kitchen, wiping his hands on a grubby cloth.

"Who gave you the blankets, boy?" Nyle towered over the lad.

The boy took a step back "I… what? What blankets?"

Nyle spoke in a low growl. "Don't play games, boy. I'll gut you slowly and prize the truth from you. You gave me blankets last night—on whose bidding?"

The boy cowered. "I don't know. I've never met you before." He winced and rubbed his temples.

Danika stepped in. Threatening the child was obviously getting them nowhere. "Are you sick?"

"My head aches. And when I try to remember last night, a pain shoots through…"

Danika raised her hand to the boy's brow; his temperature was fine. She delved deeper, reaching out her magic-like tiny branches into his mind. She pulled her hand back suddenly—such pain!

"What is it?" Nyle was standing over her, lines of concern etched upon his face.

She rubbed her hand, but it was unharmed. "A spell of some kind. I'm not sure, but something has meddled in this boy's mind—a magic I don't recognize."

The boy turned pale. "I don't feel well. I might go and lie down if that's okay?" He looked at the innkeeper, who gave a reluctant nod, and the boy left clutching his head.

"I'm a pair of hands down thanks to you." The old man scowled.

Danika spoke. "We have just been attacked, in your establishment, by massive dogs, and you worry about the dishes not getting done!"

The innkeeper's frown deepened, his watery eyes narrowed. "My security is adequate for most people. Perhaps it's your friend,"—he gestured towards Nyle—"who brings trouble here. I would appreciate it if your party found alternative lodgings."

Danika boiled at the innkeeper's words and began to protest, but Nyle stopped her. He turned to the innkeeper. "We'll be away by noon."

The innkeeper nodded. "And expect a charge for cleaning up the room." He headed back to the kitchen.

Down in the bar they found Torin snoozing on a sofa in the corner, his clothes rumpled, his golden hair ruffled, light stubble shadowing his chin. Alyssa joined them, having gone scouting at first light.

Danika watched him jump awake as Nyle nudged him with his foot.

"We could have done with you earlier, archer," said Nyle.

"Why?" Torin stared blearily at the others.

"Hunters," replied Nyle "They were after her." He jerked his head towards Danika. "They were tracking a marked blanket."

"Where did the blanket come from?" Torin looked fully alert now and addressed the question to Danika.

"A boy delivered it to my quarters last night," replied

the healer. "He was compelled by some kind of mind magic."

"In the name of the Goddess, how did you manage to escape?"

Danika looked away. "I wasn't in my bed at the time of the attack."

Torin looked from Danika to Nyle and smiled. "Well, that was lucky," he said and stretched languorously.

Danika caught just a flicker of Alyssa's eye. Was it surprise? Condemnation? She couldn't tell.

"Did you scope out the embassy?" asked Nyle sharply.

"Yes, but I had to interrogate a barmaid fairly rigorously to get directions." Torin ran his hand over his stubbly jaw and winked at Danika.

She rolled her eyes but failed to suppress a smile, saying, "I thought you knew the city well."

"I had a rough idea how to get there but to be sure."

"Spare us the details!" snapped Nyle. "And show us the way."

∽

OF ALL THE BEAUTIFUL BUILDINGS IN SHALLAHA, THE FAE embassy was by far the most impressive. A smooth white stone wall encircled four spiraling towers, each capped with a silver dome. Morning sunlight reflected off the domes in a blazing display of dancing colors, so bright that Danika had to hold her hands up to shield her eyes from the reflected glare.

She tried to calm her nerves as the company approached a large set of gates. Next to the main entrance was a much smaller door set into the pale stone, and to the side of that was a booth with a thick window of glass that had obviously had a glamour spell placed upon it, making it appear to shimmer like moving water.

Sitting in the booth was a stunningly attractive woman. Pale and elegant, with delicately braided hair and a flawless complexion. Not Fae, thought Danika, and from what she had been told, she doubted any of the hedonistic immortals had actual jobs, but even so, as humans went, this woman was remarkable. She looked out of the booth window at the band of journey-sore travelers with undisguised disdain.

Danika smoothed down her hair and spoke to the gatekeeper through the hatch. "We need to speak to the ambassador. It is a matter of national importance."

The woman looked at her coolly, and Danika detected a smirk lurking beneath her cultivated expression. "I'm sorry. The ambassador is not accepting visitors today. I can make you an appointment for—" She flicked through a large book on the ledge in front of her. "—early next year?"

Danika looked back at the others. Nyle was frowning, hand resting on the hilt of his sword, Torin looked at the gatekeeper with ill-concealed desire, and Alyssa gazed straight ahead, as impassive, and as cold as ever. Frustration gnawed at Danika. So much was at stake.

She rolled up her sleeve and presented her tattoo to the gatekeeper. "This is the seal of Elfain. It was presented to me by Fae royalty, and I demand that you grant me access so that I may petition the prince." She kept her tone firm as her heart was thumping in her chest.

"Oooh, that is pretty," the gatekeeper smiled, "but it looks like the kind of glamour one can pick up in the souks for a few copper coins. I repeat, the ambassador is accepting no visitors, and as for petitioning the prince." The woman laughed prettily. "I doubt that very much."

She was already closing the glamour glass barrier.

Danika panicked. "The ambassador is expecting me. I'm a healer from the university—He sent for me." The words were out of her mouth before she knew what she was saying. She tried to look confident, but she was sure she would be called on her lie. The woman paused, her eyes darting to the book in front of her, and for a moment Danika saw the woman's groomed facade crack and confusion take its place.

"You're not in my diary," the woman replied, shuffling through the papers on her desk.

"My job here is of a... discrete nature." Danika lowered her voice and leant in towards the other woman. "I doubt the ambassador would have told many people about it."

The woman looked from side to side, her elegant features drained of color. She leant in and whispered to Danika. "You may be too late. His daughter's mind weakens by the day."

Fae and madness: the unspoken curse of the immortals, inferred but never confirmed, rumors, obscure references in textbooks. Danika quickly warmed to her lie. "You must allow us access. Her sanity depends on it. If you prevent us from entering, you'll answer to the ambassador—or even the prince."

The woman stared at Danika for a moment, her eyes

wide with fear. She turned to the three warriors. "But I cannot let these soldiers—"

"We are her protectors," said Torin, flashing the gatekeeper a devastating smile. "This Shaman is a powerful healer, and many seek to use her power for their own ends."

The woman hesitated, then picked up a large silver key. "Come to the door."

Danika and the others waited for a moment, and the door in the wall opened. Behind it stood half a dozen tall guards dressed in black silk and carrying curved swords. Each wore a turban of blood-red silk, which added to their already impressive height. The woman addressed them. "Formak," she said, and one of the guards bowed, "show them to the ambassador's waiting chamber."

The guard straightened, spun on his heel, and without a word set off towards the largest of the towers. Danika followed with the three warriors in formation behind. Danika, almost breathless with nerves, turned to catch a look of approval from Alyssa. Well, that's something, she thought wryly. They probably wouldn't be braiding each other's hair any time soon but that might be considered a small thaw.

As they walked, Nyle sidled up to Danika and spoke quietly in her ear. "What's your plan?"

"I'm going to try to treat the ambassador's daughter," she whispered.

"The ambassador's daughter is a Fae. Does your magic even work on their kind?"

"Not my healing powers, but I've studied some

compounds that have succeeded in treating delirium," Danika replied under her breath.

Nyle leant closer, his breath tickling Danika's ear. "Won't their healers have tried this?"

"Elder Sha Ameena guided me in a particular preparation—she claimed it was for migraines, but I now suspect it was the Fae curse I was treating."

"You... suspect?"

Danika half turned to Nyle. "A Fae doesn't get migraines. What else would she need my help for?"

They were led into the base of the tower and up a long, winding staircase. Vibrant portraits and opulent tapestries adorned the walls, and a densely woven rug carpeted the stairs. Danika marveled at the way her feet sank into the soft fabric, leaving indented footprints where she walked. They were shown to a large bright room with one curved wall and a window that looked out over the whole city.

The guard turned to them. "You will disarm all weaponry before you can see the ambassador," he said, opening a deep wooden chest and gesturing for the warriors to place their swords within. Danika noticed Nyle and Torin exchange pointed looks as they gave up their swords and knives. Alyssa reluctantly surrendered her whip. The guard locked the lid and pocketed the key, then disappeared into an adjoining room, closing the door behind him.

Danika sat on a chaise longue and rubbed her hands over its plush velvet upholstery. Everything in the room was rich and colorful, from the deep purple sofas and gleaming mahogany tables to the colorful curtains and exotic looking green plants. Sunshine streamed through the large window and reflected off the highly polished wooden floor. It smelt of vanilla and roses and, despite her nerves, Danika couldn't help but bask in the full-scale assault on her senses.

Torin found a leather easy chair to slouch in, Alyssa stood and gazed out of the window, whilst Nyle paced around the room, stopping by the wooden chest and sizing up the lock.

"If we get any trouble, Torin, you need to use your power and shoot our way out," Nyle said to his archer.

"No problem. I don't think the Fae know much about our weaponry, otherwise they might not have let me in."

Nyle nodded and continued his restless pacing.

Eventually, the door opened, and the guard entered, followed by the tallest and most lavishly dressed man Danika had ever seen. He was almost as tall as Nyle but of slender build with waves of white-blond hair curling over his shoulders clasped at his nape by a silver jeweled clip. He wore blood-red robes, which swished and billowed as he entered the room. Danika tried to pull her eyes away from his perfect golden complexion and his pale-blue eyes but couldn't, not for a moment, he was too... beautiful.

When she finally did manage to look away, she caught the eye of Alyssa, and for a moment the female warrior's spellbound expression matched her own. Alyssa quickly dropped her gaze, her features settling back into their usual stony facade.

The tall stranger spoke to Danika. "You are from the university? You are a healer?"

"Yes. I have a message for the prince. I must deliver it in person."

"I was told you were here to heal my daughter. They said nothing about a message."

Danika chose her words carefully. "I will do what I can for your daughter, but I must also speak with his highness. There are dangers he must hear of, some of which will affect the Fae."

"See to my Marian, then we will discuss the message," the ambassador said dismissively.

"Do I have your bond, Ambassador, that if I treat your daughter, I can convey the message to the prince of Elfain?" It was rumored that a Fae could not break a bonded oath, that to do so would cause excruciating pain. Danika hoped it was true.

The Fae's light face darkened, and his eyes glinted like chips of ice. "I could make you do it, girl," he snarled. "I could cause such terrifying hallucinations that you would beg for a way to please me, just to make the horror stop."

Nyle growled deep in his chest. "Harm her and I will rip you apart, dreamweaver."

The ambassador spun to face the warrior. "Savage! You dare threaten—"

Danika interrupted. "I will not tend Marian without your bond." She lowered her voice and approached the ambassador. "Just promise me you'll plead our case for an audience, and I will do everything I can to help her."

"Fine!" snapped the ambassador. "I swear to request an audience with the prince in return for your help." He moved forward, towering over the little healer. "But if you hurt her further, I will torture you with visions until your mind bleeds from your ears and you claw out your own eyes."

Nyle advanced on the ambassador, but Danika stopped him. "I commit to deliver the full benefit of all the learning I possess to save her."

The ambassador turned. "Follow me."

∽

As he followed, Nyle struggled to suppress the rage that bubbled up inside of him. When the Fae had threatened Danika, it had taken every ounce of discipline he possessed to keep from crushing the conceited swine. Only the soft plea in the healer's eyes had stayed his arm.

They were led through several living chambers, each packed with the same finery and trappings as the first, and up a small flight of stairs into a huge circular bedchamber.

A fire roared in the grate, and the room was uncomfortably warm. In the middle stood a massive round bed draped in gold silk and piled high with quilts and blankets.

Nyle followed Danika as she approached the bed. Amongst the heap of covers lay a thin, pale girl of about nineteen. She had her father's high cheekbones and pale-blue eyes, the same blonde hair fanned out against the silken pillows. Her chalk-like pallor, however, was pale even by Fae standards.

Nyle watched the girl struggle to focus on the people around the bed, but her eyes kept rolling upwards. She could barely speak for shivering as she held her slender arms across her chest.

"They come and there is nought but death." Her voice was a whisper. "The blood runs in rivers in the streets and down the chins of his children." She writhed on the bed, her back arching against the covers.

Danika leant over the girl and pushed her gently back to the silken cushions. "Where are her healers?" she said to the ambassador.

"Their magic was useless. I sent them away." He moved forward and brushed a strand of hair from his daughter's brow with a trembling hand. "She worsens by the day." The tall ambassador then knelt by the bed and spoke quietly, gazing down at the girl. "Marian has been everything to me since her mother died. Her light has been the only beacon in my grief. She is one of only a handful of children born to the Fae in the last twenty years. My wife was so happy when she discovered we had been chosen, that she would be a vessel." The ambassador hung his head. "When Marian became sick, it was like my beloved Laxmi all over again. I begged the prince to remove my daughter to the palace in Elfain, but he would not allow it." His voice became a hoarse whisper. "Madness is shameful in our lands, and the prince fears she will… taint others."

Danika knelt beside the ambassador and took the young woman's arm in her own. She turned to the ambassador. "I need to know a little about your physiology."

"We keep our physiology secret, to protect ourselves. By revealing such information, I could be tried for treason."

"I think I can help Marian, but I need that information. I ask, not to endanger you but to save her." Danika ran her hands over the girl's forehead, and she stilled, her face softening. As Danika raised her hand, the girl resumed her agitated state.

The ambassador stood up and moved to the end of the bed. He ran his hand through his silvery hair. "We are not immortal, as other races believe. When we reach maturity, at the age of twenty, our ageing slows." The ambassador paused and looked around the room nervously, as if frightened of being overheard, but eventually he continued, "The oldest Fae are near a thousand years old, and it is rumored that some have lived longer than that. But eventually we do succumb to time. We can be killed the same as others—by a large trauma or losing blood, by burning or drowning or poison. But we never fall prey to disease, and the injuries we survive are usually repaired quickly.

"This mind disease, however, is not unknown amongst the Fae." The ambassador looked up again and lowered his voice. "Our minds differ from yours. Due to our powers of glamour and our long life spans, we are far more vulnerable to paranoia, hallucinations and—" He paused. "—insanity. It happens most when we spend too long among mortals. Your imaginations, your emotions, they overload us."

This information surprised Nyle; he'd been taught that the Fae were impervious to anything but physical violence. His race lived about eighty years, most of which one would expect to be able to fight, hunt, or work the land. He wondered what it would be like to live to a thousand. Would it make time more precious or less? One thing was certain, the reputation of the Fae as cruel and heartless was disproved to him here as the ambassador bent over his daughter and gently stroked the poor girl's cheek.

The prince, on the other hand.

The girl squeezed her eyes shut and moaned. "The soles of my feet burn. They roast in a slow fire as everything burns around me. I can smell the cooking flesh. I feel it blister and crack."

Danika rolled up her sleeves and examined the girl. "I'm going to need specific herbs and compounds."

The ambassador nodded eagerly. "Just tell me what you need."

∼

Nyle watched Danika work. She'd labored throughout the night in her makeshift workshop. She'd spoken seldom, only to tell him that the preparation was a difficult blend, and without her notes, she would have to retry it a number of times before she achieved the correct balance.

Finally, she'd turned to him in the early hours of the morning, holding a flask, a look of triumph on her delightful face. He'd never seen anyone look quite so beautiful.

And here they were in the Fae girl's bedchamber.

The girl thrashed as the ambassador held her tightly. She would not drink the preparation.

Danika tried to calm her using the same tone he'd

heard her use on the injured boy at the inn. The girl snarled, and suddenly Danika cried out and sat back heavily, clutching her head. Nyle instinctively moved towards her and touched her shoulder. "What is it, Danika?"

She took a deep, shaking breath and opened her eyes. "She's afraid, and she is lashing out with her body—" Danika frowned deeply. "—and with her mind."

"Danika, be careful." He didn't care that Alyssa and Torin were swapping arched looks at his expense.

"It's okay, Nyle, I'm okay."

Danika sat back on her heels. Nyle saw her hands tremble, and when she looked around, her eyes were bloodshot.

She spoke to the ambassador. "We must get her to drink the potion."

The ambassador nodded. "My people see the invasion of another Fae's mind as the worst kind of assault, but in this case I must, for her own good. I will compel her to drink." The ambassador closed his eyes, and the girl stilled. She moaned softly but didn't fight when Danika held the cup to her lips.

The young girl fell into a faint after finishing the last of the liquid.

"Is she cured?" The ambassador clutched his daughter's arm.

"She has been left untreated for such a long time. It will take many more treatments before she is restored,"— Danika's voice wavered— "when she wakes, she should be stable - for a while."

"Thank you, healer." The ambassador's voice cracked. "I will keep my end of our bargain."

Danika tried to stand. Nyle ran to her side and caught her just as she collapsed into his arms. She groaned. "My head, it hurts."

"She needs a place to rest," barked Nyle to the ambassador. "Now!"

"Of course, I will have Formak show you to your quarters. Let him know what you require. I am in the healer's debt." The ambassador bowed stiffly to Danika before turning back to his daughter on the bed and tenderly clasping her hand.

Without any signal that Nyle could see, the guard from earlier entered the room and bade them follow. Nyle carried the healer easily, pausing when he passed the trunk containing their weapons.

"We need back our armory," said Nyle to the guard.

"They will be returned to you on your departure, not before."

Nyle grunted but didn't argue. He was more concerned by Danika's pale face and the dark smudges under her eyes.

They were taken down many stairs and shown into their two rooms. He laid Danika on the large plush bed. "Bring her food and wine," he demanded. The guard nodded and left.

He removed her boots and jacket and lay down next to her on the bed, wrapping his arms around her small frame. He listened to her breathing and stroked her hair as she murmured restlessly in her sleep.

She shouldn't have made herself vulnerable to the Fae girl. Didn't she know how vital she was? Always rescuing lost causes and risking herself for others—she needed protecting from herself! She was too important to go around saving every waif and half-drowned sparrow. *Too important to the mission or too important to you?* He ignored the voice in his head as best he could. He brushed away a wisp of hair that trembled on her cheek. To the mission of course!

CHAPTER 12

*D*anika sat up in bed and sipped her tea. A few days ago, she would have reveled in the feeling of cool silk against her skin and the comfort of a proper mattress. But she was finding it hard to get comfortable. Perhaps she'd got used to sleeping on muddy floors and tavern beds stuffed with straw. Nyle had gone to see the ambassador and ask if there was any news on an audience with the prince. He hadn't wanted to go, and she'd had to remind him that they were on a mission and talking to the prince right now was kind of a big deal. He'd left, promising to return within the hour.

There was no denying that she felt more for the warrior than a passing attraction. He made her feel safe, even in this new, crazy world of monsters, mental attacks, and assassination attempts. She'd never met someone so focused and disciplined, but he had shown her that he wasn't cold and heartless. She thought back to the way he had held her, how he had worried about her when she was healing the ambassador's daughter.

She liked his company when he wasn't commanding her to obey him. He seemed to care for her. But would he ever admit it? And if he did, where would it go? She was a healer committed to the protection of life. He was a warrior, a killer—a clever and sometimes charming killer—but still.

She mentally rolled her eyes at her own rambling thoughts. Even if they were perfect for each other, even if there were no differences in their cultures of beliefs, there was a failing rift that threatened everything. What future existed if they failed to engage the assistance of the Fae? Here she was deciding if she and Nyle would settle in a mountain war camp or Shaman city, or if they should bring up their children believing in the Goddess or the Shaman mother of life. The world was crumbling around them. She was one of a handful of healers in this region. What would happen when creatures ravished half the city?

Alyssa entered, her face a thundercloud.

"What's wrong?" Danika asked.

"I've been told to tell you that the ambassador's daughter remains stable."

"That's a good thing! Why the frown?" She'd check on the girl right away. Hopefully, Marian would be lucid and wouldn't lash out.

"We're invited to a ball. Here. Tonight."

"What?" Danika stared in confusion at Alyssa. "We are in the grip of disaster and the ambassador wants to throw a party?" The healer sighed. "I can't go. I have work to do. I need to lobby for an audience with the prince, even if I have to sneak into Elfain in disguise, I—"

"You have to go."
"What—why?"
"It's being held in your honor."

~

Danika tried to bend her arm in an impossible direction and stretch backwards to fasten yet another clasp. There were hundreds, all carved from pearl and ivory, all as small as a grain of rice and hand-stitched to glorious yellow silk with gossamer-thin thread. Danika tried not to think about how much such a dress was worth. She would have to be very careful and not eat anything with the potential to drip.

The ambassador had been touchingly grateful for his daughter's improvement when Danika had checked on her patient earlier. But when she'd tried to press her advantage and seek a royal audience, he'd dismissed her with "All in good time, healer." Danika stretched to reach a button in the center of her back but finally gave up, again bemoaning her lack of physical magic. Layla would have just clicked her fingers and the clasps would have fastened themselves. What a ridiculous waste of time this was.

She'd tried to convey her unease at all this fuss to the ambassador, but he'd had a very persuasive manner. In fact, after their short conversation earlier, she'd found herself wholeheartedly agreeing to the notion that she deserved some luxury after such a long and uncomfortable journey and that one evening of good food and music was just the thing to unwind.

She'd allowed herself to be bathed and pampered, her hair washed with expensive herbs, all the while feeling that she deserved a break. The effect of his light glamouring, however, had faded, and here she was, fumbling with thousands of tiny pearl clasps, and facing the daunting prospect of being the guest of honor at a party that included all of Shallaha's glitterati.

When she was well and truly clasped in, she turned her attention to the lacings. They tied at the back in an intricate zigzag of sashes and ribbons, and since she was unwilling to dislocate her shoulders, she was at a loss as to what to do. She walked over to the window and gazed out onto the city below. Rivers of people jostled to and fro, a bobbing mass of anonymity. Perhaps she could just slip out undetected and sneak back later when the party was over.

"I've already tried it. There are guards at every exit and servants are on hand to escort you to the party."

Danika jumped away from the window as Alyssa entered, resplendent in an amethyst satin dress, high necked and sleeveless, and fitted exactly to her lean, tall form. Her blue eyes picked up the tone of the dress and seemed to glow from within, creating a devastating effect. The warrior looked wild and beautiful, and for a moment, Danika was struck speechless.

"You!" Alyssa glared at Danika. "This party is for you, and I have been ordered—*ordered* to attend."

Danika squirmed. "It might not be so bad. We might be able to find out some information—"

"I sent two dresses back—they seemed to expect me to flaunt my flesh for all of Shallaha." She looked down at

Danika's cleavage. Danika self-consciously pulled the bodice up as Alyssa continued, "It took me an hour to find the opening for this thing." She gestured to the dress. "I had to call Torin to help in the end. And the stuff they put on my hair has made it move on its own! Look. I go one way and my hair swoops in the other direction. It's ridiculous!" Alyssa's honey-blonde hair did look somewhat pouffy.

"I need you to do something with it." She thrust a handful of grips and clips at Danika, some of which scattered on the floor before Danika could grab them."

"Didn't your hairdresser have time to finish?" Danika's hairdresser had spent a very long time threading sparkly things into her fringe and lacing tiny ribbons into the back. Despite the tiresome process, Danika liked the effect. It made her look like an exotic bird.

Alyssa gave a snort. "I sent her away. She talked nonsense, and I've had all the nonsense I can take. Someone tried to rub coconut oil into my skin. A complete stranger—no, thank you! And the shoes they have given me have stalks on the bottom. Look!" She hitched up the dress and shoved her pointed heels in Danika's direction. "Who walks on stalks? What happens if you need to run? Or fight?"

Danika suppressed a smile. "I don't think you'll be required to fight tonight, Alyssa. We're in one of the most well-guarded buildings in the entire realm. And we're going to a ball."

Alyssa drew herself up to her full height and loomed over Danika. "I am a warrior of the elite guard, sworn to protect the Shaman territories—from the northern mountains right down to the southern isles—from the forces of Gehenna. Even though I hate this Goddess-forsaken city and this ridiculously pompous embassy, I will defend it to the death, as is my oath. I am always prepared to fight!" She turned to the mirror and frowned, brushing her voluminous locks away from her face.

Danika just stood still in shock. She had never heard the taciturn warrioress speak so many words at one time.

Nor had she finished. "You are responsible for this, healer. You must make my hair less… willful." Alyssa, usually so controlled and purposeful, looked totally red-faced. Her fingers shook as she tried repeatedly to stroke down her tousled locks.

Danika, when she could collect her wits, climbed onto a velvet stool and gathered the warrior's flowing mane into a golden tail, then braided it with ribbons. A few tendrils escaped and curled softly onto the warrior's face. She coiled the thick braid and pinned it on top of Alyssa's head. Satisfied, Danika secured her creation with an ivory clasp.

Alyssa grunted at her reflection in the mirror but didn't comment, which, in the circumstances, Danika took as a good sign.

There was a knock on the door.

"I come bearing gifts," called Torin from the other side.

As Danika let him in, she saw him pause at the sight of Alyssa. He swallowed and blinked twice.

"You both look very nice," he said, his voice a tiny bit higher than usual.

Torin continued to stare, his eyes locked on Alyssa. Then he shook his head and held out two pairs of sparkling pumps, both with low heels. Alyssa grabbed hers eagerly and kicked off her others. "Thank you," she muttered.

Danika hesitated; she'd practiced earlier and was able, if not proficient, in walking in the high heels. Besides, she'd been five-foot-two all her life; it might be nice to be a bit taller, at least for an evening. "I'll keep these."

Danika ignored Alyssa's look of scorn.

"What's wrong with the back of your dress? It has holes and stringy things all over the back." Alyssa pointed to Danika's failed attempt to lace the back of her bodice.

"Allow me." Torin moved behind Danika and, in a whirr of knotting and threading, had Danika professionally trussed up, clinched in at the waist, and elegantly wrapped in delicate silk in a matter of moments.

"How did you know how to do that?" asked Danika, admiring her elegant silhouette in a full-length mirror.

"I just reversed the process I usually employ." Torin smiled and winked at Danika, who rolled her eyes and turned back to the mirror.

She liked how elegant and grown-up she felt in the sleek dress and pointy shoes.

This was not the case half an hour later when it was time to enter the banqueting hall. Torin had walked both women to a large pair of ornate doors, and the walk down had been fraught with skimmed hems and wobbling steps. Nyle was due to meet them in the hall, and Danika's tummy fluttered at the thought of what he might think of her so dressed up. Although, looking at Alyssa, she doubted she would get the lion's share of the attention. The female warrior was a sublime vision, marred only by the frown that was currently plastered on her face. Danika tried surreptitiously to hitch up her low-cut bodice again; she was not used to showing quite so much... skin.

The doors opened and there was a hush from the multitude of voices within. The room was set with a long table sitting at least fifty people on both sides. A band of musicians played a subtle melody, and two great chandeliers sprayed a glitter of tiny lights around the room. Candles lit the table, and the whole elegant vision looked like something from another world.

Every scrutinizing gaze was on them. Danika met the stare of Nyle, his eyes unwavering and intense—it didn't leave her for a second. He was clean-shaven and dressed in a loose-fitting white shirt and black trousers. The light shirt made his skin seem darker, Ilandish almost, and with his tousled hair, he managed to look both elegant and roguish at the same time. Many eyes, Danika noted, were drawn to the imposing warrior. As she passed him, she felt studied. She was suddenly keenly aware of how low her bodice was cut. She inclined her head to him in greeting, but he barely smiled in response. A pretty, if heavily painted, woman on his left was whispering in his ear, placing her hand on his bicep. Danika looked away.

The ambassador rose from his seat as the two women were led to their places. Danika sat to the ambassador's right. Alyssa and Torin were seated at the other end of the table, so far away that Danika could hardly see them. Nyle was seated halfway down the table on the opposite side. She found herself stealing glances at him and his brazen companion out of the corner of her eye.

The ambassador remained standing and made a speech. He spoke about the Fae and Shaman relationship. He extolled the merits of repairing relations with the people of the mountain lands. Danika imagined Nyle raising an eyebrow at this, but she stopped herself from looking to see. He finished with heartfelt thanks to Danika for helping Marian, his daughter. At the end of his speech, many of the Shaman dignitaries were nodding and smiling and whispering their agreement. Danika suspected it was more due to good wine and glamour than a fundamental shift in policy. Still, the fact that they had convinced the ambassador of their cause was a blessing.

The moment the ambassador sat down, an army of handsome waiters arrived with trays of delicacies. Danika discovered she was starving and had to stop herself from gobbling up every one of the delicious fancies on the table before her in one go. Taking her lead from the starched lady on her left, she daintily nibbled at the pastries.

She turned to the ambassador. "Alyssa tells me you have requested an audience for us, with the prince."

"Yes, I am waiting on the prince's decision." The ambassador's courteous demeanor faltered for a moment, and he leant in closer to Danika. "I fear the prince will be unmoved by the plight of the Shaman. I have been recalled to the palace. They are preparing to cut all ties with this realm, to abandon the Shaman to the hordes of Gehenna."

Danika's heart sank. "Why haven't you gone?" she asked.

"They would not allow Marian passage. I will not leave

without her," replied the ambassador, his pale-blue eyes cast downwards as he spoke of his daughter.

Danika nodded. "If I can speak to the prince, I may be able to convince him." She thought about Elder-Sha Ameena's message. Would the prince agree to help in answer to his dead sister's plea? Or would he cut off Shaman and allow the daemons free rein?

"As a race, we do not feel compassion as the Shaman do, so do not rely on frothy emotional appeals to sway his majesty. I have spent many years in Shaman lands. I see my own people as they are: cold and selfish and without passion."

Danika nodded and only picked at the food she had moments before wanted to devour.

The ambassador sighed, watching Danika fiddling with her food he said, "Let us not dwell on sad times for this evening, Danika." His voice grew louder so that those close could hear. "May I introduce you to Conleth? He is a silk merchant from the Southern lands. You should get to know each other, but be careful, Danika, he is a terrible flirt."

Danika turned to face the dark stranger, who gave her a gleaming pearly smile. He bowed his head and placed his hand on his heart.

"Excuse me, Ambassador, but that is just not true. I am an excellent flirt!" His dark eyes glittered in the light of the chandelier. "And if I had known the yellow silk, you wear could look so stunning, I would have filled my ships with nothing else." His voice was husky and heavily accented.

Danika blushed. "It's very pretty… the color I mean."

Conleth's smile widened. "It becomes more beautiful the deeper you blush. I will make it my mission to flatter you all evening." He leant a fraction closer, his softly spoken words brushing Danika's neck. "You are good for business. Tomorrow orders will come flooding in for the yellow silk that was worn by the beautiful healer." Danika giggled despite herself and allowed the trader to serve her some tartlets.

She sneaked a sly glance over in Nyle's direction; his companion was still talking low into his ear, and he was doing nothing, it seemed, to discourage her attention. Obsessing on everything Nyle might be thinking or feeling was exhausting. Perhaps she should forget about the surly warrior, if only for one evening—it certainly looked as if he'd forgotten about her. Ignoring the sharp stab of jealousy in her chest, she turned back to the merchant and allowed him to fill her goblet.

"I bring this wine from the Ruby Islands, many sailing days west of the port of Shallaha." A jeweled bracelet glittered on his tanned wrist as he poured the dark red liquid for Danika.

Danika smiled and took a sip. A warm glow began in her mouth and flowed into her chest as she swallowed. Hot spices and a gently sweet taste remained on her tongue, bringing to mind summer afternoons spent basking in sunshine. "It's wonderful," she said, taking another mouthful and drawing in the heady flavors.

"The Islanders drink it to honor their Sun Gods. They drink it all evening on the longest day of the year as they feast and dance and offer prayers to the Gods. Then, when the sun finally sets—" He leant closer to Danika, so close that his lips almost touched her ear. "—they make love with each other on the beach until the morning rays break over the eastern rim and the sea mists wash away their memories of the night."

Danika didn't know whether to laugh or blush. She swallowed hard. "What do they do for the rest of the year?

The merchant paused a moment, then he laughed, a deep booming sound, and sat back in his chair. "I do not know. Go fishing, raise little islanders, make wine for me to ply beautiful young women with."

Danika laughed and allowed the merchant to refresh her glass.

The noise of conversation and laughter hung in the air. She found Conleth to be very entertaining company. Soon they were chatting like old friends, and he was regaling her with hair-raising stories of his time at sea. Danika became so caught up in her conversation that she barely registered when, farther along the table, some blockhead accidentally spilt wine everywhere, diverted, as she was, by the handsome merchant.

CHAPTER 13

Nyle frantically mopped at the spill with his napkin before it dribbled all over his neighbor's silken frippery. The overly painted, overly talkative woman to his right, who had spent the last half an hour attempting to flirt with him, was helping him to clear up the mess. Dabbing at the wine with her own napkin, she started to covertly dab him, under the pretense of cleaning up wine that had spilt on his trousers. He politely and firmly placed her cool, grasping hands in her own lap, telling her he would clear up his own mess, before returning to his brooding.

Tonight was becoming more than a chore. He was hungry and all the food seemed to be in minute portions. Conversations were loaded with subtle innuendo and backhanded compliments: *How brave of you to opt against formal dress. I didn't realize a warrior could be so sophisticated.* Despite the ambassador's diplomatic sentiments, the Shaman's attitude towards him was that of polite disdain, as if he were a wild ape who was demonstrating himself to be surprisingly well behaved.

Except for the woman next to him, who showed no subtlety in communicating her curiosity. Is it true that a mountain male's sexual appetite forces him to mate for many hours, days even? My goodness, that must be beastly! He again removed her cold, clawed hand from his thigh and politely declined her invitation to view some rare and recently imported tapestries.

He allowed more mini food to be delivered to his plate and ignored the urge to scoop it all up in his meaty paw and swallow it in one go. The place settings were also small. This was fine for the Shamans and even the willowy ambassador, but Nyle was broad as well as tall, and he had to keep his arms tightly at his sides to avoid knocking into his neighbors.

But the thing that was really making the evening unbearable was the sound of Danika's giggles from farther down the table. Nyle was not, despite this company's suggestion to the contrary, a barbarian. He was not about to leap on the table and remove the slimy sailor's slippery tongue from his mouth and smash in his gleaming white teeth—oh, but he *wanted* to! Danika was brave and clever, but she had grown up in the safety and seclusion of the university; she didn't know the kind of trouble the trader represented.

He knew well how rich traders away from home often behaved. They were notorious in the northern villages when they traded for fleeces and ores. No self-respecting clansman would let his daughters anywhere near them. And here was one working his snake charms on Danika.

What was worse—she was lapping it up! Her tinkling laughter reached his ears again, and he put down the crystal goblet he was holding to avoid crushing it in annoyance.

The vampish woman squealed loudly in his ear, "Oh, the music is starting. Let me show you the latest dances we have in the city."

Nyle tried to prize her taloned fingers from his wrist and politely excuse himself, but she clung on. Short of making a scene, he didn't know what he could do, so he allowed himself to be dragged from his seat and marshalled towards the ballroom. Nyle mournfully looked back as waiters collected whole plates of uneaten, bite-sized pastries.

Many other couples were already dancing; a cluster of musicians on various stringed instruments filled the air with elegant harmonies. In his home village, Nyle had enjoyed dancing, but the tribal beats of the skin-drums and the pipes and whistles of the clans were leagues away from these delicate melodies. The dance was intricate and formal, with couples meeting and bowing and walking in complicated circles around each other. Danika was being led around by the snake-hipped trader, pushed and pulled this way and that, color high on her cheeks and her form moving seductively in the sinuous yellow dress. She looked stunning.

The painted woman left in a huff when it became obvious that Nyle was not going to give in to her incessant mewling and dance with her. He was sitting at the side, tapping his foot irritably, when Torin approached.

"Danika seems to be enjoying herself," said the archer mildly.

"She is her own agent. If she wants to carry on like a strumpet, it's her choice."

"Well, that's a bit harsh. Also, I think perhaps if you showed her the same attention."

"What do you mean?"

"Have you ever complimented her?"

"I don't have the style for compliments."

"Hmmmm."

"Anyway, she's not the type to go for that kind of piffle."

"All women like piffle." Torin pointed to the edge of the room where, to Nyle's amazement, Alyssa was allowing herself to be led onto the dance floor by a swarthy, and to Nyle's mind, foolhardy Shaman. She was flushed and her expression was less glowering than usual, although her eyes were narrow, and she seemed to be eyeing her suitor with suspicion.

He watched Alyssa awkwardly bob and weave in time to the music mirroring the Shaman. At one point, she went the wrong way and bumped into her partner; the Shaman leant in and whispered something in her ear and... *Goddess in sunlight! Is my third-in-command giggling?*

As he watched, Danika came twirling into his line of sight, being swung around energetically by her partner. The silk merchant had not let her out of his presence all evening, demanding every dance from the healer, and when she eventually begged to be allowed to rest, he had stayed by her side and supplied her with generous amounts of wine. Nyle had witnessed the whole affair whilst pretending to look in another direction, and he was imagining how it would feel to thrash the look of shiny smugness from the slippery scoundrel's face. Getting her drunk, just to try to seduce her in some dark, secluded corner. It was outrageous!

Torin interrupted his mutterings. "Relax, pretend you don't care that she's having a good time with another man. If you act indifferent, a woman suddenly finds you irresistible in my experience. Or pretend you're having a wonderful time with another woman—that can be very effective. Women soon flutter back if you start having fun of your own."

"I'd rather go over and hit the mongrel repeatedly with something heavy," mumbled Nyle.

"I don't recommend it," replied Torin, smiling. "Anyway, I need to leave."

"What's the emergency?"

"Oh nothing. I've been invited to see some tapestries."

"Since when have you been an admirer of tapestries?" Nyle's eyes narrowed.

"These are not any old tapestries. These are rare tapestries, owned by the daughter of an influential Shaman politician. I am forging diplomatic relationships."

He skipped off before Nyle could reply, saying casually over his shoulder, "Be indifferent—or tell her how you really feel."

Nyle grunted and turned back to face the dance floor.

Suddenly Danika appeared before him in a swirl of yellow silk. Her face glowing and slightly pink, her chest heaving with the exertion of dancing, she was smiling broadly, her eyes wide and perhaps, thought Nyle, a little glazed from wine. Merchant scoundrel!

"I'm having such a wonderful time. Are you having a good time? The music, the dancing, it's all so exhilarating!"

Nyle looked down at Danika, so alive and sparkling, and he softened. She was so happy, and after all the misery of the past few days, didn't she deserve a little joy? He was about to tell her how pretty she looked and perhaps suggest she show him one of the dances she had learnt, but as he opened his mouth to speak, the silk merchant slithered over to join them.

The merchant placed his hand on the small of Danika's back possessively. Nyle felt an almost uncontrollable urge to break his wrist.

"Dannnnnika." His thick accent made the name sound like an erotic invitation. Nyle squeezed his hands into tight fists. "I returned to find you had vanished, and we are missing the best dances." He mock grimaced.

Danika smiled at the merchant, and Nyle's blood boiled in his veins. She looked from the merchant to Nyle and frowned as if confused. "I'm sorry. How rude of me. I haven't introduced you. This is Nyle, the captain of the warrior elite, and this is Conleth, a silk merchant from the south lands."

The merchant gave Nyle a theatrical bow. "An honor to meet one of the nation's protectors."

Nyle inclined his head slightly but didn't answer; what could he say? That it was an honor to meet a man who sold ribbons and bobbins? It really wasn't.

There was an awkward silence until Conleth spoke. "So, Danika, are you coming again to dance?"

"I um don't... er..." Danika looked at Nyle.

"Don't mind me. I have more important things that need attending to," said Nyle, more sharply than he meant to.

Danika frowned and looked a little hurt. "Okay, well maybe I should turn in too. I have a lot to sort out tomorrow as well."

Conleth looked horrified at the idea. "No, Danika, stay and dance. There will be much time for work tomorrow."

Danika hesitated and looked from Nyle to Conleth and back again, her expression unsure. "I don't know. Should I come with you?" She addressed the question to Nyle.

"Stay or go, Danika," he snapped. "It's your choice." He strode away before he said something stupid or flattened the sly merchant for the way his eyes kept flicking over Danika's low-cut bodice. She was a grown woman, clearly. She could take care of herself, and if she wanted to take Conleth as a temporary lover, well, that was her choice. He was done with the whole messy issue. The fact that the idea of her in another man's arms made him want to disembowel such a man with a rusty fork was neither here nor there.

He heard hurried footsteps on the wooden floor behind him and turned to see Danika approaching, kicking off her pointy shoes so she could walk quickly. Nyle noted uneasily that her face was thunderous, her eyes flashing. Well, he thought, bring it on; if she wanted to take him to task on his behavior, he had some choice comments about hers.

"What is wrong with you tonight?" She stopped opposite him and stared him square in the face.

"What is wrong with me? I am not the one acting like a brazen wench in a dockside tavern!" He looked pointedly at her cleavage and then back up at her face.

Danika's eyes widened, and she blushed. "I didn't... I just wanted to have some..." Fat tears began to edge from her eyes to her cheeks. "... fun... and... the dress was there for me. I didn't choose..." She looked to be holding back a sob and finding it hard to speak. "Conleth was... funny, and I only danced... and..." She raised her big watery eyes to Nyle, making him look away uncomfortably. When he looked back, her face had changed. It had become harder and angrier. "Don't you tell me what I should and should not wear or who I should and should not dance with! You're such a mean, miserable ox sometimes. I hate you. I really hate you!" She hitched her skirts up and pattered off towards her quarters, leaving Nyle leaning broodingly against the wall, considering the possibility that he might not have said quite what he'd meant.

∼

DANIKA STRUGGLED UNSUCCESSFULLY TO GET OUT OF HER dress. The opinionated, sanctimonious, judgmental, bigoted idiot! He could jump off the tower for all she cared. She was done with him.

She'd tried, for expediency's sake, to take the dress off without undoing all the buttons, but had just succeeded in becoming squashed, half in, half out of the bodice. When she finally managed to wriggle free, her hair was a tangle of beads and pins, her face paints had smeared into a sticky mess, and her eyes were red from intermittent and irrepressible bouts of crying. She washed herself and brushed her hair, her mind absorbed by alternately cursing her hateful warrior and feeling the sting of his hurtful words.

Finally, dressed in a linen shift and flopped on the large double bed in her room, she gazed up at the ceiling. Despite her best efforts, her thoughts returned to Nyle. He was a soldier; she knew that. He was rough and practical and was used to getting his own way. He'd looked so elegant this evening in his white shirt and tailored trousers, so much bigger and more powerful than the other men at the ball. Had she flirted with Conleth to provoke a reaction from him? No. What kind of reaction did she want from him? Not the one she got, clearly.

He could be so wonderful. She remembered how they had flirted and laughed and cuddled, but then he could turn like he did tonight. Danika's thoughts rolled around and around in her mind; she was never going to get to sleep at this rate. One thing she did know, despite her parting words, she didn't hate him. She sighed in frustration. Whatever it was, this nest of feelings and thoughts, it wasn't hatred. How could she understand so much about the workings of the human heart and yet so little of the feelings it produced?

There was a firm knock on the door. Her heart raced immediately. She tried to stay calm. He'd been an ass, after all.

She slipped off the bed and walked across the room, smoothing down her hair.

"Who is it?" she asked through the door.

There was a pause, then a low cough. "It's me. It's er… Nyle." His voice was husky.

"What do you want?" She forced her voice to sound colder than she felt.

"I wanted to—" Another cough. "—to talk to you for a minute."

Danika opened the door. Nyle leant up against the door surround, his hair tousled and spiky, his eyes were downcast. She felt the unmistakable kick of excitement she always felt when she saw him.

But he'd hurt her, badly. "You had no right to say those things to me."

He sighed. "Can I come in?"

CHAPTER 14

He paced up and down, seemingly working himself up to something.

When he finally stopped pacing and faced Danika, she hardly recognized the hesitation in his eyes.

"You're not a wench. I know that." He ran his hand through his hair. "I shouldn't have been so…"

"Rude? Petulant? Mean? Petty?" Danika raised her eyebrows in mock innocence; she was damned if she was going to make this easy for him.

His mouth tightened, and his eyes narrowed. For a moment, she thought he was going to storm off, but he took a deep breath instead. "Yes. All them."

"And jealous?" She was enjoying herself now, her mouth softening into a playful smile.

Nyle didn't smile back; instead, he pinned Danika with his intense stare. His voice was low. "Aye, I won't lie. I was jealous."

Danika's smile slipped from her face, and she swallowed hard. Nyle eyed her like a starving wolf eyes a rabbit, and the hairs on the back of her neck prickled with energy. A primal warning that she was being… hunted.

Nyle kept staring at her. A part of her screamed for her to flee, but another, deeper force had her rooted to the spot. He surprised her by gently reaching around and running his fingers down her sensitive nape. He pulled her firmly towards him, leaning down so their faces were close.

"I wanted to break the merchant's arm for daring to touch you. I wanted to rip his eyes from their sockets for ogling your breasts." He leant farther towards her. "Forgive me, Danika," he whispered into her ear, sending a rash of tingles down her spine and across her back. "I've not fought or trained for days. I am wound up tight and —" He pulled her hair slightly, forcing her to tip her head back farther. "—you are well and truly under my skin, healer."

Danika's eyes widened as he spoke. A moment ago, she had been enjoying watching him mumble an uncomfortable apology. Now she was trembling in a dangerous warrior's arms as he told her she was under his skin. What did that even mean? Was this seduction, or did he mean he felt something for her? She tried to think straight, but all she could think about was the effect his stare was having on her ability to see reason and the exquisite sensations his soft breath was causing on her ear.

He spoke again, "Do you want me to go, healer?" His voice was rough, as if he were forcing the words out. "Is that what you want?"

Danika felt afraid. How could she have possibly

thought she could handle this? Held up against him, she could feel his need for release, and it made her ache between her thighs. "It will hurt…" she murmured.

He nodded. "I'll try to make it easier, but aye, it'll hurt the first time."

She gazed into his blue eyes and read his need and his hesitation. She wasn't naïve. She understood the physiology. This was the moment of decision. Could she do this? Tonight? Now? He gently brushed the nape of her neck as he held her, and a network of tiny nerves came to life. She wanted it. She wanted it all, but there was so much to think about. It was overwhelming her.

He stilled. "Say the word and I'll stop."

He was giving her the power and relinquishing control. He trusted her to know what she was ready for, what she could handle. A fierce rush of pride and desire surged through her. "Don't stop." The moment the words had left her lips, he drew her into a breath-stealing kiss. Holding her head in his large hand, he plunged his tongue into her mouth, filling her and forcing her to take him.

He released her and she panted, trying to regain her breath as he picked her up and carried her to the bed, where he placed her on the cool silken sheets. He slipped off his shirt and knelt over her, his thick arms on either side of her shoulders. He looked down at her and paused, just watching her.

Her heart was beating so fast she felt as if it would beat right through her chest. Her courage began to falter, too much, too intense. She ran her hands up his arms and over his massive shoulders, ignoring the voices of doubt in her mind and just relishing the feel of his bunching muscles under her palms. His eyes narrowed as she worked her way over his chest. When she reached down to his abdomen, he hissed in his breath through clenched teeth. He grabbed both of her hands and placed them above her head. He smiled. "You're making it very difficult to concentrate, woman!" She was reminded for a moment of the playful side of Nyle as he said softly, "I want to be in charge in bed for a while, if nowhere else."

"Okay," she replied, smiling back, "for a while."

Nyle leant in to kiss her neck. He then ran his lips and tongue along her collarbone, making her squirm in delight.

He moved down to her breasts and suckled each nipple through the stiff linen shift. She arched herself into him, allowing him to slide the shift over her head. Completely naked, her back and thighs caressed by soft silk, Nyle leisurely lapped and suckled her breasts, running his teeth up and over her responsive nipples and making them into firm buds. He slowly moved down over her stomach, leaving a damp trail across her body. When he blew on her warm skin, the trail seared like a brand. He licked his way down across her abdomen and along the line where her skin became covered with coppery curls. Then he stopped and raised his head. "Are you holding your breath, Danika?"

She realized she was and gave a long shaking exhale. Nyle smiled at her, the lazy smile of a man who was exactly where he wanted to be.

Danika thought back to the tavern and the peaks of screaming pleasure that Nyle had wrenched from her body. Her eyes fluttered shut as she remembered, and her hand clenched tightly on the silk above her head.

Nyle teased her, kissing softly between her legs, running his tongue up the inside of her thighs until she groaned in frustration. Although she couldn't see his face, she could almost feel him smiling. When he blew a thin stream of air directly over her most sensitive spot, she almost lost her mind. She felt her inner core clench as a million tiny shivers coursed through her whole body.

Finally, when she felt like she was nearing her limit of endurance, the warrior held her thighs open to him and licked up her core with force. Her back arched, and she moaned deep in her throat. He was relentless, slowing only when she neared an orgasm, slipping a finger into her and stroking her from the inside whilst lapping gently between her slick folds. The building pleasure made her gasp deeply, her face and chest beading with sweat as her hands crushed the silk. Nyle worked in a second finger and began to move both fingers in and out of her as he had before, working at a steady rhythm, slowly stretching her in readiness for him. When she could bear it no longer, she raised herself up on the bed, balanced on her elbows, and looked down. "Now, Nyle, please!" Her voice came out rasping and desperate. He looked up from his task and met her stare, all hint of his earlier playfulness gone, now replaced by an intensity that was both frightening and erotic.

Nyle withdrew his fingers, making Danika whimper. He stood and stripped off his trousers, releasing his hard shaft and making her draw in a quick breath. When she'd taken him in her hand, she'd been shocked at how large he was. The idea of it fitting inside her raised goosebumps over her arms and back, and her mind reeled with a heady mixture of excitement and fear. On instinct, she leant forward and reached for him, wrapping her hand around his wide shaft. He was so hot, so hard; she felt the blood pumping through him like blasts of molten iron. He hissed through clenched teeth. "You play with fire, healer."

∼

GODDESS, GRANT ME STRENGTH! HE WOULD COME IF SHE moved her hand but an inch. To see her flushed and naked before him, her eyes lusty, her lips slack and wanton, to taste her sweetness, to have her reach for him in need, and plead with him to take her. It was more than he'd prepared for, more than he could take without going mad or releasing too early. "You can do anything you want to me..." he growled, taking her hands and placing them by her sides, "later."

He watched her as she waited for him to continue. Her breathing was as ragged as his, and she was nibbling her bottom lip—so damned adorable. He knelt between her legs on the bed and kissed her gently on the mouth; the taste of her lips mingling with the spice of her dew sent a pleasure dart into his groin. His shaft ached harder. He forced himself to go slowly, nudging the tip between her folds and pushing forwards. She was wet, he'd made sure of it, but despite his earlier efforts, she was still so very tight. The feeling of her soaking little sheath squeezing over his shaft made his chest heave with the exertion of not coming.

Agonizing pleasure flooded the root of his shaft, making his ballocks tighten. He eased inside, and she gasped. He paused when he reached her maidenhood. "Are you okay, Danika?" He was wound up so tightly, he could hardly get the words out.

Danika nodded, but her eyes were wide and a little afraid. "It hurts a little."

"Do you want me to stop?" The thought was unbearable, but he couldn't face hurting his brave little healer.

Danika shook her head. "Just wait a few seconds."

Nyle nodded, relieved. He used the pad of his thumb to gently rub her just above where his shaft entered. After a moment's search, he found the magic spot and watched as she arched her back, driving him slightly deeper. When he was convinced she was on the brink of coming, he pushed his whole length into her and rubbed his thumb firmly over her sensitive bud. Her eyes widened with pain as he broke through, then the instant her orgasm took hold, she clung to Nyle's shoulders, riding out the waves he felt coursing through her, crying out her release. To feel her sheath rhythmically squeezing him and feel her bucking onto his shaft was too much, and he bellowed his own release loudly, coming and coming deeply into her, wanting her and needing her like he had never needed anything in his life.

When he had nothing more to give, he collapsed breathless at Danika's side, surprised at how weak his arms and legs felt. He turned on his side to face Danika, anxious to see if she was all right. Her eyes were closed, her breathing labored. He stroked her face with his fingers until she finally relaxed. She opened her eyes.

"Danika... did it hurt very much, lass?"

She gazed at him and stayed silent for a long moment. "No."

"What is it? Did you not like it? Did I do something you didn't enjoy? You must tell me." Goddess, what if he'd put her off for life?

"It's just... you're so bossy! I wasn't allowed to do anything."

Nyle's face went from concern to shock, and then a sly smile spread across his face. He wiped himself down, then picked up Danika by the waist and plonked her down across his naked body so she was astride and facing him. "Fine, lass." He laced his fingers behind his head and sprawled out on the huge bed. "Do what you will."

∽

Danika wriggled down Nyle and ran her hands down the length of his torso, luxuriating in the feel of his taut muscles, hard and lean, under her hands.

"So, I can do anything?" She dipped down and ran her tongue over his chest, over his nipple, as he'd done to her so many times. She noted with satisfaction how he tensed, his hands clutching the bed rail above his head. "And you promise not to let go of that rail? Not to flip me over and have your way with me?" She flicked over the other nipple, and this time his breath came out as a hiss.

"Aye. I think—"

"You think?" She was warming to this game now. To have him before her, this massive warrior bound by his own promise to the bed. A light sweat broke across her chest. "Let me see that famous warrior discipline, Nyle. Do you swear to let me do what I will, without interfering?"

He was hard again. His shaft, hot and heavy, pushed against her naked thigh as she leant over him. "I swear," his words were forced through gritted teeth, "not to touch you, lass... but know this, little witch—" he paused a moment, unable to speak as she leisurely ran her fingers over the tip of his swollen shaft. When he could finally continue, his voice was raw, "I'm marking score."

She held him firmly and pumped her fist a few times, making him groan low. Oh, to have this battle-hardened warrior under her spell, to make him groan and buck with just a squeeze of her fingers, it was divine. She could feel the breathless rush of her own desire returning.

He raised his gaze and fixed her with it. "You will pay dearly for every moment of torture."

Danika smiled. She felt brave and wild and wicked. What could she do to bring her savage warrior to heel? Some of the more graphic manuscripts from her studies sprang to mind. Images of heathen feasts and carnal festivals. She lowered her head, keeping her eyes locked on his. She ran her tongue slowly around the large head of his cock, relishing how he raised his hips from the bed to meet her. His breathing became shallow, and he clutched the bedrail. "You will be the death of me, witch—" But his words were cut short when she made her mouth tight around him and drew him in. He groaned and dug his hands into the bedding above his head. She dipped down again and sucked at his shaft. The hot, hard taste of him reminded her of how glorious he had felt plunging into her moments ago.

She looked up, expecting to see hunger and need and desperation, but her warrior's eyes were closed, his breathing measured, his face without expression. *He is thinking about something else!*

She released him and blew softly on his swollen shaft. "That's cheating," she said.

Opening one eye, he smiled. "Aye." He exhaled slowly and deliberately. "I'm running battle tactics in my head."

Danika narrowed her eyes. "I guess I need to up my game." She wiggled up Nyle's tall frame, brushing her moist core over him as she went. She noted with satisfaction how he grasped the bed rail tighter when she drew herself over his shaft. She paused a moment and rubbed against him. He pursed his lips tightly, but true to his word, he didn't move his hands.

It was a dangerous game. She reveled in the control she had—it was heady, intoxicating. It made her want to ride him, to take her pleasure and to come on him. But that would mean giving up her advantage.

She raised herself up and fed him into her, sinking onto his cock, inch by aching inch. His breathing became labored, as did hers. She was sore, but she was slick, and she needed him. When he was fully inside her, she paused, savoring the overwhelming feeling of fullness.

"What now, little witch?" His voice was even, but she could see that his knuckles were white with the effort of holding on to the rail.

"Now—I want my warrior to beg me for mercy." She ran her hands over his chest and ground down onto him.

Nyle groaned, then his lips curved into a sensual smile. "Never."

Danika raised her hand and took her breast in her palm, rolling her nipple between her fingers, her eyes never leaving his.

"Goddess, yes, woman!" Nyle's hips met hers as she began to ride him; she palmed her other breast and took him into her, hard and fast, giving in to her need. She stared into his face, his mouth open, eyes hooded; he was watching her every movement, mesmerized. She reached down and caressed herself as he had done, between her thighs, right where she moved on him.

"Please, Danika, don't stop. You're so damned beautiful!"

He was going to come, but she was going to get there first. She could feel it rising within her, the swelling of him inside her, the screaming bliss, the feeling of power. She was helpless to stop the climax surging towards her.

She would not be denied. She locked onto his gaze and reached back to cup the base of his shaft, feeding her power into his sensitive flesh, forcing his seed to rise.

She could see the defeat in his eyes as he realized what she was doing.

"Mercy, Danika!" he roared, and bucked from the bed as he came. She could feel him thrusting into her, spending within her, violent and hot. She clung to him as her own climax hit, plunging her into a screaming abyss where only pleasure existed—wave upon wave of scalding, dark pleasure.

CHAPTER 15

Danika stretched. The ache between her legs was a sweet kind of pain. She curled up next to Nyle and watched rays of early morning light filter through the drapes and cast shapes on the floor. So many things were racing through her mind that sleep had become impossible. Nyle had no such qualms, and after their third, rather gentler bout of lovemaking, he'd drifted off. He was currently uttering small grunting snores, much to Danika's amusement.

In the soft light, he looked like a different man than the fierce warrior she'd grown to know. The lines and angles of his face were less pronounced, the furrows in his brow, an almost constant feature, relaxed. He looked younger than she'd ever seen him, kind of like she expected he'd looked as a boy. If he had a son, would he look like this? She brought herself up sharply at the notion and reminded herself that there were some herbal preparations she would need to take in the next few hours to prevent a pregnancy. Danika thought back to their energetic antics of the past few hours. She should probably double the dose, just to be sure.

She watched the warrior sleep. He was handsome and stoic, and she respected him. He made her laugh when he wasn't making her crazy, and he was the most honorable man she had ever met. But she couldn't allow herself to look deeper into her feelings. She couldn't allow herself to start imagining a future life, or a family. Even if they were able to convince the Fae of the need to help and save the Shaman lands, they were from different cultures, different castes. She would not fit in his world the same as he wouldn't fit into hers. She would see how far this could go, take her pleasure while she could—she owed herself that much. But she must prepare herself for the inevitable. That they would, one day soon, walk their paths separately.

Danika shuddered at the idea and snuggled closer to Nyle. Despite her concerns, she felt safer and happier than she had in a long time. I don't care; she thought. I don't care if this is only for a short while, only a way to cope with the horror of what's happening. I have this now. The warrior mumbled in his sleep and wrapped one muscular arm around her, pulling her to his side. Danika drifted off to sleep.

～

WHEN HAD IT HAPPENED? HE DIDN'T KNOW. POSSIBLY when she'd raised her hand to cup her breast, thrown her head back, and ridden him to the most powerful orgasm he'd ever experienced. Or when he'd woken to find her curled up against him, small and warm in the nook of his arm? No, earlier—a vision of her, staring up at him in defiant fury, in the middle of a sporca nest, flashed through his mind. *I saw the nest and decided to jump in anyway!* He smiled.

He'd woken with her beside him, fitting perfectly into his side, and he'd made the decision then and there. He would keep his healer—end of the world be damned! *And if she doesn't feel the same?* He looked at her beside him, standing in the throne room, her face pale, her arms crossed. *Well, if she doesn't, I am a hell of a tactician—I'll use every trick in the book to make her change her mind.*

Nyle dragged his attention away from his healer and listened as the ambassador addressed the room.

"The Prince Jamal has made it clear that he is ready to sever all ties with this realm. The situation is becoming unstable. He has agreed to this audience only at my behest and because your party… interests him." The Ambassador's eyes flicked to Alyssa and then quickly back. "But do not believe for a moment that he will be swayed by an appeal to his conscience or by pleading."

Nyle saw Danika clutch her arm through her shirt. It was time to get his mind in the game. If he was to have any future with Danika, they needed this to work.

The images reflected in the huge mirror opposite began to stretch and drift. They were replaced by the image of another room, a much grander room, and in the center of the image, seated on an ornate ivory throne, sat the prince of the Fae. The ambassador stood stiffly as the apparition crystallized, then bent low, balancing his weight on his knees. Danika, after a moment's pause, did the same. Torin and Alyssa looked at Nyle.

Traditionally, his warriors bowed to no one, not even clan chieftains. Nyle caught Danika's pleading look and forced himself into a quick bow, keeping his eyes on the prince at all times. The other two warriors did the same.

The prince motioned to the ambassador to rise and inclined his head slightly to Nyle. Fae were known for their belief in their own superiority, that the other races should pay homage. Although Nyle had heard reports recently that the decline in the Fae population had led to arguments amongst the population about diluting the bloodlines of the minor casts with other races.

The prince was pure Fae, from his long flaxen hair and perfect features to his arched eyebrows and pale blue eyes. His mouth twisted into a haughty scowl as his eyes fixed on Nyle.

"My ambassador has begged an audience, and I am here. Who is it that feels important enough to address Elfain aristocracy?"

"We have a message for you, your highness." Nyle spoke through clenched teeth. Uncomfortable as he was to pandering in this manner, he would do everything in his power to help Danika, even if that meant sucking up to a spoiled prince.

"I know all about your problems, mountain man. My agents tell me of the rift at the university. Your warriors have failed most spectacularly in your mission to hold the rift against the hoards. This is, of course, inconsequential to us." The warriors stiffened.

Danika quickly got to her feet. "This is not the

warrior's fault. There are other forces at work, forces that threaten even Elfain." Her voice was calm, but Nyle detected an edge to her tone—he realized she was defending him against the prince's barbed words. The idea of her rising up to his aid lessened the sting.

"Why am I in the presence of a Shaman commoner? My ambassador has told me that many of your university elder's council succumbed to the attack—perhaps the students now run the show. Are you the new head of the university?" The prince laughed, and Danika blushed. Nyle took a step forward, furious that the pompous ass would dare mock her. This peacock! Danika closed her hand around Nyle's arm and looked at him pleadingly. Using all his discipline, he kept his silence, though it cost him to do so. He burned with anger and squeezed his hands—imagining he was closing them around the prince's willowy neck.

Danika continued in a calm, even tone. "I have a message, your highness."

"From whom? The student union?"

"From your sister, your highness."

The prince's smile froze, his expression betraying a flash of pain. Then his expression hardened. "My sister died three hundred years ago," he hissed. "How dare you speak of her to me, you little witch. I should render you insane for such insolence!" The prince was out of his seat and peering out of the mirrored wall, his eyes sparkling like icicles. Nyle took a step towards the mirror.

Danika continued bravely, but her voice quavered as she spoke. "My teacher, Elder-Sha Ameena, was murdered by the ażote a few days ago. Before she died, she gave me a message for Prince Jamal of Elfain. She asked me to show you this. She hoped it might convince you to help those that fight for the Shaman." She rolled up her sleeve to bare her forearm and held it up to the glass.

Prince Jamal stumbled backwards when he saw the markings on her flesh. The tattoos glowed soft amber and seemed to dance and move in the air above Danika's arm.

"That is my sister's signature. This is not possible. This is some kind of trick." The prince's eyes darkened, the fire in the throne room rose and bellowed smoke, his voice grew louder, a low rumble born of power and anger. It was as if the prince were speaking from inside Nyle's own head.

"Come to me, red hair, and I will rip the truth from you along with every memory you hold dear. How did you come by this mark?"

The room in which they stood hummed with a strange energy. Blue and white sparks crackled along the ceiling and walls. Danika, her irises alive with a pale, alien light, walked towards the opening, towards the prince, spell-dazed. Nyle sprung in front of Danika, shielding her with his body.

"Release her or I will twist your royal head from its shoulders."

"Move away from her, barbarian. I need the truth. I will not be denied."

Danika groaned and clutched Nyle's arm. Desperation welled up inside him. This was a fight he could not win. He couldn't reach his enemy, let alone fight him. "Take it from me. I was there. I watched your sister die!" Nyle lunged at the mirror, bellowing at the prince.

He felt something plunge icy fingers into his mind and tear out pieces of his very soul. "Get her somewhere safe!" Had he spoken out loud? It didn't sound like his voice. He felt himself teetering on the edge of an abyss. He fought to stay aware; his one desire was to protect Danika until the others could get to her. It was his one thought, as all-around was fading and drifting into fragments of memories. He felt rather than saw someone drag Danika away. The healer's fingers were wrapped tightly around his arm, anchoring him. And a moment later, she was gone. The connection was broken.

He crumpled to his knees as his mind screamed in protest against the probing, scraping agony of the prince's assault. Then he pitched forward into the silence of the darkest, deepest void.

∼

Danika could feel the confusion, the chaos and rupture where there should be harmony and flow. She gently pushed deeper into the wounded psyche, trying to manipulate the energy into channels, encouraging unity. It was like unpicking a giant bundle of snagged yarn. She carefully worked each little knot, coaxing it into release, then moving on to the next, struggling with the almost unbearable concentration required to untangle such complexities. She rested her head on Nyle's silent form as she worked, aware only of the deep rise and fall of her lover's chest. He lived still, and that thought gave her courage.

"Rest a while, Danika. You have been working for hours." It was Alyssa.

"I can't. If he wakes before I finish, the damage might be permanent."

There was a pause, then Danika felt a light touch on her shoulder. "May the Goddess walk with you." Alyssa's voice, usually so cool, wavered.

Danika took strength from the female warrior's gesture and returned to her work.

There were people speaking in low murmurs, but she was buried in her task and paid them no heed, just as she ignored the cramping in her arms and the numbness in her legs. As for the pain she felt in her very marrow, the cold aching loss that settled in her bones—that was a simple diagnosis: She was in love with this man.

The moment she'd been pulled away from him, it had become an obvious truth, as if it had always been there. Like the compulsion to heal—it was so deep in her she couldn't remember what it had been like without it.

She opened her eyes and took in his pale, sleeping form. His face, bereft of concern, was that of a young man. His features softened and calm, his brow unfurrowed. If she failed in her task, Nyle might awaken a different man—a simpler man. Not the surly, arrogant warrior she'd fallen in love with, the man whose face was alive with each moment, working through options and strategy, planning his next move.

Would she still love him? She dismissed her fears as they served no purpose now. She would fight for her warrior in the only way she left open to her—dogged stubbornness.

She dragged her hands through her hair and rested her palms on his chest, remembering how she'd come back to consciousness to find herself shielded by his hulking form from the prince's fury. How he'd taken the brunt of the prince's mental assault and paid the price. Nyle had sworn to protect her, to give her the opportunity to deliver the Elder-Sha's message, and he had performed his duty faultlessly, even though it may have cost him his mind. When the prince had finished, he had left the portal, but what part of Nyle had he taken with him? It was too early to tell.

She paused as she reached a particularly gnarly group of strands; her energy waned, but she ploughed on regardless, calmly using her magic as a focus point and rubbing the fibers gently apart. Weariness weighed heavy upon her, and she struggled to think clearly. She could hear the background mumbling increasing in volume; there were exclamations and angry exchanges. It was all happening beyond her, she told herself—in another time and place, it was not her concern. She was here with Nyle, feeling his heartbeat, a heavy thud in her palms, healing his fractured mind and praying to any deity that might help her to bring this man back to her as he was—fierce and clever and intense.

She came to the last knot, a bunch of coppery red, amber, and ivory strands, twisted and kinked. She could do this. Just one more. Come on, Danika. Dig in, girl. Stay sharp. But it was drifting away from her. She struggled to recapture the vision but knew her power was almost completely depleted. She fought back, mustering her last reserves of energy, feeding herself into her magic, remembering how it felt to lie in Nyle's arms, to have his hands caress her skin. She undid a little more of the knot and then a little more, cheering herself along every moment. But it was too complex. It slipped away from her, and she reached out after it as it drifted off into darkness. She, too, drifted for a moment before collapsing into an exhausted heap over her beloved warrior.

Perhaps she felt him move—she couldn't be sure. She thought she heard him speak, but again, she couldn't be sure. She just wanted to sleep here with Nyle, safe and warm in the arms of the man she loved. Loved? Really? It was an overwhelming notion, but here in this moment, with her mind wandering the abyss, she knew it was true. She could stay here with him, silent and at peace. But his voice kept coming back to her, persistent and unyielding, preventing her from truly resting. Words she couldn't understand as they rolled around in her mind. Words she didn't want to understand; she was just too tired. She would listen later when they'd woken and made love, and eaten and made love some more. Then she would listen. So she ignored the words vibrating through his chest and the strong hands moving her aside.

"In the name of the Goddess, will someone remove this strange wench and tell me what's going on!"

CHAPTER 16

What a mess. Nyle sat at the desk in his room, trying to think, but the fire was too warm. His head ached, and he couldn't concentrate. He could remember most of the events of the last few days in a vague way. The magic containing the gates was draining away. He and his soldiers had failed to reach the herb witch in time. He'd been sent on a mission to petition for the assistance of the Fae prince. Then the prince had... had refused to help—he, Nyle, had become... enraged? Nyle shook his head in an attempt to clear it.

Whenever he tried to look too closely at his recent memories, they drifted from him, like the details of dreams on waking. And then there was the sleeping girl. Nyle's eyes flicked to the sleeping chambers where Torin and Alyssa had taken her. She'd been with them on the journey, apparently. A sharp stabbing pain shot through his mind when he tried to recall anything about the young woman, a flash of amber and red behind his eyes rendering him unable to think.

His soldiers returned. "What have you done with the woman?"

"She sleeps," replied Alyssa, not meeting his eyes. "She's been through a great deal. I'll check on her in a while."

Curious, thought Nyle, he'd only ever seen Alyssa show contempt for civilians. She seemed quite moved by the Shaman's endeavors. He shrugged off the notion. "Tell me when she wakes. I will need to interrogate her as my memory—" He paused. "—is somewhat fragmented." Again, Alyssa looked away as if he had offended her in some way. He continued regardless. He had no time for one of his best soldiers to develop a misplaced infatuation with some university girl. The pain in his head made him wince. "Have we had word from the prince?"

"The ambassador is petitioning him on our behalf—in light of the information your… er… memory provided," mumbled Alyssa in reply.

"And news from the university?"

This time it was Torin that answered, his usual easy-going expression replaced by a haggard and weary look. "Nothing yet. The last we heard was from a villager four days past. At an inn we stayed at." Now Torin was looking shifty. What was wrong with his troops?

Nyle grimaced; all reinforcements were dealing with the ever-increasing number of incursions throughout the land. Except for the large contingent of fighting men that were stationed here—to protect the fat politicians and guard the city, no doubt. Damned fools! If they sent their best men to the university, they stood a chance of defeating the army at the rift, at least geography would still be on their side, but if the hoards breached that narrow channel, they would spread en masse over the land—it would be too late to protect the city then. The prince would be safe back in Elfain, and the Shaman lands dammed to hell.

"We need our weapons," he snarled, turning to Alyssa and Torin, who both stood pale and still.

In the doorway stood the ambassador; he too looked like he hadn't slept in some time. His pale skin looked grey in the afternoon sunlight.

"That won't be possible at this time, Captain."

"Then we need Fae aid, Ambassador. Or more troops." He was running out of patience and energy—the pressure of only having part of the information. He felt like if he could only unlock the rest, he would know what to do. He had never felt such indecision and impotence.

"The prince has agreed to your request. He will provide you with the blood-magic you require—at least for now."

Torin drew in a sharp breath, and even Alyssa looked taken aback.

Finally, some good news! "Tell the prince we are extremely grateful. We will swear to his protection—"

"The prince cannot leave his land at this time. There are political issues to which he needs to attend."

The ambassador, Nyle noted, was trying very hard to keep his emotions in check. "Then who?—whose magic is strong enough to heal the rift—yours?"

The ambassador closed his eyes, his shoulders bowed, and Nyle realized just how much effort it was taking the

Fae to stand and deliver this message—the man was in torment.

"No. I have been... ordered... to stay with the embassy and help organize the defense of the city." His slender fingers curled into fists, and he shook slightly as he spoke. "My daughter, Marian, will carry this... honor."

An image flashed in Nyle's mind. A pale, fragile girl wracked with visions. A beautiful woman bent over her, whispering comforting words. Another shooting pain burst through his head. Nyle paused, afraid he would lose his balance. He recovered after a moment and chose his words to the ambassador carefully. "Your daughter is weak, and her mind is troubled. Is there no one else that can bear this... honor?"

The ambassador looked to the floor and shook his head. "The prince was adamant. I cannot be spared here, and he will not permit another Fae to enter Shaman lands. She is the best candidate."

"But it will be dangerous."

"That is why it will be your responsibility, warrior, to ensure her safety. You must protect her!"

A memory tugged at the back of Nyle's mind, another Fae, this time an old woman: "It is your responsibility to protect her. In this, you must not fail." But he couldn't reach it, and it drifted away from him—damn this memory loss. What had the prince taken from him?

Nyle sighed and nodded. "I will ensure she is protected. I will see to it personally that she returns to you."

The ambassador bowed. When he stood up straight,

his face had softened slightly. "Thank you," he paused. "There is one more condition."

The damned Fae and their code of recompense.

The ambassador's eyes shifted nervously around the room. "The prince demands an exchange. It is our law that all favors must be answered, and you will owe a considerable debt."

"What," Nyle hissed through gritted teeth, "does he want?"

"The female warrior." The ambassador inclined his head towards Alyssa.

Her expression didn't change, but she raised her head slightly, and her eyes flicked towards Nyle.

"Unacceptable." Nyle hated the idea of leaving one of his soldiers behind. He thought for a moment, considering his options. "I'll need all my warriors to protect your daughter. Take the Shaman girl when she wakes."

Alyssa gasped. "Danika has no means of protection. You cannot expect her to go alone into the clutches of the man who nearly killed you. At least I can fight—"

"No!" Torin interrupted, his voice uncharacteristically grim. "Only I am equipped—" He held up his hands, a reminder of his archer's status. "—to deal with whatever is on the other side of that portal. I will not allow Alyssa or Danika to risk their lives."

The ambassador began to speak. "I don't think you understand—"

"Enough squabbling! I am in command here." Nyle faced his warriors, his face thunderous. "The woman with red hair—Danika—is the logical choice. She is of no further use to the mission now she has delivered the message. She is of the least value, so it makes sense that she goes." Why were his soldiers looking so shocked? Couldn't they see that the witch was their best chip to play—with the least downside? Pain shot through Nyle; something was crushing him like a vice. He had to forcibly stop himself from doubling over and crying out. He rubbed his forehead in a vain attempt to clear his thinking.

"I'll go." A woman spoke from the doorway. "Nyle is right. I'm the logical choice." The redheaded woman stared at Nyle, her amber eyes fixed on him, unflinching. Nyle felt a strange jolt when she spoke and struggled to break away from her gaze. Pain consumed his mind, an almost constant throb.

The ambassador cleared his throat. "I'm sorry. You all misunderstood me. The prince requires the presence of that female warrior." He nodded to Alyssa. "He will not accept a substitution."

"And why her exactly?" demanded Torin.

The ambassador turned and looked out of the window, out to the patchwork of thatched roofs and stone towers that made up Shallaha. "The prince has asked me to assure you that she will be unharmed, and that whilst under his care, her wishes will be… respected. She will be a guest and will be treated as such."

Nyle pursed his lips. "Do I have his bond?"

The ambassador looked back at Nyle but wouldn't meet his eye. "You have his word."

"Nyle, you can't do this!" Torin turned to Nyle. "We can't deliver up one of our own like a goat to be slaughtered. We have no way of knowing what plans the prince has for Alyssa, although I suspect he has some underhand motives—"

"We need help, Torin." Nyle cut the archer off. He looked at Alyssa.

She wore her usual mask of cold indifference: her eyes just a fraction wider than usual, her lips pulled into a grim line of acceptance. She met Nyle's eyes and nodded once. "I'll make my preparations." She turned to Torin and spoke quietly to the archer. Nyle only just caught her words.

"Fear not. Whatever plans the prince has regarding me, he'll soon find out I'm more trouble than he bargained for." Her final words were aimed at Danika. "Keep these two in line while I'm gone." She gave the healer a half-smile.

"You can count on it." Danika smiled back, but her face was pale as ash. When did Alyssa get so friendly with this woman? thought Nyle, but kept the question to himself. There were large gaps in his memory of the last few days; perhaps the women had bonded on the journey here. Perhaps they were lovers. Another wave of pain flashed behind his eyes.

Nyle walked over to the window. He watched the usual hustle of the street below, rivers of people weaving in and out, horses with high-laden carts, and street vendors clutching trays piled with refreshments. The pain in his mind quietened, and he rested his eyes by looking into the distance.

"How is your head?" The woman stood beside him, looking up at him with those bewitching amber eyes. He felt vulnerable under her gaze, unnerved. He shifted uncomfortably as he answered, "Fine—a little hazy, perhaps."

"Can I… examine you? There may be some residual healing that requires—"

"You're a healer? That is why you were with me when I awoke?"

The woman took a slow breath in. "Don't you remember me at all, Nyle?"

Did he remember her? He felt like he did. When he looked at her, he felt something. But he couldn't pin down anything specific. He shrugged. "No, I have no memory of you. The others told me that you carried a message from the university to the Prince to aid our cause, for which I offer you my thanks."

"Please." Danika gestured for Nyle to sit down. He sat and allowed the little redhead to place her hands on his head. She closed her eyes and breathed deeply. Being this close to her, Nyle could smell the scent of her skin; her soft breath skimmed his neck, and he shuddered. *Am I bewitched? Why such a reaction? It must have been too long since I have lain with a woman.* His senses seemed confused and overly keen. Was this woman the cause of his befuddlement?

For a while nothing happened; he gave himself up to the pleasant sensation of being close to this beguiling woman. He continued to bask in the woman's scent and her closeness, feeling his tension drain as he did so. He drifted; there was warmth, the mere shadow of a memory, of morning sun and coppery hair.

The most excruciating pain he had ever endured ripped through his entire body, reaching an unbearable crescendo in his head. Nothing mattered except the agony in his mind. It was more than any man could endure. Nyle roared. "What are you doing to me, witch?" He jerked away from her hold and moved swiftly away, holding his head in his hands. The woman looked at him, her eyes wide. She swallowed. "If I could just isolate the problem, I could—"

"No! I have the information I need. I will get Torin to fill me in on the rest. Your services as a healer are no longer required."

"But Nyle—"

"I must return to the university at once. You may accompany us if you will, but I insist that you refrain from attempting that again. In fact—" Nyle's eyes narrowed as he regarded the young woman, and he tried to ignore his pounding head. "—stay away from me in general."

He turned on his heel and exited the room, motioning for Torin to follow, leaving her alone in the fading afternoon light.

CHAPTER 17

"Stay away from me!" So reminiscent of her father's words. The pain of her father's rejection felt all over again. Don't think about it Danika—focus.

Marian opened her eyes.

"I know you!" The Fae girl smiled at Danika. "You are in my dreams, a golden light," she paused, "keeping away the darkness."

Danika smiled and offered Marian a sip of the same concoction with which she had treated her earlier.

The teenage girl frowned and wrinkled her nose at the smell but took the drink without complaint.

"You are overcome by your dreams and visions, Marian. We need to find a way for you to filter your gift." Danika straightened up her back, stiff from leaning over the pale young woman.

"It never used to be such a problem. I could see my visions without pain . . . but never such dire things."

"Something has changed, Marian, there are forces that

seek to manipulate the future in unnatural ways. I suspect that is what is causing you so much distress." Danika dabbed the girl's mouth with a cloth. "Also, some Fae can pick up too much psychic feedback from others: Central Shamans, Islanders, and clans-folk for example."

Marian nodded. "I think so too. These visions get worse when I am in contact with the Shaman courtiers at the embassy. Their constant plotting and social manipulations are . . . wearying."

Danika smoothed her patient's hair from her eyes. This poor woman would be forced on a journey, one that she would find difficult to endure. "Do you know you are to come with us to use your royal blood magic to heal the rift at the university? That the prince has requested it."

Marian nodded. "My father explained. Although when he did so, I became ill with another vision, one involving the large warrior with the blue eyes."

"Nyle?" Danika felt a cold sweat develop on her neck and back. "Can you remember anything about it?"

Marian looked away from Danika and stared for a long moment at the wall, then shook her head. "I'm sorry. It's all muddled."

Danika managed a smile. "No matter. If you remember later then let me know."

"You love him?"

"What?"

"The large warrior, Nyle. You love him." This time it wasn't a question. "My gift—I can sense things."

Danika sat still and silent for a moment then sighed. What was the point of denying it? "Yes, I do, deeply, but he no longer remembers me. It just . . . hurts."

Marian sat up and raised a slender hand and softly cupped Danika's cheek for a moment. "Such pain in your heart. I could make you forget him too if you would like me to." She regarded Danika with her light-blue eyes, innocent and kind, the gift was without guile.

Danika drew away. Did she want to forget him? An image of Nyle leaning over her, his breath on her warm skin as he spoke gently onto her neck, floated up from her memory. "You are well and truly under my skin healer." A small shiver travelled down her spine. "No thank you, Marian, but . . . it was a kind offer."

The Fae nodded then her eyes seemed to focus on something in the corner of the room. She frowned, her eyes narrowing. Danika turned around to look but could see nothing, just blank walls.

"What is it?" Danika asked.

"Nothing just . . . nothing." Marian closed her eyes tightly and lay back down. "I think I'll sleep for a while, work up my strength for the journey.

Marian was making good progress, and under Danika's care her periods of lucidity were increasing. But Danika suspected the young Fae was not letting on the full extent of her affliction. She stroked the young woman's forehead and stood and turned to leave.

Nyle entered the room. His features were dark in the low light, but his shape, the bulk of his shoulders, his ruffled hair, was so familiar now to Danika, yet so unattainable. She wanted nothing more than to run to him and bury herself in his arms. But she was a stranger to him, nothing but an annoyance. He walked into the room, lean and supple, his boots making little noise on the marble floor

"Is she ready to go?"

Danika thought that his voice sounded deeper than usual.

"In an hour or so." She readied herself for an argument. He would want to leave as soon as possible. To Danika's surprise the tall warrior didn't argue. He just nodded and looked down at the girl on the bed.

"We'll leave in a few hours."

He stood a few feet away, but his presence felt much closer. Danika caught the scent of wood smoke and cloves. Memories of his touch and the taste of his naked skin flooded her senses. She fought the urge to move towards him, to reach out and touch his face.

Danika instead busied herself with her patient, making a big show of noting both pulse and temperature. She sighed. "She cannot ride, Nyle. She'll not make a day on horseback, and she can't sleep in the open; she's just not strong enough."

Nyle nodded. "I've explained this to the ambassador. He has given us a carriage and four horses. It is large enough for the both of you. You can sleep in there too."

Danika nodded, relieved for Marian, and for herself. Her limbs still complained of her journey here.

"Alyssa?"

"She left for Elfain a few hours ago."

"And Torin?"

"He's okay. Alyssa is tough, she can take care of herself—Torin knows this."

"It can't be easy for him, he feels deeply for her,

although she doesn't seem to return his affection . . ." Danika trailed off wishing she hadn't brought the subject up.

"They are both warriors, wedded to this life. They know that relationships of that kind are untenable." He spoke quickly, almost snapping out the words.

Danika nodded and held Nyle's stare.

The warrior looked down and began to pace around the chamber. "Torin tells me that, well, he suspected that, we . . . I mean you and I . . . spent some time together, and that you might be feeling confused." Nyle looked to the door.

Danika could feel his discomfort, it radiated from him. He wanted to be as far away as possible from her, from this conversation—he was feeling guilty.

"Anyway," he dragged his gaze back to her own, "I'm sorry, and I hope you won't feel . . . er . . . too badly of me. I mean we will be together these next three days, and I would like us to be . . ."

Friends? Any moment he was going to say "friends," and she would want to throw herself at his broad chest and beat upon him with her fists. Remember me, damn you! We were a hell of a lot more than friends. Fighting is what you do. Fight for us!

Even now, as he ran his large hand through his short dark hair and stuttered and struggled to find a nice way to tell her he was indifferent to her, that he was embarrassed to be near her, whilst his eyes darted wildly around the room for an escape route, even now—she wanted him. She hated herself for wanting him, but she couldn't bring herself to hate him.

She turned away from Nyle, squeezing her eyes shut to prevent tears from escaping. She would never put herself in this position again, she thought bitterly. Firstly her father and now Nyle. She'd been dismissed without thought. Well—she was through with it! Done! She made an internal vow to never again allow a man to make her feel so superfluous, and it was as if her blood transformed into iced water. She shivered slightly and clenched her fist tight. Turning back to face the warrior, she arranged her face into a mask of cordiality.

"Nyle, what we had was a flirtation—nothing more. Torin may have misinterpreted what he saw." She spoke lightly. The lie slipped easily from her now that her feelings were safely locked behind her tight smile. She stepped back from the warrior, ignoring the cold ache in her very core.

Nyle frowned. "Oh, well I'm sorry. I must have misunderstood. I thought perhaps we . . . that it was more, but . . ."

"I'm sorry to disappoint you, Nyle, but it was just a few shared jokes. You need to lighten up. Don't take Torin too seriously, and anyway—" She took a deep breath. "—do I seem like the kind of woman who would just jump into bed with a mountain warrior after knowing him a scant few days?" She didn't know why she had said the last few words, she'd never had much time for the whole "virtuous virgin" nonsense, but she was angry, and she wanted to regain control. She arched her eyebrow at Nyle, a silent challenge.

There was a pause wherein Nyle seemed at a loss of what to say. He stood with his mouth slightly open, looking like he was searching for a memory. Eventually, he inclined his head and said in a formal tone, "I'm sorry to have caused you any embarrassment, Danika. I realize that by suggesting that we were more than friends it may have been interpreted that way. Of course, I meant no insult. I did not mean to imply that you would ever—" He cleared his throat. "Social graces and views on virtue are viewed differently in the clans. I apologize for any offence." He spoke with a rigidity she had never heard before.

The cold earnestness cut like a blade, but she bore it without allowing her mask to slip. "Let us concentrate on the job in hand: getting Marian safely to the University." Danika gestured to the sleeping Fae and without raising her eyes to Nyle said, "You have not offended me, and I expect us to work together without distractions." This time she did look up. "We have a responsibility, Nyle. Let's concentrate our energies on that."

Nyle gave a curt nod, his face unreadable, turned on his heel, and left quickly.

∽

THEY MOVED TOGETHER IN A POUNDING RHYTHM TOWARDS what Danika knew would be an exquisite release. Her warrior, lean and strong, crushing her to him, again and again, their hot bodies entwined so that her entire length was pressed against him. They were so close she could feel his racing heart pounding in her own chest, and when he whispered her name, it was as if she was hearing him from inside her own mind. He was making her body scream for him, keeping her at the perfect place. Just a moment longer and she would break apart. She crested towards her orgasm consumed by Nyle's touch, his need for her. She was wrapped within him, crushed against him.

Then, he just wasn't there—she was holding nothing, without anchor, within a void. Falling, the dark ground rushing up towards her, she landed with a jarring thud.

Danika opened her eyes, face down in a soft fur throw.

Marian was sitting up beside her on the carriage bed. "I think the carriage went over a hole in the road." The Fae's pale-blue eyes regarded Danika with sympathy. "You dreamt of him."

It wasn't a question.

Danika blushed hotly and struggled to sit up. "You read my mind! While I was asleep! Why would you do that? I can't believe you would—"

"No! Of course not. You cried out . . . and, and . . ." Marian looked down at the bed. "The sense of loss was so powerful I couldn't help picking it up. I'm sorry I couldn't filter it out." Marian's pale face twisted into a mask of dismay.

Danika took a deep breath. "It's okay. I thought for a moment . . . Never mind, it's fine." She shivered and rubbed her arms, trying not to think of her fading dream.

The carriage was jogging along briskly. The ambassador had had the inside modified for his daughter's comfort. An elevated mattress draped with thick pillows, furs, fine quilts, and soft cotton sheets took up most of the space.

Danika and Marian had been sole occupants of this

rich boudoir for the past two days. Nyle and Torin rode nonstop towards the university. My homeward journey, thought Danika, running her hand over a silk cushion, is a far cry from the hard, outbound ride to Shallaha. I would trade all the silk sheets in Shallaha to ride again in Nyle's arms. She immediately squashed the errant thought and forced her mind away from... him.

The outside of the carriage had also been modified, stripped of all the ambassador's gilding and jewels. The rich carvings now covered by old wood and grease, it had been changed from royal coach to a farmer's wagon, the sort that transported livestock. It had been Nyle's idea to avoid attention.

Danika leant over and checked on her patient. Marian remained sitting up, surrounded by pillows. Her face was as pale as ever, and her delicate fingers worked the blanket before her nervously. But her eyes were focused, and she seemed lucid. The fever that had previously wracked her body had eased. Danika smiled and Marian smiled back.

"We will arrive soon, at your university. Are you are looking forward to it?"

Danika nodded. "It will be wonderful to see Layla, to be home, to sleep in my own room."

"It has been a hard few days."

Is that all it had been, a few days? It felt like an age. When she thought back to the night before the attack on the university, Danika hardly recognized the naïve student she'd been. Before everything... before him.

Again, she crushed the urge to brood; she needed to concentrate on what had to be done, here and now, and leave the past alone. She'd lost enough sleep over a certain warrior.

She gently pressed on Marian's neck to check her pulse; it was stronger than it had been—good, she was recovering. "We've not heard word of any further attacks. Hopefully, the university has held fast this past week."

As Danika spoke the words, Marian's pulse quickened under her fingers, and the Fae pulled away.

"What's wrong? Are you in pain? Did I hurt you?" Danika drew her fingers from Marian's neck.

Marian looked into Danika's eyes, fear etched onto her face. "The university is . . . is . . . breached."

"What!" Danika clutched the pale girl's arms. "What do you mean? How do you know?"

"A vision, I see . . . a monster holding aloft the heart from one you love dearly."

"Please, Marian, speak plainly. What do you see? Who is being hurt? Whose heart is being held?"

"I do not know these people, but there is danger at the university." Marian's eyes glazed, she sighed, and then in a distant voice muttered, "But it is the way it must be."

Danika tried to break the girl's trance, but the Fae started to convulse. The healer banged hard on the roof, and the carriage slowed then stopped. Nyle appeared at the door frowning.

"What is it?" he demanded. "We cannot afford unnecessary delays." But as his eyes turned to Marian, his expression changed to one of concern. His voice softened. "What ails the girl?"

Marian turned to Nyle—the same eerie blankness in her stare. "You will face your greatest challenge, warrior."

"What do you mean, girl? Don't offer muddy words! Tell me—what do you see?"

"Be soft with her, Captain," ground out Danika as she struggled with Marian, "she's sick." Danika cradled the young girl in her arms and tried to sooth her. She could feel the poor girl trembling, the stiffness in her arms and legs. She caressed the girl's face and murmured softly into her ear.

As the girl curled up next to Danika, the healer could feel the girl's heartbeat slow and her breathing steady.

As she drifted off, she spoke in a soft drowsy voice laced with sadness, "I see you, Nyle, standing on a pile of ashes; the remains of everything you believed in." And with that, the pale girl drifted into sleep, her tiny frame huddled into the tightest, smallest ball she could manage.

CHAPTER 18

Nyle wanted to wake the girl, but he knew the civilian healer wouldn't allow it. She would wake soon, he told himself, and then he could question her... gently.

When had he become such a sentimentalist? For that matter—when had he cared about the opinions of civilians? Short, beautiful, red-haired civilians with eyes that seemed to know what he was thinking and pale skin that made him want to reach out and feel it beneath his fingers. She knelt in the carriage amongst the silk and pillows tending the sick girl, her soft features blurred by weariness and stress. He wanted to stroke her hair, to soothe her, to tell her it would be fine—he would make it fine.

He shook his head and turned away. He wasn't himself—he was missing an edge. Instead of planning the mission, going over every minute detail of the blood magic ceremony in his mind, visualizing the terrain and testing his plans for weaknesses, he was thinking of the healer, of Danika, of what she would think of him if he shook the young patient awake and demanded answers. Over the last two days, he had constantly caught himself wondering what Danika was doing—what she was thinking when she turned from him with a quiet sadness in her expression.

He was all over the place. His instincts were clouded like never before. And in his gut, twisting like a nest of serpents, was a feeling he'd had to try hard to identify, one he had successfully controlled since he was a cadet. He felt true fear. But fear of what? Of losing something? Of being blindsided? By what?

"Everything okay?" Torin turned to Nyle as Nyle climbed up to the carriage seat. "I heard shouting."

"Fine—just the ravings of a sick young woman. Let's move on."

Torin paused for a moment and raised a questioning eyebrow.

"Move!"

Torin shrugged and geed the horses. Nyle leant back and crossed his arms across his chest. So much doubt, so much questioning. He hated all this complicated second-guessing; he needed facts, not dubious predictions and rumors. He couldn't turn back, despite the unease crawling over his skin. He could not plan a defence based on insecurities and vague prophecies. He had a mission, and he had to deliver the Fae to the university to end this battle before it became a war.

And if Sabre had let the defences fall? He would cross that ford when he came to it.

He would secure the healer at the university. She

belonged there, continuing her studies, building a life with her student friends, finding a husband maybe… The idea made him clench his hands so that his nails bit into his palms.

Nyle sensed Torin's sharp sideways glances, pity laced with concern.

"Rumours, conjecture, hearsay. Don't think on it, Captain. Sabre would have kept the university secure. Even with a bare platoon of academics and farmhands," said Torin.

Nyle felt a pang of guilt. "Aye, I trust him to have done his job." Surely he should be planning what to do if his second in command had been captured, not pondering the fate of one Shaman witch.

You will face your greatest challenge, warrior!

If he must face his greatest challenge, he wanted to do it with Sabre at his side. Not second-guessing everything he trusted and knew.

～

DANIKA STRETCHED HER CRAMPED ARMS AND TURNED HER face upwards. She noted that the leaves on the trees were tinged with brown. There was a chill in the evening breeze that heralded the changing of the season. Danika rubbed her bare arms to try to warm them. She bent down to gather a few fiery milk thistles that had made their home at the root of the old oak.

"I thought lasses preferred daisies and honey-cups." Nyle stepped out from a nearby copse.

For a heart-stopping moment Danika thought he was referring to their experience with the sporcas, but then realized he'd spoken without irony. He really didn't remember.

She smiled sadly and looked away. "You can't make an effective analgesic from a honey-cup."

He shrugged. There was a moment of silence between them. Nyle cleared his throat. "How's the girl?"

"She's improving. She'll be strong enough to complete the task before her."

"I didn't mean... I mean, I wasn't asking," Nyle paused and took a breath—his voice was soft. "And you, Danika? How are you?"

Danika was surprised by the question but tried not to let it show. "I'm fine. I'll be glad when this whole business is over, and I can go home." A sharp gust of wind made the leaves rustle, and she shivered.

Nyle immediately took a step closer and rubbed her bare arms to warm them. "You didn't bring a cloak with you," he said.

He was so close and so familiar. She ached to have him touch her. She wanted him to pull her to him, to let him pet her and kiss her, to be enveloped by his musky warmth and come alive under his soft caress. She nibbled her lip with her teeth and raised her eyes to his.

His hands stilled upon her arms.

Suddenly, he was covering her mouth with his own, her back pressed against the tree. The feelings she had tried so hard to suppress flooding back.

Nyle grazed his teeth over her shoulder and neck, and

she leant in towards him, feeling his desire for her with every kiss. She reached for him and met his lips with her own, greedily tasting him, feeding her need for him. He groaned deep in his chest and lifted her off her feet, allowing her to wrap her legs around him.

"Aye, lass." His breath brushed across her ear.

She clung to him as their kisses became desperate. His hands supported her as she ground herself into him. He dug his fingers into her hair and eased her head back so he could devour her neck with rough, punishing kisses. She was undone and spinning away into a place where nothing mattered but having the man she loved buried inside her, wrenching pleasure from her without mercy, hearing him bellow her name as he came.

The man she loved… who barely remembered who she was. Who'd almost destroyed the world with the word "friends."

She paused a moment and loosened her grip on his arms.

He slowed his kisses and raised his head, his breath labored, his eyes glazed with need. "Danika?"

"Do you remember me, Nyle?"

Nyle narrowed his eyes and licked his lips. His voice was like gravel. "I want you, lass, more than I've ever wanted anything before. You're all I ever think about—at the embassy, driving here. I can't get you out of my head."

"But do you know me?"

"I… I think," She saw the frustration in his eyes and a flash of confusion. He took a deep breath and lowered her to the floor. "No, I don't remember you."

Danika leant against the trunk behind her and looked away.

He raised his hand and touched her face, gently turned her to face him. "But I know we had more than a fling, Danika. I want to…"

"What?" She held his gaze, his fierce blue eyes piercing her heart. "What do you want, Nyle?" She held her breath. Was it possible that this tough, cool-headed warrior could trust his feelings—rely on his emotion?

It was his turn to look away. "I'm a soldier, Danika. If you know me, as I suspect you do, you know that it is my life. I can only offer you what I have right now. This." He caressed her neck with the tips of his fingers, running his thumb up over her cheek and across her lips.

A few short days ago it would have been enough—his body, his touch, and a vague and unknown future. She would have taken that deal in a heartbeat. But that had stopped being an option when she'd fallen deeply in love with this man. The feel of his fingers gently tracing the shape of her mouth was blissful and wretched. She pulled away. "I can't."

Nyle placed his hands on the tree behind her and let his head hang down. "I'm sorry. I shouldn't have."

"It's not your fault." She fought the urge to reach up and clasp her arms around his neck. He was hurting, and she wanted to make that pain stop. But she had her own pain to think about, and she couldn't risk another dismissal like the one at the palace. He'd wanted to send her away for Goddess's sake. Nyle felt for her, but he didn't love her. Perhaps he couldn't love her.

He turned and began to walk back to the carriage, his shoulders hunched.

A stiff breeze made the trees sway. Danika began the walk back to camp as the first leaves of autumn fluttered to the forest floor.

CHAPTER 19

Danika began to recognize her surroundings. The villages she'd visited to perform healings, the forest she and her students had combed for supplies. The university loomed on the horizon, grey stone on grey sky. She shivered.

Marian sat quietly, her face pale and set, her hands folded in her lap. When she'd woken up, both Nyle and Danika had tried to question her about her earlier vision in the wagon, but Marian had refused to elaborate, saying only, "It is done now—there is nowhere to go but forward."

The young girl's silent detachment and the cloaking dampness in the air set Danika's teeth on edge. She needed to see Layla and to make sure her friend was okay. She longed for the warmth of the dining hall and the familiar chatter of students to chase away her chills. But the nearer they came to her home, the nearer came the time that Nyle would leave her forever.

If they succeeded in their mission, he would disappear

—back to his barracks, his life of fighting and organizing defenses. He would go without a backward glance, and she would spend the rest of her life clutching onto the memories of the last few days, reliving every moment they'd had together like rereading the same story over and over. And she'd be the only one that remembered! It was a pitiful thought.

Danika felt a cool hand cover hers. She turned to find Marian looking at her. It was the first time the girl had really focused on anything since her seizure.

"I feel your sadness, Danika, I'm sorry."

"Thank you, Marian. I just, I don't know how I'll… keep going."

"It may all be well yet. Nyle's feelings for you remain I think—it is his memories that are shrouded."

Danika felt heartened at the idea that Nyle still felt for her, but she knew it was in vain. "Nyle never acts on unknowns. He trusts facts. If he doesn't remember me, he'll dismiss his feelings as baseless." Danika sighed. "We'll both be sad—only he won't know why."

Marian gave her hand a squeeze. "Nyle may change."

Danika gave a sad smile. "In another realm perhaps."

The carriage stopped, and Danika heard a couple of thuds as the two men jumped down. Danika opened the door and climbed out into the foggy evening before turning and helping Marian. She stood looking up at the grey walls of the university, once the center of her world, but now it seemed only desolate and bleak.

"Stay here," Nyle told the two girls without turning to them. He and Torin approached the massive wooden gates of the entrance and rang the iron.

It was a long time before movement could be heard from the other side, but eventually, the doors opened a crack. Danika was too far away to hear the conversation, but when Nyle raised his voice in anger, the doors opened wider, and Nyle motioned for her to lead Marian inside. Marian clutched her arm tight enough so that Danika could feel nails bite through her soft leather sleeve. The Fae moaned softly as she shuffled beside her and sagged against Danika.

In a flash Torin stood beside them; he picked up Marian and held her gently in his arms. "If I may, lass, I will support you and let you rest a moment."

Marion nodded, but her eyes were dull and unfocussed as Torin carefully proceeded to carry the girl through the gates.

Danika thought she recognized the two students standing guard as a couple of second years. The taller one was particularly talented with mineral magic. They were no more than sixteen years old, but they looked so different from the two cheeky teenage boys she'd often seen in the refectory. Something had changed them. Their eyes shifted as if they couldn't look directly at her or her company.

Nyle turned to the students. "Take me to Sabre, immediately, and debrief me on what has been happening since we left." His commands echoed off the great stone walls.

The boys flinched, and Danika noticed a furtive glance pass between them. One of the students, the shorter one, spoke, "We'll take you to Sabre. He will explain." When he spoke, it was in a dry whisper, as if afraid of the sound of his own voice. The other student looked as if he were about to speak. He looked behind him into the darkened corridor, then seemed to change his mind. He motioned for the company to follow.

The company was led along the main passage, past the dining hall, and up towards the elder chambers. On the way, they passed other students, many of which Danika knew. They didn't meet her eyes either; most turned away as she approached.

Nyle fell back in step with Danika. Momentarily, she caught his scent, woodsy and familiar.

He leant in towards her and whispered in her ear. "I remember the students as more spirited when I was here before."

Danika turned away, his breath so soft on her neck, yet so painful to her heart. "There's something wrong. They're afraid."

The students must have been through a lot with the attack and the strain of not knowing if the company would make it back in time with the Fae. But they were back in time—they'd succeeded, hadn't they? The halls were not full of blood-drinking monsters. Surely this was an opportunity for happiness or relief rather than this tense quietness. Something was wrong. And where was Layla? Why wasn't she coming to greet them?

Nyle reached for his sword but didn't draw it, resting his hand on the hilt. Danika just caught the glance between Nyle and Torin. The lean warrior shifted Marian's weight, so he'd be ready to defend her if necessary. The mood here was all… wrong.

"In here," one of the students said, as he and his companion backed away at the entrance to the Elder quarters. They exchanged glances, and Danika thought she saw the shorter boy give a tiny shake of his head.

Nyle tensed and held his hand to stay the others. "Stay here a moment."

He drew his sword and parted the thick wooden doors.

"Friends!"

In the center of the circular chamber, behind a large covered banqueting table, stood the hulking form of Sabre, his arms on his hips, a broad smile on his rugged face. Nyle's shoulders visibly relaxed; he sheathed his weapon, turned, and nodded at the others to enter. Torin, holding Marian, followed in behind with Danika.

"Hello, comrade, I see you have kept the university from falling into chaos," said Nyle, approaching the table.

"Aye, I have, brother, and you have brought a Fae," replied Sabre, his eyes flicking to Marian, then back to Nyle.

"Does the rift hold?" asked Nyle.

"It does, but it will not for long."

Nyle nodded. "Then there is no time to lose. We must perform the rites now, and then we must—"

"Brother, there is no rush. Sit with me and eat. I found some wine in the cellar. I think you'll agree, Nyle, it is a particularly good grape." Sabre sat back down at the table and poured a goblet of wine, which he offered to Nyle.

Nyle frowned and waved the drink away. "Sabre, we may have little time. I insist we take Marian to the rift so she may cast the necessary magic."

"And I insist we do not," said Sabre, spearing some chicken and stuffing his mouth with the meat.

"Are you ill, Sabre? Are the rumors true? Has your mind become tangled?"

"I am not insane, clansman." Sabre lounged back in his chair, smiling at Nyle, bits of chicken spitting from his mouth as he spoke.

There was a growl, a low, menacing, guttural sound that raised the hairs on Danika's arms—a sound she recognized and had hoped never to hear again.

Nyle froze. His gaze fell to the covered table, then back to Sabre.

The seated warrior was smiling, but his voice was suddenly harsh. "Now, now, Nyle, no sudden movements."

The tablecloth parted, revealing a pair of massive ugly hounds, crouched and ready to pounce. Two sets of red eyes burning with bloodlust.

Danika couldn't believe what she was seeing. Had Sabre betrayed them? For what?

Nyle drew his sword instantly and pulled Danika behind him. "Torin!"

In one flowing motion, Torin placed Marian on the floor and raised his hands, placing himself between the Fae girl and the hunters.

"Deal with Sabre!" Nyle shouted to Torin as he advanced on the dogs.

Torin fired twice at Sabre, who dived to avoid the shots.

Danika ran to Marian and crouched down next to her, then watched in horror as the archer was lifted from his feet and carried to the wall as if by some massive invisible hand. Struggling against the stone, he was unable to break free, his arms pinned behind him. Nyle followed, helplessly picked up as if he weighed nothing and pinned by an unseen force.

"Cutting it a little fine, my beautiful witch." Sabre got to his feet and turned to a tall figure emerging from the farthest entrance.

Walking towards them, arms raised and power pulsing from her hands in blood-red waves, was a young woman, her brown hair coiling wildly around her shoulders, her eyes gleaming, and her mouth set in a grim line.

Danika whispered her name in disbelief, "Layla?"

～

NYLE STRUGGLED IN VAIN. THE WITCH HAD HIM TIGHT against the wall. He could barely breathe, but he managed to force out his words. "What… madness… Sabre?"

The man Nyle knew as Sabre approached, his eyes gleaming with bitter scorn. "Lucky the villager only had rumors to go on. I feared they'd worked out my true nature, but it seems they just thought I'd gone insane."

"You sent the dogs that attacked the young man?" Nyle could not believe that his old friend would have done such a thing.

"Of course! We couldn't have you racing back here with reinforcements now, could we?" Sabre turned towards Marian and Danika. "It is unfortunate that the hunters were unable to nip this little problem in the bud, you see—" He turned back to Nyle. "—I am very keen for the rift to open. I have some friends that I would like to come and visit—I'm sure you understand." Sabre's face twisted into an almost unrecognizable snarl.

"There is not much fun to be had in Gehenna. Not like here."

Rage built in Nyle's chest, but he was unable to break free. Powerless to stop this insanity, he could just watch as the man he called brother threatened to destroy everything he'd sworn to protect. It was the one betrayal he could never have foreseen. "You're not Sabre." He spat the words at the beast before him.

"But I am, that is, Sabre is in here with me."

Nyle frowned.

"He has such faith in you, Nyle, he cries out to you, but he is weak, just a whisper in my ear, a petty annoyance."

"You're a Vorm?" Could it be possible? Could his friend be possessed by a mind spirit of the abyss?

"Well done, warrior." The creature stretched languidly.

"But then Sabre is dead?" The thought hit Nyle like a club. The Vorm could only latch onto dead hosts.

"No," the Vorm sighed, "he is still in here, screaming and bellowing like a wounded bear. It seems that in this realm, I can inhabit the living. The lack of decomposing is a relief… the constant yapping is a bore."

"Sabre—I will rip this creature from you!" Nyle called out to his friend, but the Vorm just laughed.

"I'm sure he'd be grateful for your words were I not torturing him with visions of what I plan to do to you." The creature came close and smiled. "I got here by tagging along with a bunch of ażote when they found passage. It was just luck that I was inhabiting one of them back in Gehenna—luck on my part, not so lucky for the new host I found. I must say, however, didn't I do well?" It stepped back and held out its arms, Sabre's arms, and admired its muscular physique. "He put up quite a fight mind. He fought me off for days; of course, that witch, Layla, was on his mind, distracting him, which helped me. And it was worth it. It's been a long time since I have been in human form."

"It was you that controlled the ażote, led them here, and sent the hunters." Nyle tried to wriggle free, but he was held fast. If only he could reach his sword. "But why here?"

The Vorm grinned. "I heard her - the herb witch. I felt her failing magic, and I followed the scent." He ran his hands over his body, over Sabre's body. "I've been busy over the last few days, but when my companions arrive, I intend to fully enjoy the pleasures of such well-formed flesh." The Vorm turned to Danika, reached over and stroked her cheek, and she flinched and turned away.

The thought of this monster enjoying Danika made every fiber in Nyle's body scream in protest. The past few days were a blur, but of one thing he was suddenly sure, Danika was his. He would shred anything that threatened to hurt her. He struggled to think clearly; he needed to assess his enemy. "And the witch, is she Vorm too?" Nyle flicked his eyes to Layla.

"No." Sabre's form leant in closer to Nyle. "She helps me of her own volition." He lowered his voice. "I think she does it because she lusts for me." He gave Nyle a boorish wink.

Nyle grimaced in disgust and turned towards Layla. The young witch looked straight ahead, her face guarded and blank. "Why do you do his bidding, girl? You could crush him with your power, yet you let him treat us thus."

Nyle jerked his head towards his former friend. "This is not Sabre! Any loyalty you owe my arms-man is forfeit now."

Danika spoke. "Yes, Layla, turn on him—on it… and—"

"Don't judge me!" Layla spat the words without turning. "I'm as trapped as you."

The Vorm grinned and turned to Layla. "Hold the warriors and the Fae still while I bind them."

The possessed warrior approached, but Nyle could do nothing, pinned as he was by the witch's force. The thing that looked like his friend snapped heavy irons onto Nyle's wrists and ankles, and the bound warrior slumped to the floor, released from the witch's spell. For whatever reason, Danika's friend was indeed doing the daemon's bidding. His arms were bound fast. He looked over at Torin. His archer's hands were also trapped behind his back. The archer shook his head, indicating he could do nothing.

He struggled as Danika was taken away, but the chains held fast. "If you harm her, Vorm, I swear to you, I will tear out your soul!"

"You are hardly in a position to offer threats, warrior. I'm keeping you alive only because there may be some more Vorm coming through when the gate fails." He slapped Nyle's muscular shoulder. "Clansmen make good hosts."

"I will die before…"

"Yes, yes, that's what Sabre said, but he did what he was told when I threatened his woman." The Vorm leant close to Nyle's face. "I see how you lust after the redhead. Fear not, I will give her to you to play with when one of my brothers has full control over you. You will get to watch it all!"

Nyle felt a surge of power rise through him at the thought of watching Danika being used at his own hand. A red haze settled over his vision, and his heart pumped loudly in his chest.

His bonds began to give a little.

∼

Danika couldn't believe what her friend was doing as she was guided through the doorway and into the hallway. A group of students scuttled past, eyes fixed on the floor.

She stopped and turned to her best friend. It seemed Layla had aged a decade in just a few days.

"Layla, what's going on? Why are you helping him?"

Layla continued walking, head down. Danika grabbed her and pulled her back. Layla stared down at the hands wrapped around her arms, and Danika could feel her friend tremble. What had happened here? How had her friend changed so dramatically in just a few days? The Layla she knew would never be a part of this—she would fight—but there was nothing but defeat and pain in Layla's eyes.

Finally, her friend spoke in a quiet, thin voice that Danika hardly recognized. "In a moment you'll understand." She pushed open the heavy wooden doors to the altar room.

The carnage of the ażote attack had been cleared away, and the altar stood, as it always had, in the center of the chamber. Behind it, however, was a group of new structures. Three roughly wrought pens lined the back wall, each holding a cluster of young and frightened children.

"The youngest students, kitchen boys, village children!" said Danika as realization dawned. Next to each pen sat an ażote, and each one held its feeler near the throat of a child.

Danika was about to go to her when a young voice cried out. "Danika!"

She recognized the boy Micah as one of the hostages. An ażote was holding a feeler to his neck, and as the child cried out to her, the creature tightened its grip.

Micah scowled but didn't speak again.

Danika rushed to the gate and held onto the bars. "It's okay, Micah. Nyle is here and all will be well."

The ażote cackled. "When the rift fails, some of these children are promised to us as a reward. I plan to eat mine… slowly."

Some of the children began to cry softly. The blood boiled in Danika's veins as she turned to Layla.

Her friend shrugged and hung her head, and she spoke in a flat whisper, "I cannot use my magic to free them all at the same time. My energy is always depleted. I could fight two maybe, but not three, and I couldn't neutralize three ażote in the time it took one to kill a child. I could not sacrifice any of them, so… I do Sabre's bidding." She turned to Danika, her eyes moist with tears. "If I disobey him, they burn them to punish me."

Danika gasped and turned to the children. Some had angry red feeler marks on their arms and neck. On instinct, she moved towards the nearest cage, but the ażote hissed, making the children cringe and whimper.

"The creatures feed off livestock for now, but when the rift fails..." Layla trailed off.

Danika turned to Layla and saw the fear and exhaustion on her friend's face.

"You've done all you can, my friend, more than anyone else could have done. You have kept these children from being slaughtered. You've had nothing but difficult choices." Danika felt her friend's pain. Her voice was low and full of emotion when she added, "You've been tested, and you have endured."

Layla sobbed once—a desperate, throaty gasp for air. "And when the rift opens and I can no longer protect them, what then?"

Danika shook her head. "I don't know—we must just keep faith. Nyle may yet come through this. Sabre may be able to battle the daemon inside him. Until the rift breaks open, we'll just have to hope that there is a way to defeat them." But even as she spoke, she felt hope draining from her. They could not risk an open attack without also risking the children. The daemon had them neatly tied into his plan, and she could see no escape.

Well, at least she could do something. She approached the nearest ażote. "Your master has ordered that I heal the children of their burns." She spoke as confidently as she could. "You must admit me access to the cages immediately!"

The ażote snarled and coiled its feeler in the air. "Why would our master care about these snotty little Sha babies?"

Danika drew herself up to her full five feet two inches and used her sternest voice. "Some of these Shamans will be hosts for Sabre's important guests. They must be in pristine condition, and I am to ensure that is the case!" Many of the children cried out at Danika's words. She hated scaring them this way, but she hated the idea of the burns becoming infected more.

The ażote recoiled and hissed but drew the cage door open. Danika entered quickly and began treating the injuries. The children whimpered and moaned when she laid her hands on them, but they soon calmed when their pain was removed. Some cowered away from her, afraid that she was in league with Sabre, but a few soft words of encouragement and they allowed her to soothe their sore limbs.

As she was healing, she started forming a plan—what was it Layla had said? Two maybe, but not three. *I couldn't neutralize three ażote in the time it took one to kill a child.* But she could down one, if she channeled her healing power and avoided its whip—she'd done it before in the library. She turned to Layla, who sat next to her, soothing a child in her arms, and whispered, "My healing has a strong effect on the creatures. If I eliminated one, could you manage the other two?"

Layla looked at her friend for a long moment. "Are you sure?" she whispered.

Danika nodded. If the last week had taught her anything, it was that she was no longer a passenger—she was capable. *This is the plan. This is what needs to be done. Breathe, Danika, control your power, your adrenaline, walk through the plan in your mind, and see the* outcome clearly. You will not fail. Danika clutched her shaking arms, forcing herself to relax.

Danika gritted her teeth. "Let's do it."

~

Nyle had never felt strength like it, it buzzed along his limbs, fueling him with a surge of white-hot power. And each time he pictured Danika in danger, the feeling increased. The lanvi. The ancient gift of the clans. Proof that he loved the healer. As if he needed its proof. He'd known deep down in his soul that he loved her, even when he didn't remember her. She'd somehow wedged herself into his heart, and he constantly felt her. And now he knew it—he'd been blessed, like his grandfather—granted double strength at the mere thought of his kish'la.

He'd been blessed—and now he was going to find her even if it killed him.

He could feel the iron on his wrists flexing under his grip. He concentrated on the healer's face, her amber eyes, her creamy skin—the way she called his name when she came. He remembered! They'd been more than colleagues, more than just lovers! He had fallen for her—her strength, her curiosity, her wit—he loved her without hesitation, and she was in danger! He had to—

There was a noise from the direction she'd been taken, a bang. The walls of the hall trembled, and dust fell from the cracks in the stone.

"They're here!" The Vorm turned to the prisoners. "Forgive my rudeness, but I must leave you now. My pets here will look after you." He gestured to the three snarling hunters prowling the hall. "They have orders to attack if you try to escape, so don't make any sudden movements." The Vorm smiled. "I'll be back soon, with some of my friends." He stopped in front of Marian and leant down. "I know your race's secret, little Fae, your people's blood extends life—you will be my greatest gift to my brothers." And with that, the Vorm left the hall towards the altar chamber.

Nyle looked at the Fae girl. The idea that immortality could be stolen from them—no wonder they kept it a closely guarded secret. Elfain would be under constant attack if the truth were known.

Marian turned to look at Nyle, her face pale and drawn. "It is true. Our blood is the source of our longevity and our power. To share it is to dilute it. That is why we keep to our own realm."

Torin struggled with his bindings. "We need to get to the gate and stop the other Vorm from entering."

Nyle closed his eyes and concentrated on Danika, his Danika, and this time focused his rage, harnessing the power her memory generated in him. He gathered all the anger into one place and felt the energy pulsating in his arms. He snapped the chains as if they were made of twine. One of the hunters bounded over, dripping a foul-smelling drool in its wake. Nyle caught the dog by the throat and smashed it against the stone wall, but before he could return to his fighting stance, the other two dogs launched themselves at Nyle.

∽

Layla shuffled forward so she was in sight of the two ażote farthest away.

Danika got up and walked around the cage until she was in touching distance of the nearest. It was the one that held Micah. The creature hissed at her but didn't move. She placed her hands on the boy and looked him in the eye. He looked back. She inclined her head slightly, and he nodded once.

"Now!" she cried and clutched the creature's arm, forcing a large dose of healing power into its body, but it screamed and pulled away before she could deliver it all.

As the creature leapt back, Danika was aware that there was a battle raging behind her. Layla had the two other creatures pressed against the wall, suffocating them with the weight of her force. But the third was strengthening its grip on Micah. It would crush the life from him in an instant. Danika threw herself at the creature and drove home another jolt; the creature wrapped its claw around her throat and began to squeeze. Just as she thought she could take no more, as her vision began to fade and her power wane, the creature fell slack and released her. She scrambled upright, and her eyes met Micah's. She ran her hands over his neck. The boy was unharmed.

Layla was standing over the lifeless forms of the two other creatures.

She ran to her friend, and they embraced.

"We need to get the children to safety, then I need to confront Sabre," said Layla, a grim look on her face.

Danika was already unlocking the cages and guiding the children to freedom, praying that Sabre hadn't harmed Marian—or Nyle. "If we can get Marian down here, she'll be able to heal the rift." She ushered the children past the fallen bodies of the ażote. "If not for good, at least until we can garner more support from the Fae royal family. We will be able to—"

A loud crack, like a clap of thunder, echoed around the chamber.

The stone altar in the middle of the room split down the middle, and each half fell away. Layla looked at Danika, her eyes wide, her face pale.

The floor shook.

The rift was breaking open.

CHAPTER 20

The warrior fought like fury itself, fending off the powerful beasts with his bare hands, but without a sword it was a hard task. He had one dog in a hold, about to break its neck when the other took Nyle's arm in its powerful jaws and crushed through skin and bone. Nyle rode out the pain and dispatched the dog in his arms, but not until the second dog had inflicted another deep gash in the warrior's abdomen with its claws.

Blood rushed from the wound as the second dog rounded on Nyle. The warrior held his bloody arm tightly against his stomach; he could feel the warm blood flowing onto his thighs. He feigned left, and sent the dog that way, then leapt, grimacing at the pain, to land astride the beast. He slammed his good arm down, quickly breaking the dog's back with his elbow and collapsing with it to the floor.

He crawled over to the archer, clutching his wounds.

"How in the Goddess's name did you break iron?"

asked Torin, his eyes wide.

Nyle grunted. Again, a vision of his brave healer formed in his mind—his pain ceased for a moment, and a great force thrummed through his body. He clutched the archer's cuffs and broke them apart.

Torin rubbed his wrists. "The lanvi?"

Nyle nodded. "I don't know how long it will last..." He moved to Marian and freed her in the same way. The moment her chains fell away, however, the pain returned, and he felt a weakness he did not recognize. He leant against the wall and brushed his palm across his stomach. It was warm and sticky.

Marian spoke. "We need to get to the rift. There may still be time." Then she turned to Nyle and whispered in his ear, "Danika needs you now, more than ever." Nyle was quickly on his feet. He had one thought now—not the rift, nor his duty, nor revenge, nor Sabre—he needed to find Danika. He needed to tell her that he loved her, that he needed her, that he was sorry, and would never forget it again, and that she was his kish'la. He lurched towards the door.

∽

Danika watched in awe as her friend kept the rift from breaking apart. She could see in Layla's expression what a struggle it was to maintain the barrier between this world and the next. She glimpsed ominous shadows and gnarled shapes through the red haze, throwing themselves against the blockade. She moved to the stairs. They needed Marian, and fast.

If only she could free Nyle, perhaps they could…

"Going somewhere, little one?" The Vorm in Sabre's form came bounding down the staircase towards her. "You must stay. I have some friends I would like you to meet." His attention flicked to Layla, and his leer turned into a snarl. "You tiresome witch! I have no idea why my host sets such a store by you. He began to make his way over to where Layla was casting her spell. Danika knew that Layla could not maintain the wall and fight Sabre. There was only one thing she could think to do.

Danika launched herself at Sabre's broad chest and pushed a dart of anesthetic power into his chest, enough energy to down two large men. Sabre was strong, but his physiology was human. The Vorm stumbled, and for a glorious moment, Danika thought it had worked, but he regained his footing and grabbed Danika by the arm.

Leaning in close to the healer, he hissed in her face, "Not this time, girl. My spirit protects this body. But for that little stunt, I will make sure the daemon that owns you is the most brutal creature to ever walk the plains of Gehenna. You will beg to please him if only to stop the torture that he will force upon you."

Danika felt hatred rise from her guts. Anger and frustration burned through her as she stared into the sneering face before her. "Burn in Gehenna!" Her free hand came up fast and slapped the Vorm hard across his cheek.

The creature snarled. "You will submit!" He hit her back, much harder, with the back of his hand. The room swam and danced before her eyes and bile rose from her stomach. She fell backwards, clutching her throbbing jaw.

There was a roar from the doorway, and a large blur of

muscle and brawn launched itself at the Vorm, knocking it to the floor.

Danika saw Marian and Torin rush to Layla's side and began the blood casting ritual to close the rift—Torin shooting back any creature that came too close to the barrier. But Danika's attention was drawn to the fighting —it was Nyle. At the sight of her warrior, alive, her chest ached with a sweet pain. The warriors rolled on the floor, each trying to gain purchase on the other. Could Nyle outwrestle the Vorm? He was strong, with more heart than any man had the right to have, but he was struggling. There was an injury to his stomach and one on his leg, too.

Her healer's training kicked in. She assessed the wounds.

They were bad.

Really bad.

∼

HE'D FOUGHT SABRE MANY TIMES ON THE TRAINING FIELDS and knew well his strength and speed. But his friend was possessed with an animal fury, and Nyle could feel his own lifeblood draining away.

Despite the lanvi still pulsing through him, Nyle's strength began to wane, and Sabre was gaining purchase. Nyle caught sight of Danika a few feet away. He remembered it all now—the way she shuddered when he caressed her back, the flash of laughter in her warm amber eyes, the defiant tilt of her chin when she disagreed with him.

He fought for her—he would die for her.

A last surge of power coursed through him, the desperation of a dying man. He flipped his opponent onto his back and wrapped his hands around the Vorm's neck, squeezing. The Vorm pushed back hard, but Nyle held his position and stared down into his best friend's face. He was dimly aware that the rift was shrinking. Torin and Marian must have completed the rites. The powerful witch, Layla, was backing off. Nothing was coming through now.

The Vorm stopped struggling and laid still.

Nyle loosened his hold a fraction.

Sabre's eyes opened and looked up at him. "The Vorm is weakened for a moment. You must finish this, Nyle." It was his friend, the man he had grown to love as a brother. "I will not watch this creature debase everything I hold dear." Sabre's eyes flicked over to the witch. Nyle suspected a bond had grown between them before the Vorm had—

"Now, Nyle!" His friend looked up at him, his eyes wild. "He wakes, and I cannot hold him back."

"No!" Layla threw herself upon Sabre's chest. "We can find a way to release the daemon. You must not kill him. I will not allow it!" Layla's hands began to glow. "I will take him from here, and I will ensure he does not hurt anyone. I will find a way to expel the daemon. I will—"

Sabre lurched upward and pushed back Nyle. "You should have killed me when you had the chance, Captain." He grabbed Layla before anyone could react. "And you, witch, will be of use in hell!" With that the Vorm plunged through the portal, dragging Layla with him.

∽

DANIKA CRIED OUT AS THE RIFT CLOSED BEHIND HER friend. Alone in the wilderness of Gehenna! But as Nyle groaned and slumped onto his back, Danika was by his side in an instant. She laid her hands upon him. His heartbeat was weak, his circulation sluggish. He was near death.

"Danika, I must—" He coughed, and his face screwed up in pain.

"Shhhh for now, my love." Danika eased open his sodden shirt to view his wounds. As she feared, they were very deep. She ripped open his trousers—the blood gushed from him as she pressed her hands to his thigh.

"Danika!" He reached up and caught a lock of her red hair as she bent over him.

"You must stay still."

"No, you must listen to me woman!" He clutched her arm and wheezed a moment before continuing, "I must say the words, before I—"

"I will not let you die."

"Let me speak."

Danika paused for a moment and looked up into the rugged face of her warrior.

"If I must go from this world, I will go with your name on my lips, for you are my kish'la."

Danika felt tears rise in her throat, but she choked them back. "You will not die, soldier. You owe me, Nyle. You have a whole lot of making up to do, and I swear to you I will not be denied."

Despite his obvious pain, Nyle laughed softly. He closed his eyes and whispered one word, "Danika—"

His chest fell, then moved no more.

No! Danika felt a surge within her. She thrust her palms upon his cool skin and unloaded as much power as she had left as deep into his wracked flesh as she could. Everything she'd ever learnt about healing raced through her mind.

She prepared herself for the longest night of her life.

∼

DANIKA WOKE TO THE SOFT LIGHT OF DAWN. SHE TURNED immediately to check on Nyle. The bed she'd laid him in was empty. What had happened as she slept? It had been a long healing, taking her to the point of exhaustion and beyond, but she'd repaired the worst of his wounds. He'd been stable when she finally succumbed to the necessity of sleep, but definitely not well enough to get up and walk. Had he died in the night? Goddess no!

She swung her legs over the edge of the bed and sat up. The room swam a little, and her eyes had trouble focusing. Despite her dizziness, she got unsteadily to her feet and pulled on some boots.

On leaving her room, she was caught up in a bustle in the corridors and carried along for a moment with the pushing crowd.

"What is it? What is happening?" She turned to the nearest excited student.

"Royal riders bring word from Elfain,"

Danika didn't care—the whole damned lot could go to

Gehenna. She grabbed the student. "The captain of the warriors, Nyle—do you know where he is?"

The student shrugged and shook his head. He pulled free, eager to follow the crowd thrusting towards the great hall.

She turned back and forced her way through the throng, heading for the back entrance of the university. She needed to find Torin or Marian. They might know what had happened. She rushed through the kitchen and out through the service exit into the backyard.

The sunlight was so bright she had to squint and shield her eyes with the palm of her hand, but ahead she saw a hulking shape her heart would have recognized anywhere.

Danika felt weak as she saw him, tall and hale, dismounting his horse and giving the reins to the stable lad. She leant against the rough wall for a moment to regain her strength. The world was tilting, and she had to close her eyes. When she opened them, he was there beside her, concern etched into his rugged face.

"What are you doing out of bed?" His voice was stern, but his touch was soft as he pulled her to him.

"What am I doing out of bed? How are you walking around? I left you close to death not three hours ago." Danika straightened up and pushed against the firm shoulders of her warrior—he towered above her.

"Aye, lass, but that was near on three days ago. You've slept all that time. He pulled her in towards him and tucked her into his embrace.

She breathed in his scent, leather and smoke and warm sunshine.

He shook his head. "I've been gone but for an hour. I was coming straight back to you. I didn't want to leave you but… there was something that couldn't wait."

"I've been asleep for three days?" No wonder she was dizzy. She allowed Nyle to guide her to a seat and gazed up at him.

"Aye. They told me you near killed yourself saving my skin." He smiled and brushed an unruly lock of hair from her brow. He spoke softly, "You must never do that again, kish'la. You must not risk your life for mine."

Kish'la. It was the sweetest sound. As the word brushed over her, she knew she'd do it over and over for him, for the man she loved, but now was not the time for that conversation. She smiled. "The prince's cousin has arrived."

Nyle nodded. "He's come to discuss the rift. I hope he'll give support to our cause, and…" he hesitated, "I shall ask him to open a temporary portal that we may look for Layla and Sabre."

Layla, alone in Gehenna. Danika shuddered at the thought.

Nyle noticed her fear. "Your friend has much power, Danika. I believe she'll be okay when we find her, and Sabre too, once we rid him of his daemon."

Danika leant farther into Nyle's embrace. The last of the summer sunshine warmed her. A soft breeze ruffled her tunic. "This is just the beginning, isn't it, Nyle? There is so much that needs to be done."

"Aye, lass, but we'll face it together." Nyle turned towards Danika. His usual look of stern intensity had been replaced with something else. Was he nervous?

He cleared his throat. "I've just come back from the local blacksmith."

Danika looked at him blankly and waited for him to continue.

Nyle sighed. "In the mountains that would mean more to a lass." He dug in his pocket and pulled out a small round branding iron carved with the shape of a flower.

Danika took it and studied the design. No, not a flower... "A thistle!" she gasped. "You remembered!"

Nyle smiled. "Some but not all." His voice softened. "I remember how much I love you, and that'll be enough." Then he spoke to Danika in the language of his forefathers:

"Sire do aoibh gháire—take me as your husband and I will sire your smiles forever."

She paused a moment and beheld her warrior as he stood before her, his face reflecting love and just a hint of uncertainty. There was much that she was uncertain about—about Layla trapped in Gehenna, about the future of the university, about the rift, and how they would convince the Fae to work with the Shaman. But there was one thing about which she was certain, a thing that she would cleave to through raging wars and attacks from the forces of hell—the love she felt for this brusque, dismissive, stubborn, battle-hardened warrior. Any doubts she'd had were banished, any pain from the past slain.

She flung her arms around his neck, clutching the brand tightly in her fist, and burying her face in his chest.

"Forever."

LAYLA'S DESIRE

BOOK 3 OF WARRIORS, WITCHES AND FAE

She was being hunted.

A hungry gaze slid down the back of her neck along with rivulets of sweat and grime. She turned sharply and paused, a statue in the dimness. But all was as before—just dense, hot jungle and shadows, no eyes glowing from the gloom, no ragged teeth, white and cold, waiting to tear into her.

She was alone.

Well, not quite alone.

Layla eased back on her magic and gently lowered the unconscious warrior to the ground in the clearing. As his massive bulk connected with the floor, a host of insects, some uncomfortably large and befanged, jumped and scuttled out of the way. He made no sound, no sign of waking.

Layla scraped a few damp curls from her eyes and slumped at the foot of a tree. She looked up; the top of the tree disappeared into the canopy above. So high, so big, so wild. She longed for the gentle plains and tame forests of

Shaman. The smells were too rich here, and every breath was baking hot. She could protect them both with her magic, but if she couldn't rest and recharge, her power would fail - soon. Then what? They'd be vulnerable to every creature that walked Gehenna, this hellish realm in which she now found herself. Found herself—*ha!* In which she'd jumped, feet first, to save this... this... *brute!* She rubbed her face in an attempt to sharpen her wits. And now everything depended on him.

The mocking calls of unseen birds continued, as did the incessant chatter of insects. Something bigger screamed down at her from from the canopy above, a high shriek, which made her turn startled and bump her heel into the prone warrior. She waited with her hands raised, ready to summon the last of her magic and blast the creature from the trees. Nothing came swooping down. After a few moments, she lowered her hands—keep it together, Layla. This place attacks the mind as well as the flesh. She calmed her breathing by going through an exercise drilled into her at the university. She visualized a blue calming tonic in her mind, a lapping ocean of calm, cooling her hot, fevered thoughts. If only Danika was here, she thought bitterly; the healer's presence alone would revive her. But the last image she had of her friend was that of her pale-faced, crouching over a fallen warrior, before Layla had dived through a portal which had transported her to Gehenna, the realm of dark spirits and damned souls.

She beheld the man on the floor, a man possessed by the darkest of spirits. He was immense, big even for a warrior. Without her dwindling supplies of magic, she wouldn't have been able to move his muscular frame an inch. His sandy copper braids were dark with sweat and mud. His skin, once clear and softly tanned, was pale with a greyish tinge, and his wide handsome face, a face she'd seen light up when she'd laughed at his jokes, was now drawn into a pained snarl. What sick tortures was the dark spirit, the Vorm daemon, inflicting on his mind right at this minute? What fetid dreams was the monster cooking up to torment the brave warrior she'd begun to know, only a few short while ago? A fierce hatred for the creature buzzed through her body and a tiny trickle of magic wisped unbidden from her fingertips, singing a nearby branch. She sunk onto her haunches and wiped her sweaty hand over her face. What now?

She was thirsty and hungry, but it was the thirst that she couldn't ignore. Her mouth was bone dry despite the moisture in the air, and her head was pounding. How to get water when you've been kidnapped by a possessed warrior and taken to hell... Yes—she must have missed that particular lecture. At the university, water was provided in earthenware cups, often laced with a little sugared lemon for flavor. Presumably, it was drawn from a well, although coming from a privileged family, she'd never actually drawn any herself. She tried not to think about the university, about her friends, and her teachers, about the attack.

Sabre would know how to get water. This man who'd tortured her, who'd ordered her to betray her friends and threatened to harm children if she disobeyed. This man who'd left her no choice but to come here to die of heat exhaustion, while he—she looked down at his prone form

—remained unconscious! Anger bubbled up again, but this time, she couldn't quite separate the monster within Sabre from the warrior himself. Did she even want him to wake? Then she'd know if the Vorm, the mind daemon, was still in there—still twisting the easy-going warrior she'd once known into an evil creature of the abyss.

She leaned further over him. Like this, he looked like the man she'd stood beside to fight the daemons, the man she might have... had feelings for. He'd been so ready to laugh, to joke and tease. In the few days they'd worked together, she'd found herself smiling much more than usual, despite the difficult circumstances. Then he'd become distant, and finally, the Vorm had taken control, and everything she'd loved about him had been stripped away. She might have left him to rot with the Vorm, but at the rift, just for a moment, the real Sabre had returned. He'd begged his oldest and dearest friend to kill him and to rid the world of the monster within. In that moment, Layla couldn't bear the thought of Sabre dying. She'd stopped Nyle from delivering the death blow.

And ended up in hell... *Good move, Layla!*

His lips moved; he was murmuring in his sleep. Worry lines appeared on his brow. Layla fought the urge to stroke them away. She leaned in closer, trying to hear what he was saying, so close that she could feel his breath cool against her heated cheek.

His eyes flicked open, and he grabbed her roughly before she could react. She needed her hands to cast her magic, to fight him off. But he was on his feet in moments, pinning her arms to her side. She was no match for him physically.

His eyes met hers, the same leaf green eyes she remembered coaxing a smile from her by acting the clown, or making the university children squeal by pretending to be a bear and chasing them round the quad. He dragged her closer, their lips just inches apart. Was this Sabre, the warrior, who'd protected what she loved, or the daemon sworn to destroy it?

"We're being watched." His gaze flicked to the brush; Layla looked too. At first, she couldn't see anything, but then appearing from the darkness came a pair of glowing eyes, white orbs with a black slit pupil, holding within them feral intelligence. Then a wrinkled piggy snout covered in grey leathery skin—then teeth, small and sharp and dripping with spittle. Sabre's eyes returned to hers. "Do you have power here?"

Was it him, or the daemon? She half nodded, unsure how much to tell him. "Some." In truth, she was nearing her limit.

He released her, and she took a quick step away. "Strike any of them that come close."

Them? Sure enough, more sets of ghoulish eyes appeared along with snouts and jaws and teeth. They walked on all fours, with a body like a puma, but furless. they slunk out of the jungle into the clearing, avoiding any shafts of direct sunlight, circling the pair. Layla counted seven in all.

The first attack came from the left. Layla spun and pitched it back with a sharp flash of energy. The creature ran back and the other six screeched at the bright light.

"Their eyes," said Sabre. "Your light hurts their eyes."

Layla offered up another flash. The creatures backed off, but only as far as the shadows.

"Can you do a larger flash? It might scare them off." He looked at her, his face grim. "Without a weapon, I can't take them all."

If she did as he asked, it would take the last of her power - she would be defenseless against him. The creatures advanced with stealth; two had slipped round the back of them, cutting off any escape. She raised her hands and concentrated on the casting. Drawing on the last vestiges of energy within her, she allowed the power to surge up through her body and pool in her hands like a red smoking coil. She released it in one almighty flash.

She fell to the ground, her power, the only thing sustaining her, gone.

Her head rested on the dry leaves by Sabre's feet as the warrior turned in a circle. The creatures had been forced back, but not far. She could see their paws pacing around the clearing, wary but undeterred.

She didn't care. She was done. Let them claim her.

As exhaustion washed over her, she didn't fight it—hadn't she fought enough?

Her eyes closed, and the world receded. She just caught Sabre's words to the creatures before she drifted into unconsciousness.

"I am of the Vorm and she is my prisoner. Leave us, or I will bring my brothers here to feast on your souls…"

AFTERWORD

Thank you so much for reading *Danika's Touch*. I really hope you enjoyed it. If you did *please* review or rate me on Amazon and Goodreads - these reviews are my lifeline amongst a crowded market of wonderful romance books. Danika's Touch is independently published and the most important thing to this indy writer, is how you feel about my book. If you have any suggestions or would just like to reach out, email me on admin@darcyjameson.com. If you would like background information or additional content regarding the world of Warrior's, Witches and Fae, visit me at www.darcyjameson.com where you can sign up to my newsletter and be at the front of the queue for news and giveaways.

I hope you enjoyed the first chapter of the next installment, *Layla's Desire*. I loved writing it despite giving Sabre and Layla a torrid time. Keep an eye out for upcoming titles *Alyssa's Heart* and *Torin's Curse*, or sign up to the mailing list so you don't miss a thing.

ABOUT THE AUTHOR

Darcy Jameson is a mother of two from Surrey, England. She loves going for long walks with her beloved Cavachon and thinking about ways to torture her poor heroes and heroines (but making sure they always find their happy place in the end). She loves baking - the squishier and creamier the better, and spends her days reading and writing sexy romances set in worlds where there are no mobile phones. She always squeals with joy when somebody contacts her regarding her books at admin@darcyjameson.com or wanders on to her website darcyjameson.com

Printed in Poland
by Amazon Fulfillment
Poland Sp. z o.o., Wrocław